CHARISMA

CHARISMA

JEANNE RYAN

Dial Books
an imprint of Penguin Group (USA) LLC

DIAL BOOKS
Published by the Penguin Group
Penguin Group (USA) LLC, 375 Hudson Street, New York, New York 10014

USA/Canada/UK/Ireland/Australia/New Zealand/India/South Africa/China
penguin.com
A Penguin Random House Company

Library of Congress Cataloging-in-Publication Data
Ryan, Jeanne.
Charisma / by Jeanne Ryan.
pages cm
Summary: Tacoma, Washington, high school junior Aislyn's extreme shyness has
crippled her socially and cost her a college scholarship, so she jumps at the chance to
try an illegal gene therapy, but although she is finally able to date her long-term crush,
Jack, the therapy becomes a contagious disease that can be fatal.
ISBN 978-0-8037-3966-6 (hardcover)
[1. Bashfulness—Fiction. 2. Gene therapy—Fiction. 3. Virus diseases—Fiction.
4. Dating (Social customs)—Fiction. 5. Single-parent families—Fiction.
6. Cystic fibrosis—Fiction. 7. Science fiction.] I. Title.
PZ7.R9518Ch 2015
[Fic]—dc23   2014013425

Printed in the United States of America
1 3 5 7 9 10 8 6 4 2

Designed by Maya Tatsukawa
Text set in Bulmer MT Std

For Ryan and Lilia, who shine so bright

ONE

I swim varsity but know firsthand what being trapped below the surface feels like. This. Chest-crushing, head-pounding panic as you fight for just one breath. Fingernails clawing into my palms, I struggle for air on this dry-as-dust stage, in front of science fair judges, strangers from across Washington State, my family, and Jack, who also qualified for this competition.

Dr. Lin, the head judge, and physics teacher at my school, taps his clipboard as he waits for me to convince him of my project's relevance to society.

Even though I fear a tide of hopelessness will rush in to flood my lungs, I force my mouth open a fraction. "Scientists have identified, uh, many genes associated with specific disorders, so . . ." My heart's a machine gun in my chest, my voice a lost cause.

Dr. Lin cocks his head. "Miss Hollings?" He glances at my knocking knees. "Aislyn? Are you feeling well?"

I nod, and summon the strength to finish answering his question. But my vision goes fuzzy and I struggle for another breath, which only increases my light-headedness. The books all say to "accept" a panic attack, as if there's a choice, letting it flow through and out of your psyche. Here's what they don't tell you—panic doesn't flow, it jolts your body like an earthquake, leaving you unmoored and flailing from a deep chasm intent upon sucking you in.

Dr. Lin raises his eyebrows, waits an unbearably long moment, and angles the microphone back to himself. "If you could fix genetic mutations, where would you draw the line? What about the person who claims their baldness or height must be fixed?" He's reading from the playbook of those crazies who protest in front of the Nova Genetics labs, shouting that gene therapy is "playing God," who'd halt all life-saving cures if they could.

But knowing how wrong the anti-everything folks are doesn't spark any brilliance in my next words, which limp out like refugees. "Frivolous gene alterations aren't being approved for development." I blink at the audience. In the front row, Mom leans forward, her chin nudging the air, as if that could spur me forward. Her anxiety about how to finance my college tuition has grown into an ever-present entity that

I'd hoped to chase away with tonight's hefty prize.

Dr. Lin sighs at this pathetic student who can barely describe her project, much less win a competition, no matter how many leading questions he feeds her.

There's so much more I need to say, but my knees threaten to give out at any moment. I lean against the table holding my tri-fold display. Big mistake. The table tilts and the cardboard charts teeter. I jump to stop the table's shift, but not in time to prevent the display from toppling and my handouts from flying across the stage into the person standing at the next table, who happens to be Jack. Lanky, blond, sweet-smiled Jack.

He picks up the papers and hands them to me, whispering, "You're doing fine."

No. Fine performances aren't met by gasps and snickers from the audience. And they don't lead to asphyxiation on stage.

A traitorous blush sears my face. Hundreds of eyes watch, watch, and, oh hell, did a camera just flash? I fumble with the papers, my neck burning. Every molecule in my body screams, "Run." But I will not. I convinced myself long ago that if I ever let myself flee from my anxieties, I'd never stop running. So I'll stand here and endure.

Dr. Lin scribbles onto his pad. "Anything you'd like to add?" His persistence is either due to the fact that I go to the school where he teaches or sadism. Not that it makes any difference.

I gulp a breath and glance at Mom, whose lips press white. She must wonder why I spent countless hours on this project instead of on something useful like helping her out with my brother, Sammy.

I swallow. "I hope you have a chance to read my report."

He blinks as if he hasn't heard me correctly. "We'd like you to tell us in your own voice."

Yeah, so would I. But all I can do is nod dumbly.

He says, "Okay, then. If that's your decision."

I cringe at how ominous this sounds, but can't summon the words to convince him of how important this topic is, how gene therapy's given sight to the blind and life to the dying. Someday it'll fix the genetic mutations behind cystic fibrosis, which causes Sammy to feel like he's suffocating every single day. Every single damn day.

That's what I should say. But it would be easier to fuse atoms than force another coherent sentence from my mouth.

Dr. Lin moves on to Jack's presentation. I try not to lock my knees. *Don't run, don't hide, don't crumple.* My threshold for success has dipped to this shamefully low mantra.

Avoiding Mom's and Sammy's gazes, I focus on Jack's presentation, delivered in his calm, confident, Jack-like manner. Usually I have to catch him in glimpses, often aborted when I discover him watching me first. On afternoons when we edit stories for *The Drizzle,* he always tries to strike up a conversation, which leaves me as wobbly as I feel now. It's only a matter of time before he gives up. The way every other guy has, no matter how many compliments they invent, usually along the lines of comparing my long, white-blond hair to unicorns or Nordic princesses. No, I'll end junior year the way I started, more untouched than one of those princesses locked in a tower.

Finally, the judges excuse us for now. Head down, I make my way to Mom, and Sammy, who's coughing into a tissue as quietly as possible. My brother is eleven, but like most kids with CF, looks years younger due to a body that has difficulty absorbing the nutrition it needs.

In the too-loud voice Mom uses to show houses, she says, "No one else's research is as sophisticated as yours. How many teens learn how to sequence DNA?"

I hang my head. How many DNA-sequencing teens can't get a decent word out when they most need to?

We stand there, arms crossed, feet shuffling. I check the time every twenty seconds. Waiting is always a challenge; tonight it's enough to make my head throb. Endless minutes later, they call the finalists back onstage. I stay with Mom and Sammy, who's coughing again. Dr. Lin announces that Jack's project on restoring salmon streams wins first place, and a chance to compete for an even larger prize in the national competition this summer. Somehow, I get an honorable mention, but no scholarship money.

Mom puts her hand to her mouth, but only for a moment, quickly recovering and giving me a brave shrug. Sammy's coughing increases to a red-faced gasping, something Mom and I are used to but not the people around us, who point and stare.

Mom claps Sammy's back. I dig frantically through her purse for more tissues. We shuffle as a threesome past pitying eyes. One woman offers to call for help, but we assure her that isn't necessary. This time.

Outside, when Sammy finally catches his breath, he says, "Sorry for the spectacle."

I tap his sneaker with the toe of my boot. "Don't apologize for that. Besides, my spectacle was bigger than yours, buddy. I had props and a stage."

He doesn't argue the point.

On the way home, I text my best friend, Evie, with highlights of the fiasco, even though she won't see her phone until her debate competition is over. My next text is to my mentor at Nova Genetics, Dr. Sternfield. At least the work I've done with her will count toward early college credit.

When we're inside, Mom smiles half-heartedly, which must take superhuman effort. "I know you tried your best."

If only my best were better. I rub my arms. "I'll help Sammy with his treatment tonight." It's the least I can do.

We head upstairs, where I clap his back and chest to loosen up the stuff that's doing its damnedest to destroy his lungs. Normally, he tries to sneak in jokes between the pounding, but tonight he hunkers down in silence with his sketchpad. I don't force a conversation; it would be callous to complain about college tuition to someone dealing with an average life expectancy of thirty-something years.

After I'm done, Sammy fills his nebulizer with several drugs that he'll inhale for the next thirty minutes. He doesn't need help anymore with this nightly task, but he likes the company. With his mask on and the aerosol flowing, he sits on his bed with a sketchpad while I sink onto the armchair next to him.

All around us, his bedroom walls are filled from floor to as tall as Sammy can reach with vibrant paintings of dragons and other creatures that only he knows the names of. On his pad, he adds shading to a pencil drawing of the Space Needle under attack by robots.

"That's really good," I say.

He sucks air from the mask. "Lots of time to practice."

Yeah, too much time. And, yet, maybe not enough.

Forty minutes later, I get ready for bed, nestling under the covers with my laptop on my knees, wishing I could avoid school tomorrow. But it's the last day of junior year, even though technically it's a half day and there'll be zero learning.

My phone beeps. I accept a video chat, and Evie's neon smile fills the screen. Her thick black hair is pulled up into a topknot to show off gold filigree earrings her mom bought on their annual trip to Indonesia.

She's all dimples and sparkle. "I won!"

We fist-bump our screens.

Her face settles into a more serious expression. "I totally owe you for prepping me. Wish I could've done the same for you with the science competition. Heath Roberts is an ass for posting that picture."

My gut spasms. "What picture?" Before she answers, I shift her image to check out Heath's page. Underneath a picture of me knocking over my exhibit at the science finals, he's written: "Hot? Yeah! Hopeless? Hell, yeah!"

What was he even doing there? Then I remember his little brother qualified for the middle school division. The queasy hopelessness from earlier rises again in my stomach. "Everyone's seen this?"

Evie waves dismissively. "Yesterday it was Shoshanna's butt crack. And she landed a few dates from the attention. You get major exposure therapy points for even entering the science competition. That was brave; you hear me?"

Thanks to psych class, Evie's been pushing exposure

therapy to treat my shyness. To be fair to myself, it's not like I haven't tried to get beyond this problem. So far, I've endured anti-anxiety meds (caused heart palpitations and didn't work anyway), hypnosis (put me to sleep), visualization exercises (couldn't focus), a sugar-free diet (made me grumpy), and, now, exposure therapy, which according to all the texts is the most effective way to treat social phobias. However, there's always that percentage of people, like me, who try, and try, and fail. Evie insists it's only a matter of time. But I know every bell curve needs its outliers.

She bats her eyelashes exaggeratedly. "By the way, a certain soccer player who may be the weak link on the debate team, but is mighty pretty to look at, asked me three times about Drew's party tomorrow."

My stomach drops. "You should go with Abby and Zoe."

She wags her finger. "You haven't been to a party in a month, and summer vacation is almost here. Best friends do not let best friends commit social suicide."

"Best friends do not push each other beyond their comfort zone after they tank at the one area they're supposed to be good at."

"You're better at way more than science and helping me maintain my glorious GPA. Do not be a shy-girl cliché. Starting Saturday, you'll be the blond lifeguard babe. Remember that."

I exhale a raggedy breath. My summer job, which I applied for in a fit of exposure therapy and the backing of my swim team coach, is something I've avoided thinking about, even though it starts the day after tomorrow. "I've had enough exposure therapy."

"For *today*. I'll see if I can get Heath to delete that picture." She pops offline.

Ugh. Maybe I'll break my leg before school tomorrow. Or maybe I should expose myself to a quick bout of the flu. Now there's exposure therapy that could do some good.

Dreaming of ways to avoid the reality of being, well, me, I put my laptop on the end table and fall asleep with my arms crossed tightly across my chest like a mummy. But I awake every couple of hours. As usual. Each time I do, Sammy's coughing and gasping. As usual.

It strikes me that life-as-usual for both of us is an endless struggle to simply breathe.

Group Protests In-Depth Genetic Testing

by Norman Kim, Seattle Health Blog

Marchers stormed out in force to protest the joint announcement by Seattle Reproductive Specialists and Nova Genetics, a gene therapy developer, to evaluate embryos for thousands of potential defects. Dr. Madeline Olevsky, Director of SRS, claims, "Anything we can do to fulfill our clients' dreams of having a healthy baby is progress we celebrate."

Others, however, believe that genetic testing traverses a dangerous path. Nita Farthing, President of Humans for Equality, argues, "Any thinking person should be terrified by the potential of unnatural selection. In a society where the divide between haves and have-nots is already alarming, science that differentiates us at a DNA level will thwart the American ideal of egalitarianism, this time permanently. We will do what's necessary to prevent this attack upon humanity. Developers of species-altering treatments should be prepared for whatever consequences their actions bring forth."

TWO

At school the next day, I meet Evie at our side-by-side lockers. No one's gotten between "Handojo" and "Hollings" since middle school.

A pale gold batik-print dress sizzles against her olive skin, and her waist-length hair, something we have in common despite hers being as dark as mine is light, hangs loose, save for a tiny clip on top filled with luminous green stones. Her eyes travel up and down the pink T-shirt and gray pants I've paired with ballet flats. "Cute, but I'd have gone a wee bit flashier for the last day of school. Make some memories, you know?"

"I have to meet my science mentor this afternoon."

She blinks rapidly. "Oh, no, no, no, we're all going to the mall for lunch."

"Sorry. I have to do the wrap-up with Dr. Sternfield if I want college credit."

"Ask her at the family event Sunday."

"That's for so-called fun. This is business, so she insisted on separate days." My family's attendance at the event will be on account of Sammy, who participated as a research subject in a trial at Nova Genetics. Even though Sammy wasn't helped by the drug, he, Mom, and I became part of the Nova Genetics "family," which means a ridiculous number of "bonding" events and support sessions. It's how I met Dr. Sternfield.

Evie blows upward. "Fine, then I'll pick you up tomorrow at eight for Drew's party."

My purse strap slips from my shoulder. "I might have to hang with Sammy if my mom's meeting clients."

"On Saturday night?" She pokes a freshly adorned fingernail on my collarbone. "Do not use your brother as an excuse. Last party of junior year is a big deal. Your mom'll understand. She was a sorority girl."

A sorority girl who was widowed before her second kid started kindergarten, and has had no social life since. I hike my handbag back up. "My first shift at the pool is tomorrow. I'll be wiped out afterward."

Evie rolls her eyes slowly, letting the white-whites glimmer between the black of her irises and the kohl that lines her lower lashes. Seriously, if eye-rolling were competitive, she'd score straight tens.

Fresh out of excuses, I head off to my abbreviated classes, between which I catch glimpses of Jack's dark blond hair. But I hurry out of the way before he can offer condolences on last night's showing. Five minutes after the bell rings at noon, I'm in my car heading out of the parking lot.

From our school in north Tacoma to the Nova Genetics campus near Gig Harbor takes twenty minutes. But because the drive passes over the towering Tacoma Narrows Bridge, its taut cables resembling a giant harp suspended over churning waves below, the journey to the Olympic Peninsula always feels like traveling to a distant city.

And today it's under siege.

My insides tighten as I pull up to the visitors' parking lot just outside the gated grounds. Dozens of protestors march between the lot and the guarded entrance. Their bobbing signs demand: DESIGNER JEANS, NOT GENES and KEEP FRANKENSTEIN IN THE FICTION DEPARTMENT.

My frustration with their ignorance sets off pressure in my skull. They should focus on the good news, like kids who don't have to live in sterile bubbles anymore.

A beady-eyed man scowls as I approach, backpack clutched tightly to my chest. He chants, "No justification for abominations! No justification for abominations!"

He and the others shake fists and signs, glaring as if I'm an abomination in the flesh. They block my way to the gate, where a guard speaks into a phone.

I try ducking between protesters. "Excuse me."

A middle-aged woman with Cleopatra hair snarls in my face, "There's no excuse for anything that goes on in there."

No, there's no excuse for not trying everything you can to save lives. I'll bet this woman doesn't have family members with anything more crippling than a closed mind.

The guard holds up his hands and shouts, "If you continue to block the entryway, I will be forced to call the police."

The woman and the man part a couple of inches, nowhere near enough for me to get through.

"Excuse me," I squeak again, wishing I could tell these trespassers off, or, better yet, stick their signs where they belong.

They shout, "No justification for abominations! No justification for abominations!"

I scoot to their side, desperate to slip through a gap in the swarm, but they stomp in a circle, cutting me off. Blocking my way is illegal, right? My brain fumbles to form words that my mouth won't say anyway. Maybe Dr. Sternfield will understand if I reschedule.

The guard blows a whistle, which only fires up the protesters, now hollering at an Audi that pulls up. I see my opportunity to squeeze between the bodies as the gate rises to let the car inside.

Someone yanks at my shirt. I yelp.

The car screeches to a halt and the guard barges toward us. Finally, the pressing against me lessens enough to lurch forward, but there's no way to avoid brushing against the protestors.

"You're siding with evil," the Cleopatra-haired lady hisses into my ear with oniony breath.

Shriveling, I gain another few inches. The door of the Audi opens and Dr. Sternfield jumps out, pointing her phone at the protestors. "I suggest you leave that girl alone before this video ends up with the police. You know what the penalty is for assaulting a minor?"

The crowd shrinks back. Dr. Sternfield nods to the guard and smoothes a hand against her auburn hair, pinned in an elegant knot at her aristocratic neck.

"Why don't you get in the car, Aislyn?" she says.

I hurry in and she drives to a reserved spot near the main entrance. My legs shake violently. It takes a moment to find my voice enough to thank her.

She waves me off. "Paradigm shifts always cause angst. Look at how people protested against civil rights and knee-length hemlines. Did you know hand-washing was once considered taboo?"

I want to wash my whole body after squishing between the protesters. Why couldn't I have fended off those awful people? My phone has a perfectly good camera to threaten them with. If I had a spine.

We step into a pavilion of massive wooden beams supporting walls of glass. The airy architecture is misleading, though. Belowground sprawl nests of laboratories that connect all the above-ground structures.

In the main lobby, a two-story ceramic sculpture in the shape of a double helix tempts the earthquake gods. Around it, clusters of people make their way to hallways that spoke outward. A pair of tall, muscular men stride into the north corridor. Behind them rolls a woman in a wheelchair, oxygen tubes in her nose. Nova Genetics will study her genes as intently as the "model" genes of the athletes in front of her.

Dr. Sternfield pauses to say hi to Xavier Dionisio, one of her college interns. He's Asian with a banker's haircut and the chest and shoulders of a weight lifter.

Dr. Sternfield asks, "How's the sequence for the dancer coming?"

Xavier's voice is soft, but clearer than I've heard it before. "I've identified a few interesting alleles." His thick eyebrows rise on the word *interesting*. Maybe he's discovered a mutation that explains the difference between a ballerina who's destined for stardom and one who'll never be promoted from the corps.

"Great. I'll check it out as soon as Aislyn and I are through."

I follow her past a door that requires a thumbprint scan. We end up in a corner office, where I take my usual seat across her desk and pull out a binder. After being one of her mentees the past school year, and seeing her at events for years before that, I'm more comfortable with her than with most adults, a hundred times more at ease than I was with Dr. Lin on stage, anyway.

She folds her hands on the desktop. "Your project should've been a shoo-in at the science competition."

I rub a callus on my finger. "Yeah, well, I'm not the best public presenter." Understatement so major that it borders on irony.

She nods. "Sometimes it's not enough to have the best research or work the hardest, is it?"

I slide a form across the desk. "At least I'll get some college credit."

She glances at the paper. "So many forms to consider for your family today. The group running the AV719 trial wants my recommendation on whether Sammy would be a viable candidate."

My pulse spikes. AV719 is an experimental treatment

targeted to Sammy's particular CF mutation. Preliminary results have some folks already using the M-word, and a miracle is what my brother needs before his lung capacity gets much lower.

Hands clasped, I say, "You couldn't find a kid who deserves it more. And we'd make sure he followed every protocol to the letter."

"Of course you would. It's just a matter of far fewer slots than applicants. And he participated in the NSB-12 trial. But you know how highly I think of your whole family."

Does she still, after last night? "You would not be sorry if you backed him."

"Well, I'm only evaluating suitability. The final selection would still be random."

I've never cheated at school, but I can't help wondering how a person might rig the randomness of a drug trial. Theoretically.

Dr. Sternfield scans my form, but doesn't pick up a pen to sign it. She can't deny me credit because I bombed at the science finals. Can she?

Still not signing anything, she pulls her computer over so it sits between us. With languid movements, she opens a few files that I recognize as screenshots of DNA samples I worked on. Chromosomes she taught me to identify under a microscope. Chromosomes that happen to come from a blood sample she drew from me my first day on the project.

She pulls up image after image and uses the cursor to mark off specific sequences. "Remember that gene? It's partly responsible for that stunning blond hair of yours. And this one contributes to your silver-gray eyes."

I nod. Maybe this review is necessary for the college credit. A waste of time, but, if that's what it takes. She continues, pointing out this feature and that while I dig my toes into the Oriental carpet. And then she brings up a dozen images all at once. A few are genes I recognize, many more are not. She highlights a bit from each slide and turns to me with eyebrows raised.

"This is a combination of alleles that add up to a phenotype. Can you guess what it is?"

A test? Seriously? I rack my brain, but can't recall anything about this combination or even what all the components are. Hell, I'd fail this too. I stammer, "I d-d-don't know."

She leans toward me. "Sociability."

I squint. "But wouldn't that be affected by thousands of genes? And our environment?"

"Yes, but I believe this combination is key. Alter them appropriately and a person's Q factor would explode. You know what that is?"

Thanks to Evie, I have a clue. "A score they use to measure a celebrity's likeability and fame, right?"

"Good girl."

The impact of what she's saying hits me. "Wow. If you developed a therapy to boost that, people would line up for it."

Her eyes gleam. "Oh, yes they would."

I motion my head in the direction of the front gate. "You'd also piss off those people outside even more."

She grimaces. "Yes again."

I bite my lip. "The stuff I've read says tying genes to personality traits is too complex. They can only explain a tiny bit of how we act."

She stares at the images and gently traces a slender finger along a stretch of genetic code that happens to spell C-A-T. "Most people haven't been looking in the right places. I've done preliminary work that suggests it's very possible."

"Really? You never mentioned it."

She steeples her hands. "Why do you suppose that is?"

It only takes a nanosecond to answer, "Because it's ridiculously controversial. And you wouldn't be allowed to take it past animal trials anyway."

Her finger stabs an imaginary button in the air. "Bingo."

I gaze out of her window, onto the overcast June afternoon. On the lush lawn, I spot something brown and crumpled—a bird that's crashed against the pristine glass panes. Too bad gene therapy can't raise the dead.

I quickly look away. "Um, no offense, but if you're working on stuff this advanced, why not focus on diseases?"

"Who says I'm not? But so are a thousand other research-ers." Dr. Sternfield's eyes burn despite the rest of her cool demeanor. "However, I know firsthand how crippling a so-cial disorder can be. And you do too."

I swallow. "Is that why you're sharing this with me?"

She rests her arms on the desk and takes a long breath. "I want you to know there's hope, Aislyn."

Hope. I eye the computer again. "You think you'll really be able to do something about shyness someday? By altering genes?"

Her smile is conspiratorial. "Really. But for now, let's keep this between us, okay? The party line around here is disease only, especially with my father." Her dad, Dr. Gordon, is the president of Nova Genetics.

"Of course."

She picks up a pen and signs my form. "See you at the family event on Sunday?"

"Sure." I have what I came for, plus a bit more. But I still can't stop my eyes from wandering once more to the tiny heap of brown feathers in the grass outside before I leave her office.

Feeling privy to a secret, I head past the giant helix and into a day that's become darkly overcast. Thankfully, the threat of rain has scared off the protestors.

As I drive back to Tacoma, my thoughts float into the misty air settling over the highway. Imagine what life would be like if Dr. Sternfield were allowed to develop her research. I picture myself with Jack, face to non-blushing face.

My phone buzzes. I stiffen. Even if driver's ed never forced us to watch texting-while-driving carnage films, I'd have avoided answering. I know who it is. I know what she wants. I'll tell her I have to stay home tomorrow night after all.

I wipe my forehead as the phone buzzes a few more times. Evie won't give up that easily. If only Dr. Sternfield's research were ready now. If I go to Drew's party, it'll be a repeat of the last one Evie dragged me to, everyone else knowing how to act and what to say, while I stand at the edge clutching a plastic cup of something that's supposed to put me at ease.

I drive, wishing I could deal with my own damn shyness. I should be able to stuff some nurture down nature's throat and get beyond my DNA. People change. And then they write books about it. Why can't I?

As I park in front of our hedged-in yard on a typically soggy street in Tacoma, I heave a sigh. The way I always do when reaching my hideaway from the big, bad world. My sanctuary.

Which will only provide a safe harbor until my new job tomorrow.

Nova Genetics Internal E-mail

From: Dr. Charlotte Sternfield, Principal Investigator

To: Cecily Frank, Chief Security Officer

Effective immediately, please change the security access roster for Lab 6 on B2 to myself only. This includes primate caretakers and janitorial staff. I'll schedule with their departments to escort them into the lab as necessary.

THREE

The next morning, I wish I could stay in bed, hiding away. But I need to earn money. Now more than ever. Bonus, according to Evie, is that lifeguarding is far from shy-girl cliché employment such as filing assistant or data entry clerk, and provides opportunities for exposure therapy. Many, many opportunities.

Which is why I want to puke.

Sammy hammers at my door. "Aislyn!"

I rush to get it, alarmed by the sharpness of his voice. "Are you okay?"

"Mom said to wake you up so you aren't late and get fired."

Yeah, we all know how dismal my college fund is. With heavy movements, I dress. Outside, it's shaping up to be warm, which means opening day at the pool will be crowded. Great. On the drive over, my body trembles more and more violently the closer I get. Right about now, working in a stockroom or a cave sounds way more appealing.

Janie Simpson, the pool manager, meets me at the entrance and hands me my official whistle. "Remember your training. And don't be afraid to use this."

Wait, no warm-up time? As if that would help anyway. I stuff my things into a locker and head with Janie to my assigned station. At least it'll be a short shift, since swim classes don't start until Monday.

I climb the chair, which seems higher than it does from the ground. Okay, I can do this, keep an eye on swimmers, and whistle if there's a problem. Way less complicated than sequencing DNA.

Within minutes, I spot Asher Johnson and his buddy Zeke goofing around as they climb the water slide. Both of these boys tease Sammy for being the smallest kid in his grade. I grit my teeth, keeping an eye on them. Asher bounces at the top of the slide, staring at me, the hint of a grin flickering.

I swallow. Asher's friends on the sidelines dart glances between him and me. Shakily, I raise the whistle to my lips, just in case. Asher rests all of his weight on the arm rails so his feet swing an inch above the bright yellow slide. Back and forth, while he stares at me. Not doing anything I can flag, but clearly with trouble on his mind.

Then, in a flash, he plops his belly on the slide and whooshes down facefirst. The kids around us spring wild with glee. I squeeze up courage to get air from my lungs through my lips. *Breeeeep.*

Another whistle screeches and Janie Simpson yells, "Strike one."

But it's me, not Asher, she glares at, drawing the attention of all pool-goers my way. Uh-oh. The blood rushes to my face. I blink, trying to look anywhere but at Janie as she marches toward me.

She halts beneath the lifeguard chair. "I know you saw him, Aislyn."

I nod. "As soon as he went down, I whistled."

"Barely. Look, I'm sure you'd swim faster than lightning if someone were struggling in the water, but you need to step up if you see a potential problem. You're the first defense."

"I know. Sorry." There should be a tattoo on my forehead that says sorry.

She heaves a big breath and looks to heaven. "As much as your swim coach raved about you, I won't be able to let you work here if I can't rely upon you totally."

"I'll whistle louder next time."

With a theatrical sigh, she strides back to the club house.

Damn. My pulse races. I scan the pool, biting my lip. Everyone still stares.

The chair beneath me groans as I suffer through the rest of my watch, the knot in my stomach growing with the fear someone will slip on deck and crack a bone. Somehow the clock ticks forward to noon and I get a five-minute break before I have to start maintenance duty, a euphemism for collecting trash.

Instead of grabbing a soda with the other staff, I plunge into the emptiest corner of the deep end. A bolt of cool water rushes over my body, freezing my scalp in a way that makes me feel instantly clean. For the minute I'm submerged, my world is replaced with something bordering on calm, a break from the frequent sensation of drowning I feel on land. White noise fills my ears as I release gentle bubbles around my face. Everything within sight takes on a blunted, gentle edge no more threatening than cotton. I understand what drew my dad to water, even if his passion for it went too far.

I come up for air only as often as necessary and immediately return to my cocoon below. All too soon my five minutes are up and I climb back into the clanging world.

Weirdly, it turns out that stabbing at litter and stuffing it into bags is a relief after my time on the chair. Kind of Zen. I get into a garbage-picking rhythm.

Near the edge of the deck, Heath, who posted that awful picture of me at the science tournament, struts by with another lifeguard. They give me a slow once-over that has me blushing and gluing my eyes to the trash bag. Somehow I resist the powerful urge to drop everything and dive back into the pool.

As they head off, Heath says, "Yeah, she looks like all that, but she's a mute or something."

The other guy groans. "What a waste."

They laugh as I try to shrink my five-nine frame a foot or two. There must be a clever comeback, but even if I came up with one, it would just be filed away along with the thousands of other comebacks I've never used.

I finish my trash picking, wash up, and get trained on the snack-bar cash register. Fortunately, I'm paired with a chatty girl named Alicia who interacts with the customers as I fetch ice-cream cones and French fries.

At two o'clock, my work day's over. Even though it's been shorter than the shifts scheduled for next week, being around so many people has drained me of every last bit of energy. No time to recover, though. As I trudge to the parking lot, my phone buzzes with another text from Evie.

YOU WILL NOT USE SAMMY AS AN EXCUSE. SEE YOU AT 8.

Crap. She won't let up until I accept my fate. I drive off,

defeated. Maybe there'll be someplace to hide at Drew's house. If only he had a pool.

At home, Sammy's cough is a bit rattly as he gives me the once-over with those wise-beyond-his-years eyes. "Sucky day?"

I remind myself that sucky is taking twelve CF meds a day and probably needing a lung transplant before graduating high school. I say, "Just getting used to the new job."

If only I could tell him about the chance he'll be admitted into the pool of AV719 candidates. But I don't want to get his hopes up yet. When hope's your most precious commodity, you learn to treat it with care.

And fear.

Evie, fresh in a neon-green dress and matching headband, picks me up at eight p.m. As we get into her car, she says, "If you just relax, the party could be super-fun. And it's not like you have to worry about driving."

"Maybe I *should* drive. If we take separate cars, then—"

She revs the engine. "That's not environmental. If you need to leave early, use the code."

At the other two parties she forced me into this year, which earned major exposure therapy points, I hadn't resorted to the code, since I saw that as running away, and Evie knew it.

She tugs at her necklaces. "I should actually make you go more often. For the therapy to work."

"What if all you're exposing me to is an ulcer?" I pull an elastic band from my wrist.

She shoots out an arm to snatch the band from me. "How many times do I have to tell you? Girls with Rapunzel hair should flaunt it. Just like their impossibly toned bodies. That shirt bags on you."

I cross my arms. "It's comforting. Give me one small exception, okay?"

She sighs. "Aiz, if you really, really don't think you're up for it, I'll turn around and drop you off. But I really, really hope you'll get beyond this fear-of-the-world thing."

"*Thing?* It's not like I don't try. You of all people should—"

"I just don't want you to give up. Ever."

She's right. How will I be a successful advocate for kids like Sammy someday if I can't deal with talking to people? I need to suck it up.

If only my resolve could stop my bones from rattling. "Let's not stay long, okay?"

"Fair enough."

No, it isn't fair that a simple thing like going to a party makes my stomach so tight I skipped dinner, and still feel like throwing up.

The heavy bass of the song on the car radio pounds like a funeral march. I cross and re-cross my legs, hoping that'll ease my nerves in some acupressure-y way. It doesn't.

We park a block from Drew's house and run into kids laughing and shouting hundreds of feet before we reach the yard. Someone must've bribed the neighbors to sit through this. My insides drum, increasing in intensity the closer we get to ground zero.

Evie drags me by the arm through the front door, giving quick "heys" to the guys who swarm the entryway, rating all arrivals. She ignores their nods of approval and plows us through to the kitchen in less than a minute.

Before I can protest, she fills a red cup to the brim from a keg and hands it to me. "I know it's lame to rely on alcohol, but desperate times call for desperate measures. So drink up."

This must be how people become alcoholics. Trying to escape their personalities.

I guzzle down half the cup. "Enabler." That'll teach her to spew psychology crap on me all the time.

"Only enabling you to have a decent time." She tops off my cup and grabs a soda for herself. "Now let's mingle."

Does the English language have any two words more horrifying than *let's mingle*?

She pats my shoulder. "We'll start easy. There's Abby and the swim teammers."

We make our way to the sliding glass doors where they huddle. I talk to these girls at every practice, so they should fall into my "safe" territory. In theory. But something about parties—or nearly any kind of social gathering, for that matter—fills my belly with barbed wire. I gulp at my beer, arrange my facial muscles into what I hope is a smile, and gulp some more. My cup empties too soon. Evie seizes it and runs off for a refill even though I tell her not to. While she's gone, I pretend to keep up with the stories, the jokes, and the flirting with the boys who've joined us. But it's overwhelming and I feel the way I always do around a crowd—as if it's a living creature with a thousand limbs that move in sync to a rhythm I can't hear.

What is wrong with me?

When Evie returns I take another sip, hating myself for needing a crutch. Especially a stupid one. Exposure, smexposure.

Evie's shoulders abruptly pull back and her body goes on full alert. I follow her gaze to the foyer, where Rafe Sellers, a tall guy with shoulder-length black hair and the promise of a UCLA soccer scholarship, has arrived.

I tug her sleeve. "It's okay if you go talk to him." She's not the only one who can push a best friend toward progress.

She bites her lip, reminding me that much of her bravado is an act of willpower learned as a little girl, when our classmates would tease about her family eating chicken feet. Back then, she hid in corners too, but, over the years, she ventured out and has been dragging me along ever since.

She says, "Eventually, he might come over this way."

He probably would. Evie and Rafe have been flirting for months, even though they haven't taken things further. Which makes him brain dead as far as I'm concerned. What guy wouldn't be crazy about my amazing, gorgeous friend?

I will not be the one to spoil her fun. "Go. I'll be fine here, really." I take another swig of beer to prove it.

"You sure?"

I wipe the corner of my mouth. "If I change my mind, I've got the code, and I'm not afraid to use it."

She nods to herself, still unsure, despite the invisible tether that pulls her toward the kitchen, where Rafe and his buddies disappear.

I push her gently. "Now who's chickening out?"

She takes a deep breath and flutters off. I turn to the folks around me and try to think of something to add to their conversation about naked bicycle riders at the solstice parade. But, really, what can I say, besides maybe suggesting strategically placed talcum powder?

I sip, nod, and check my phone. We've only been here for twenty-five minutes? I burp. Hmm, better slow down on the beer.

Abby O'Keefe, twirling a red curl around her finger, asks me about working at the pool. I open my mouth to respond, and that's when I catch sight of the latest party arrivals. My breath hiccups. Jack is here.

Abby laughs. "Wow, you've got it bad."

I stand there, unable to form a rational response. Somehow, I blocked the possibility Jack would be here too. Which was stupid. Or denial. I'm a pro in that department. For years I held on to the pathetic belief that Dad didn't really die in a diving accident; it was all a massive mistake.

Abby's face gets serious. "I'm going to help you." She waves toward Jack. What is it about me that launches my friends into pimp mode?

Finally, I get a word out. "No." As much as I like Jack, when actually confronted with the real live version, all of my systems scream, "Hide!" But my protest is too late. He heads our way, his gaze locked on mine. All I can do is hope my eyes aren't too glassy and that I'm not blushing too hard. More denial.

As he approaches, I'd swear he gives me a lightning-quick head-to-toe appraisal. Only fair, since I do the same to him, taking in his slightly damp blond hair, blue-blue eyes, and swimmer's build. He leads the guys' team in butterfly.

His features soften into a slow smile. "Aislyn, you came."

"Yeah." Deep breath, get words out of mouth. "Evie forced me to."

"I hoped she would."

"Um, yeah." I swallow a beer burp. Why is this so hard? Jack and I have what pass for interesting conversations online, and we've e-mailed a zillion times about submissions for *The Drizzle*. But now, no matter how much I will my heart and lungs to slow down, my knees to hold up, and my brain to focus, my body resists on all counts.

I say, "Um, congrats on the science competition."

"I thought for sure you'd win. Your stuff is always way beyond the rest of ours." He pulls at his shirt. "This place is crazy hot."

I resist the urge to tell him exactly what, or who, is crazy hot, and point toward the glass door like a robot.

"Good idea." He opens it, letting in the evening breeze.

Ah, that's delicious against my burning face. A few minutes of this and I could cool down enough to avoid fainting or puking. With major luck.

He starts through the door. "You coming?"

Oh, no, he wants me to go outside with him. Actually make these feet move.

There's a hand at my back. Abby says, "Way to work fast," and gives me a push.

I stumble outside behind Jack. About twenty kids hang around the yard, but Jack's able to find a couple of deck chairs. It's a relief to get off of my feet, which I don't trust to support me anyway. My belly is the next body part to fail me, turning all quivery with the thought that here I am with the object of all my—well, with Jack. I take a deep breath. God, I want to cry. Just break down and let all my anxiety out in a gushing torrent of tears. No one would ever expect me to do any kind of exposure therapy ever again.

He points to my cup. "What's in there?"

I peek inside as if I don't know. "Um, beer. There's a keg in the kitchen." I'm slurring. Great, I've finally gotten out two complete sentences and I sound drunk.

He shrugs. "Maybe later."

Guys like him don't need liquid bravery, which makes me feel more pitiful. Stop, stop, think of something to say, like a normal person would. I ask, "So you start at the radio station next week?" He scored an internship that would look great on his college app, along with dozens of other accomplishments.

"Yeah, Kids Eat Free is coming for an interview on my first day."

I shake my head. "I can't imagine doing something so… so public."

Jack shrugs those smoothly muscled shoulders that make a wide V down to his waist. "Goes with the territory."

"Still, always having to be so *on*." Oh no, a bead of sweat rolls down my face. Probably the first drop in the tsunami of misery I expect to melt into at any moment.

He laughs. "You make it sound like shoveling elephant dung."

Oh, now he thinks I'm insulting the band. "No, no, they're great. Just like you. You're always great." I blink rapidly and put a hand to my head, partly to steady my vision, partly to wipe away another drip along my temple.

He cocks his head and gives me that look he often does, which makes me feel so *seen*. Usually it causes a combination of thrill and terror, but tonight I'd rather be as unseen as possible. "Can I get you something?" he says.

"No, I'm okay. Just a little dizzy. Not used to so much beer." I stand up and lean toward a bush to dump out the rest of my cup, but stumble and spill it on his foot instead.

"Oh, God, I'm so sorry!"

He jumps up. "I'll get you some water. That'll help."

He rushes off toward the kitchen. At that moment, my belly lurches and I feel an overwhelming urge to escape from all the kids who suddenly glare my way. I remember seeing a bathroom off the entryway. Now, if I could just walk without falling over. I try. My legs are almost steady now that Jack isn't around. I make my way inside, and push through the crowd to the bathroom. But it's locked. No!

I chant under my breath, *Do not barf. Do not faint.* The seconds tick endlessly. Jack's probably back with my water. I should run and tell him I need to go home, that I'm sick, yeah, that wouldn't be hard to convince him of. My stomach cramps. Nope, not running anywhere.

Finally, the bathroom opens and out pop Jessica and Caleb. I scurry past them, slam the door, and pant as I lean on the sink to hold me up.

With shaky movements, I wipe my brow with a damp tissue. And then I make the mistake of looking in the mirror. My red-rimmed eyes glare in pain and my mouth opens and shuts repeatedly like a fish. I put a hand under my chin to stop my jaw, but it seems to fight against it. I clasp my mouth, trying to keep it shut, to avoid breathing in any more of this, this, whatever craziness this is. My eyes bulge with pressure. My head goes light. Is this when I'll completely snap with the inner turmoil that builds up every single day, from when my first conscious sensation is a bolt of fear straight through my chest? My existence is a constant struggle against the world. And now, here I am at a party, a *party,* with way too much alcohol flooding my system.

I let go of my jaw and clutch the sink with both hands. That's when the tears, mucus, and muck I've been holding in decide to explode. It's also when someone knocks at the door.

"Just a minute," I choke out.

I spend the next five minutes sobbing, trying to wipe myself up as best I can. When the knocking becomes too insistent, I splash my face, dry it off, and stagger out the door.

A girl I remember from freshman gym class pushes past me. "Bitch."

Her hostility threatens to start me crying again. Holding back tears, I make my way toward the patio.

But Jack isn't there. Or anywhere in the backyard. I slowly spin around, peering into the dark. Suddenly, a flurry of raindrops begins hitting like missiles, sending everyone rushing for the house. I join the herd. Inside, I hunt through the crammed living room, but Jack isn't there either. I hold my hands over my ears against sharp techno music that's turned up so loud the walls echo. It isn't until I reach the kitchen, where the crowd is densest, that I spot him in the far corner, laughing as if he's never heard anything so funny. At his side giggles Alexandra, editor of the school paper. Her magazine-worthy face sparkles as they engage in a high-octane tête-à-tête.

My heart does a free fall. Of course he's with Alexandra. Why has it taken my straight-A brain so long to figure it out? She and Jack are perfect for each other. Both of them seriously into writing, both naturally gorgeous, and, as much as I hate to admit it, both really sweet. I might be jealous of Alexandra's easy confidence, but she isn't one of the mean girls, not by a long shot. Which only makes me feel worse.

In that moment, the noise and motion swirl around as if I'm at the center of a vortex, being sucked into a black hole.

My breathing quickens and I feel sick to my stomach. *Don't run, don't run, don't run.* I don't have to shine, but I can't let myself flee. That's the promise to myself I have to keep.

The ghost of my tantrum in the bathroom tugs at my brain, begging to be let out again after its taste of wailing and gnashing. Trembling, I back into the living room until I spot Evie on the sofa next to Rafe, in deep conversation. Well, she is. He stares intently at her chest.

My legs seem to move of their own accord in Evie's direction. I know I should stop. Look how happy she is. But it's a choice between yielding to my legs or to the harrowing need in my chest to scream at the world. Maybe a few minutes in Evie's company will calm me down.

I sidle next to her, hating myself when she forces a smile at my miserable self. Her whole body, her whole spirit is aimed at Rafe, and I'm in the way. I should go back to the swim team girls, or the bathroom, or the kitchen. No, not the kitchen. But also not here, ruining Evie's chance. Yet my brain and body feel as if they'll lose all control at any moment.

My mouth blurts, "Cap'n Crunch." Those two small words unleash a rush of guilt and self-loathing. I want desperately to unsay them. But I can't stay in this house a second longer without imploding, or exploding, whichever is messier.

Evie's sagging shoulders make me feel like I've kicked

over a baby carriage. With a hesitant blink, she asks, "Are you sure?"

Oh hell, how can I do this? Just because I'm teetering on the edge of a cliff doesn't mean I need to destroy her night too. Barely able to meet her eye, I mumble, "If you give me your keys, I'll wait in the car until you're ready to leave. No hurry. Really."

She nods and hands me the keys. I rush out the door and into the rain. Why didn't I bring a jacket? Because I'm hopeless. My head pounding, I jog and then run down the block with my arms wrapped around myself. The rain pelts me, but I no longer care.

A sob wracks my chest and I moan into the night. This is it. I've let myself flee. Finally. There's a certain liberty in giving up that last shred of defiance against my affliction. Yet there's also a choking despair.

I keep running, past Evie's car, onto the next block, vaguely in the direction of home. The rain soaks through my clothes and runs down my scalp, mixing with my tears. When I can't run any longer, I march, shoulders hunched forward, chest heaving. There's no telling how long I've been crying when a car slows down beside me. My first thought is that this horrible night will be capped by a serial killer yanking me into his van.

But Evie leans out the window and screams, "Aislyn! Are you nuts?"

I halt, speechless. She's never, ever implied I was crazy. And now she's done so in front of Rafe, who's in the driver's seat and keeps his head pointed forward.

I wipe a hand across my face. "I said you didn't have to go."

"I wasn't going to leave my best friend sulking in my car. But when I got there, you were gone. Now get inside and we'll take you home."

What else can I do? I get inside and hand Evie her keys over the seat. "Sorry."

"We can still go back. No big deal."

My heart spasms in the second it takes to realize the "we" she's referring to includes Rafe, not me. I'm relieved not to go back to the party, but her sudden shift in allegiance jars me. Thankfully, she doesn't press for details. There's that much loyalty at least.

At my house, she insists everything'll be okay in the way you'd assure a terminal patient. I make my way to the front porch. The tipsiness from earlier has morphed into full-on exhaustion. I run a hand through my hair and blot my face with the inside of my shirt. Quietly, I open the door.

But Mom's fast asleep on the sofa, her blond hair a few shades darker than mine flapped over her cheek, computer on her lap. I stifle a groan when I see she's been checking out part-time job listings. To make up for my lost prize money, of course. There aren't any more hours in the day for her to work. Would Dad have taken the chance at his stupid free-diving if he'd known what an impossible life he'd leave her with?

Shivering, I gently lay an afghan over Mom's bony shoulders. Somehow I'll find a way to pay for college. I have to. But the heavy knowledge that I succumbed to the urge to flee tonight has me doubting whether I can follow through on anything ever again.

Upstairs, Sammy's cough has a hard edge to it that's different from his normal cough. Like bird watchers who learn to identify every warble, Mom and I are always alert for signs of lung infection. We'll need to take his temp in the morning. For now, it's best he gets all the sleep he can manage. Me too.

Once I'm tucked under my blankets, my quiet room feels safe, as if I've escaped a hurricane. But it also feels isolated, like I'm missing out on something.

I fall asleep with a deep sadness. Now that I've let myself escape once, what's to stop me from escaping everything? I sense a foreboding that my fear of the world is spiraling faster downward, past a point of no return.

Major Pharmaceutical Seeks to Block New Drug
by Harrison Makitani, *Pharma Today*

VidaLexor, one of the world's leading drug developers, is seeking to block the patent pending by Nova Genetics for a new gene therapy to treat muscular dystrophy. Dr. Geoff Gordon, owner and director of Nova Genetics, claims, "Tragically, opponents of our breakthrough drugs are motivated by profit rather than patients. There's a massive paradigm shift occurring in medicine. One that asks why we'd subject patients to a lifetime of medication when a one-time fix will do. Gene therapy's time has come."

Dr. Linda Galleon, CEO of VidaLexor, counters, "Those who are truly concerned with patient safety will demand extensive testing for drugs that could prove more lethal than the diseases they're trying to cure."

FOUR

On Sunday morning, my phone buzzes me awake with a text from Evie: OFF SAILING. GOTTA TALK THE SECOND I GET BACK!

She probably wants to rehash last night and figure out a way to "fix" things. Fix *me,* if that were possible. Well, no need to discuss that in agonizing detail right away. Her family would be on their boat all day. Head throbbing, I wobble to Sammy's room, where Mom's doing his morning back-pounding.

I slump into a chair. "His cough was sharper last night."

Sammy's voice vibrates from the thumps. "My temp's normal, so we're all systems go for today, unless you find an excuse to get out of this."

I shake my head. "Give me a break, Sammy. You know

I want us to go." And I do. Kind of. Since people with CF are advised to keep their distance from each other to avoid cross-infection, Sammy's only slated for a Nova Genetics Family Fest a couple of times a year. Even then, the CF kids in attendance will be assigned to different groups.

Mom has the last word, and, after taking his temperature three times and watching him closely over breakfast, she declares he's okay for heading out. Sammy's face flushes with relief.

On the way to Nova Genetics, he sings along with Mom to an old grunge song, and motions to me. "Sing with us!"

Disappointment fills his eyes even before I shake my head. I never join the singing, which usually causes Sammy and Mom to howl all the louder and me to feel like the odd one out.

We park at Nova Genetics, where thankfully the protesters are off to the side, supervised by extra security brought in for the event. Once we're on foot, a guard checks our credentials and lets us through to the immaculate campus. Flocks of seagulls fly overhead and dozens of lookout points offer views of the water. It should feel serene, but something about the place strikes me as too quiet, like being in school after hours.

We've barely entered the grounds when Sammy's friend Bailey limps up, her family surrounding her. She has muscular dystrophy, and even though hugging isn't encouraged here, she puts her thin arms around Sammy and squeezes.

I take a breath, readying myself for the day ahead, which will probably include sharing-your-feelings exercises that'll leave me more exhausted than hours spent rolling boulders. Unless I run away. That's what I do now, after all.

Bailey's sister, Chloe, a curvy girl with long brown hair, who's a year older than me and the person Nova assigned as my "support buddy" years ago, says "Hey, Aislyn" as she applies lip gloss. Something about her strikes me as brighter, making the full, glossy lips seem like too much glitz. She's probably fallen in love with Mr. Right 3.0.

Sally Sims, Nova Genetics' perky, petite outreach coordinator, welcomes us with an excited laugh. "Hey, you guys!" She nudges Chloe. "That was sweet of you to bring in Bailey's paperwork the other week."

Chloe shrugs. "No big deal. There's always something fun going on here."

Sally says to Chloe and me, "You girls need to meet our newest sibs group member, Shane." She points toward a tall guy with curly black hair to his chin, who yawns next to a girl in her late teens with a wide smile and elfin features. Williams Syndrome, I'd bet.

Sally puts her arm around Chloe's shoulder and leans in toward us. "You guys get to head off with Joe Firelli for some clam digging."

Chloe's mouth twists. "Why isn't Steffie going with us?"

Steffie Wong is in charge of lab animals at Nova Genetics, and therefore viewed as the perfect staff member to hang with the teens for the "party" events.

Sally sighs. "Steffie's out sick. But it should be a lovely day on the spit."

Well, at least it should be way better than gathering in a circle in one of the conference rooms and opening up about our families' challenges.

I shuffle next to Chloe and a girl named Rosa with huge brown eyes and thick shiny hair, who always seems as shy as me at the meetings. Or maybe it's because English is her second language. We smile at each other, which pretty much completes our interaction for the day.

After Sally Sims passes out BPA-free water bottles, twenty teens hike toward a beach just beyond Nova Genetics' grounds. As we haul our buckets of clam-digging gear, Joe Firelli, who normally works as a therapist, provides a mini-lecture on geoducks, which sounds like something he memorized off of Wikipedia. Every Puget Sounder could tell you that geoducks are clams, not waterfowl. And thanks to honors biology, I can map the species from family to phylum.

The siblings group spreads out to hunt for the geoducks' distinctive siphons, which look like leathery infinity signs. Although I'm afraid Chloe will go off with the guys, she ends up hunting with me. That's a relief. We've seen enough of each other over the years for me to be myself around her, such as myself is.

"Over here," I call, and press a thirty-inch-diameter section of tubing into the sand before digging within the plastic barrier.

She brushes back her dark curls. "Take your time; the poor little guy isn't going anywhere. May as well let it enjoy its last minutes."

I sigh. "I thought you gave up the vegan thing." Chloe takes on causes the way other girls collect shoes.

"I still respect the clam's existence."

My shovel halts. "You want to go wading instead?"

Chloe sniffs. "Nah. Circle of life and all that."

We take turns with the shovel and chat. Even though Chloe and I keep in touch online, we go through a recap of life since the last NG event. She's acquired a new jock boyfriend named Jesse, which explains her glow, and I got over 2200 on my SAT. Same-old, same-old. And yet it's not. After last night's fiasco, my life has sunk another notch, maybe the notch that places me too low to climb back up.

I switch from the shovel to a trowel and slowly uncover most of the clam's creamy-beige neck, which resembles an elephant's trunk.

Chloe wipes her tanned forehead with the back of her arm. "Looks like a dildo."

I scoop up some sand. "Okay, my knowledge of the male anatomy is more theoretical than actual, but this is over a foot long."

She smiles as if privy to some secret.

My phone buzzes in my pocket. I glance at my sand-encrusted hands.

Chloe says, "You can survive without a status report from your friends." Her expression is haughty, as if now that she's graduated from high school, she's eons more sophisticated than me in every way—which, okay, doesn't take much.

I stab at the rocky sand. "Yeah, well, if we hear Mr. Quarterback's ringtone, I bet you'll find a way to answer."

"He's a halfback, and I told him not to call again until tonight."

"Is that why you keep checking out the new guy, Shane?"

She laughs. "He's totally hot, but I'm not a cheater. Is he making Aizzie all sweaty?"

"I'm kind of interested in someone else." Then I remember last night and sigh.

I catch a look from Shane nearby. Did he hear what we were talking about? I shovel faster.

Chloe slaps at my arm. "Watch what you're doing."

I look down to find that I've hit the geoduck's shell. Leaning into the hole, I dig by hand. Chloe wrinkles her nose as if I'm clubbing seals.

When we've harvested our prey, I wipe my hands on a rag and pull out my phone. The text is from Evie: CAN'T WAIT ANY LONGER TO TELL YOU--RAFE AND I HOOKED UP! LOTS MORE TO TALK ABOUT!

I'm happy for her, but also, I hate to admit, a little sad. The whole odd-man-out thing again. I take a swig of water, shuddering as the events of the party replay themselves in my brain.

A few minutes later, I'm ready to resume the hunt, but a few guys from the group have glommed onto Chloe. She usually gets her share of male attention, but today it's cranked up a few notches. Something about a girl who's "taken" must send out major pheromones. Evie will enjoy that phenomenon now.

Well, I can dig alone. Alone is what I do best, after all. Me and my pheromoneless self.

I slog to where I think I see movement in the sand. But by the time I reach it, the ground's only dimpled.

"There's one," a voice behind me says.

I spin around to find Shane, in all his tall dark hotness, pointing to a spot a few feet to my left. Having a cute guy nearby, hell, *any* guy nearby, is all the cue my circulatory system needs to betray me. Crap. Maybe I'll get a break and he'll interpret my pink cheeks for sunburn.

I choke out, "You found it; it's yours."

"I've already got my limit of fresh meat." He grins expectantly.

"Well, um, thanks." I call to Chloe, but she ignores me. Is she actually going to leave me here alone with a guy I don't know? A familiar queasiness builds in my gut.

"I'll help you." Shane jogs to where Chloe left the tube. If only he'd stay there.

I take deep breaths, doing what I can to calm the panic.

When he returns, he says, "Want to shovel first? You look like you want to attack something."

I stare at him, searching for signs of mockery. Did Chloe bribe him to hang out with me? No way am I digging for geoducks with him while her dildo comment lingers fresh in my brain.

I clear my throat. "Actually, uh, I'm going to cool off for a bit. Thanks, anyway." Without waiting for him to answer or for myself to debate whether this counts as running away, I slip out of my sandals and jog along the rocky sand to the water's edge. Ouch, ouch, ouch. Finally, I reach the water. Whew. Breathe. Calm down. He's not Jack. And not somebody I'll see often, maybe never if I'm lucky. Not that I should count on luck.

The tide's coming back in and provides a soothing cushion against my feet, cold enough to numb them. If only I could eliminate every other feeling from my body too. My eyes track an eagle soaring overhead before it disappears into the surrounding trees. I wade in up to my knees and close my eyes. The waves lap against my legs without a sound, and my stomach begins to settle. I could almost forget—

"So, how long did it take to perfect the bitchy blow-off?"

I jump a few inches and turn to see that Shane's followed me. When I catch my breath, I say, "Look, I'm sorry. I'm just not feeling that great."

"Oh, so excuse B is fake cramps?"

Why is he hounding me? I blink at him, unsure of what to say, tears welling in my eyes, which he'll probably claim is another excuse or bitchy drama.

Instead he shifts gears. "Chloe says you practically live here. What a pain."

I swallow. "It's for my brother."

He runs a hand through his thick hair. "I don't think my sister cares. But my mom said she'd spring for a week of gas money if I came today."

I wrap my arms around my torso. "So it's win-win."

"Win-win, eh? Even with the digging for weird clams?"

I dip my hands in the water. A tendril of seaweed slips through my fingers. "The digging's not so bad, just a little sandy."

He licks his lips. "I like a girl who's not afraid to get dirty."

I eye him. Is that some kind of sexual crack? I should walk away again. That seems rude, but so is following someone around when she clearly isn't comfortable with it.

But I say, "Yeah, well." My thoughts stop there. Argh. I'm so bad at this, whatever *this* is.

He motions toward the beach. "So, you feel like digging before they haul us back inside?"

I glance around. Chloe and her followers have disappeared around the bluff. "Not really." Can't he leave me to my socially dysfunctional self?

He examines me in a way that feels hostile. "You know, girls who think they're worth extra effort usually aren't." Without waiting for my reply, not that I have one, he hikes off, kicking sand in front of himself.

What an ass. How dare he assume anything about me? I turn back toward the sound and wade up to my thighs. But even the water can't soothe the knot in my throat or the hammering in my chest.

By the time Joe Firelli rounds us up, my legs are stiff from the cold. I limp across the beach. Chloe appears out of nowhere, flushed and smiling, three guys in her wake. Shane sneers my way and says something under his breath to the guy next to him.

Joe bounces from bucket to bucket, examining our catch

and clapping. "Wonderful work! Let's get these back to the cafeteria for our chefs to prepare." Maybe they don't let him out of the counseling suite often enough.

We hike back toward Nova Genetics, and Joe leads us into an entrance near the kitchen to deposit the clams and wash up. "After lunch, we'll meet in the conference room for a quick session."

My heart sinks to my belly. Those sessions, where everyone's expected to contribute, slay me. Would anyone notice if I hid behind the tie-dye booth and took a nap until the "fun" day was over?

Chloe sidles up to me, all dimply. "You and Shane looked cute together."

"Your powers of observation need serious work. Why did you set me up?"

She seems startled. "I didn't, really. He just wanted to talk to you. No big deal."

I look away. By now she should know that it *is* a big deal. It shouldn't be, but it is.

She taps my arm. "I'll make it up to you, okay? When we have the stupid meeting later, I'll blab so much you won't have to take a turn sharing. That'll even us up, right?"

"I guess." I don't ask why she thinks we need to even up if she didn't sic Shane on me.

As we return to the main pavilion, I notice Dr. Sternfield

chatting with Rosa, who nods and bites her lip. Is she letting Rosa in on her newest research? A bolt of jealousy shoots through me. I start toward them.

But Sammy heads me off. He giggles and is joined by Dr. Gordon, aka Dr. Sternfield's dad and Nova Genetics' director. He stands almost twice Sammy's height and has shoulders that could probably bust through concrete, but his sandy hair and round tinted glasses make him resemble a giant koala bear.

He greets us by name with a warm hello. "How was the dig, girls?"

"Great," Chloe lies. "Except for the clams, but I'm sure they're in geoduck heaven."

He chuckles. "Charlie used to love harvesting her own clams. Did she join you?"

I can't imagine Dr. Sternfield pawing through the sand dressed in one of her impeccable outfits. "Not today."

"My girl, the workaholic." He shakes his head with pride.

Sammy launches into a fit of coughing that we wait with averted eyes for him to complete. But it keeps going. I pat his back, which feels warm through his T-shirt. His face is damp from the exertion and he pulls a tissue from his pocket.

I say, "Let's sit, huh? You feel hot."

He chokes out, "I'm okay."

Mom's already spotted us and hurries over. I sigh. Sammy

hates a commotion on his behalf. Within minutes, Mom and Dr. Gordon take him off to one of Nova Genetics' doctors for a look-see. Sammy's eyes are miserable as he's hauled away, coughing. If only it could be me enduring some of this on his behalf.

Before anyone else's mood dives into somberness, Sally Sims bounces among the crowd in her dainty flats, calling out, "We've got a scrumptious lunch for everyone."

I've feasted here often enough to guess that the buffet will include fresh crab legs and truffle risotto. Hopefully, Sammy'll finish up with the doctor soon. I scan for Chloe, but she's deep in conversation with Shane, probably telling him what a misfit I am and not to take it personally. Great, I'll have to eat alone. Not that I have much appetite. Shoulders slumped, I follow the crowd.

Near the door, I'm overtaken by a waft of jasmine cologne from behind. I whip around to find Dr. Sternfield at my side. She's dressed all in white, from her silk hairband to her shiny pumps. In that instant, a beam of sunshine flares through the large window above, lighting her up like a modern-day fairy godmother.

And, oh, do I have wishes.

Gene Doping—The End of Competitive Sports?
Or the Beginning of a Whole New Game?
by Lance Starkman, *US Sports and Leisure*

The rapid muscle gain by college senior Will Williams, starting linebacker for the Warriors football team, has opposing teams up in arms. Williams insists his fifty-pound gain in the past year is due to an intense weight-lifting regimen, high-protein diet, and "good old-fashioned growth spurt." Others point a finger to the new science of gene doping, where altered DNA is injected into an athlete's body to increase athletic performance by stimulating pain tolerance, muscle growth, and endurance.

The International Council on Sportsmanship is developing a blood test to detect altered genes. Dr. Sampson Vogler states, "Artificially introduced DNA lacks certain sequences found in naturally occurring DNA. We know where to look and we know what to look for. This test should be included in our arsenal before the end of the year."

So far, science may be able to catch up with cheaters. But others believe it's only a matter of time before those seeking to circumvent the testing process develop transgenic genes that don't include the telltale signs of manipulation. Like the perfect counterfeit currency, undetectable fakes stand to make a fortune.

FIVE

Unlike the other staff who've traded their work clothes for jeans and knit shirts today, Dr. Sternfield wears a simple linen dress with a lab coat. Yet, for the first time I can recall, her reddish-brown hair hangs loose to her shoulders beneath the hairband. She leans toward me. "Hello, Aislyn. How hungry are you?"

"Um, not very."

"Care for a visit with our long-armed friends?"

As if I'd ever say no to playing with the chimps. "Sure."

She leads us down a quiet corridor away from the cafeteria. "What a relief to get away from paperwork for a day."

I know I should make nice before getting to business, but I can't stop myself from saying, "So is Sammy a, um, viable candidate?"

She winks. "Well, I can't provide any details just yet, but the guidelines do provide a fair amount of room for discretion."

"Thanks so much for whatever you do. It would mean everything to us."

I expect to head outside to the geodesic cages, where the chimps normally play, but Dr. Sternfield waits at an unmarked elevator that requires a key. We go down two floors where the AC is on full blast, and then through a winding passageway to an area I haven't visited before. When we reach a heavy door, she raises her eye to a retinal scanner and punches in a code. No other lab I've seen here requires this much security.

The room inside glows with full spectrum lighting, but I still get a claustrophobic shudder. This room is even colder than the hallway, and smells like rubbing alcohol.

We stroll past cages to one with a sign that reads RUBY. She's my favorite chimp, and Steffie, her caretaker, used to let me feed her when she was a baby. Even though Ruby should be used to humans, she still hides if the voices around her get too loud. I can relate.

We stop at her cage. Ruby scuttles our way, and puts out a knobby hand as if she wants us to shake it. That's a first. Dr. Sternfield laughs and pats her long fingers. I'd swear Ruby smiles before she does a little twirl.

Dr. Sternfield leans toward me and even though no one else is nearby, she whispers, "Charisma."

"She totally has that. But how did you train her?"

She scratches Ruby's head. "Train? I don't think you understand. I gave her the therapy I told you about, for sociability. Charisma, or CZ88, if you prefer the official name."

Blood rushes to my head so fast I wobble. "What? You already have a treatment? I thought you were only doing a study."

Her eyes gleam. "Well, I need to be careful with how much I say to whom. But I've got a strong vibe about your trustworthiness, Aislyn. Anyway, I've been working on this since med school. The chimps are my second mammal test. The first group included the most charming rats you'd ever hope to meet."

A pounding picks up in my chest. "Wow. Wow." I let Ruby take my hand through the bars. "She's so friendly. How many chimps have you tested it on?"

"Five. It's like a primate party in here sometimes."

"I'll bet Steffie loves that."

Dr. Sternfield's eyes flash for a moment before she smiles. "Yeah, she's been enjoying herself."

I watch Ruby, who appears to be dancing. "She seems really happy. Can you measure that?"

Dr. Sternfield purses her lips. "That's subjective to assess in humans, much less animals. But we can measure stress. And Ruby's levels of norepinephrine, cortisol, and adrenaline have decreased significantly."

It wouldn't take a blood test to prove my stress hormones were off the charts at the party, despite the beer. What's my normal happiness level? When I chat with Jack online, my levels float upward for sure. But now? Low, abysmally low.

Dr. Sternfield continues, "No matter how happy the chimps are, there's a huge gap between making the jump from animal trials to human clinical trials. You know what they call that gap in the R and D business? The Valley of Death. Where perfectly good projects meet an untimely end."

She's used the term before, but never has it caused me such a pang of disappointment. "You can't let this project die. It could be so amazing."

Her smile is rueful. "I know. Believe me. Yet amazing won't be enough to get it approved via official channels any time soon. My father's adamant that Nova Genetics only targets diseases, the more life-threatening, the better."

I say in a low voice, "Sometimes I think feeling like this is worse than a disease."

She sighs. "I understand, Aislyn. And by the time the world catches up on gene enhancement, I'll probably be ready for a walker."

My breathing hitches. "So you aren't going to test it on

humans any time soon?" A fresh batch of tears brews behind my eyes, even though I'm sure I used up my quota last night.

Her face goes steely and she grinds the toe of her pump into the white tile floor. "It's ridiculous. Can you imagine how many people crippled by shyness and social phobia I could help?"

"It would be life-changing."

She gives me an appraising look. "I've seen the questionnaires you filled out for the family dynamics study. How you ache to speak up so badly, to be heard, but at the same time are terrified to. When I started college at fourteen, I was the tiniest kid in the room, with the squeakiest voice, unable to raise my hand even though I knew all the answers."

I know all about keeping my hand down. About what it's like to keep your spirit trapped at ground level. "It's hard to believe gene therapy could make someone braver."

She purses her lips. "Well, personality *is* terribly complex. Charisma, or CZ88, targets multiple genes that work in harmony, DNA that might be dismissed by other researchers. But one scientist's trash is another's treasure."

I can't picture genes as tiny packets of trash or treasure, but Dr. Sternfield never shies away from colorful descriptions. One of the first explanations she gave me of how gene therapy works was to imagine the viral vector as a shipping box addressed to specific tissues in the body. Inside the box was altered DNA that could take the place of faulty genes or instruct them to behave differently. The virus could hold so much DNA before ripping apart, but if you had too little DNA in it, you'd need to include stuffer DNA, like packing peanuts.

I kick at the tile, mirroring Dr. Sternfield. "If you were able to get approval, how long before you had something you could test in humans?"

She cocks her head and stares at me for a long moment. "It's ready now."

My vision goes blurry. "As in *today* now?"

"Today now," she says with as much of a grin as she'll allow.

I shiver. "And it's safe?"

She bristles. "I've tested drugs for years, with a stellar safety record." She exhales loudly. "But no matter how safe I know Charisma to be, the FDA will prevent this from going to clinical trials. Which is why my days at Nova Genetics are numbered."

A surge of panic races through me. My voice squeaks out, "What?"

"I've got to go where I can help the most people. Right now, that's not the US."

No, this can't be happening. To get so close to a dream, and have it snatched away before I could grab it. Without thinking of what's coming out of my mouth, I say, "What if you performed a pre-trial before you left? On someone who really needs it?"

Her brow furrows. "Are you proposing what I think you are?"

I don't know. Am I?

She says, "It's okay to say no. Not everyone is up to making monumental changes in their lives."

She's actually offering it to me. Well, what better guinea pig than someone whose life is a monumental disaster? "When would I have to decide and get the paperwork in?"

She shakes her head. "I'm afraid there isn't the luxury of a long decision. Or paperwork. But if you're serious about improving your life, I could help you today, as in *today* today."

My insides freeze. "Don't you need to track things so you can publish your findings?"

She reaches into Ruby's cage to stroke her head. "Here I thought we were on the same page, damn the official channels. By the time you come back for the next family meeting, I'll have moved on."

The walls around me seem to hum, or maybe that's my veins throbbing. I rub at my temples. "Sorry. I'm just getting used to the idea. Doing things in secret could get you into a lot of trouble, couldn't it?"

"Only if people found out. But I trust you, Aislyn. And

I want to help you and others *now*. Just like I want to help Sammy get into the AV719 trial even though he's had more infections and exhibits less lung capacity than the average eleven-year-old with CF. The business interests behind that trial want kids who have the best chance of improving, to yield the highest success rate."

The panic I felt a moment earlier over losing out on a miracle drug doubles when it comes to Sammy losing out. "That's so unfair. They should help those who need it most."

She puts her hands on my shoulders, the first time she's ever touched me beyond a handshake. I feel her fingernails through my sleeves. "I'm willing to support him, even if that means not adhering so strictly to black-and-white regulations. Are you with me, Aislyn?"

Everything around me seems blurry, except her eyes, which shine like crystals. I say, "If I agree, how would I take it?"

"An injection, clean and simple. Probably only one dose, but no guarantees. We don't know how quickly the viral vector that delivers the treatment will propagate and how much of your DNA will be affected. Of course, you would be in total control of whether you received any further doses."

Next to us, Ruby rocks on the floor and seems content in a way I've never felt. I contemplate. "Can I talk to my mom? She'd keep this quiet since her kids are more important than any regulations."

Dr. Sternfield drops her hands from my shoulders. "Wow, I thought with your IQ— Look, let's forget the whole thing, okay?" Brushing her palms against each other as if they're dirty, she starts toward the door.

Wait. What? My body freezes. Sammy and I could both change our lives thanks to Nova Genetics, and Dr. Sternfield. Getting over my shyness would even help me advocate for him. How could I pass up this chance? Mom, of anyone, would understand.

Gulping a deep breath that leaves me dizzy, I say, "No, listen. I totally get why you need to keep this secret, especially with those crazy protesters outside. I'm in. I'm in."

She eyes me for what seems like a full minute and then finally nods. "Okay, Aislyn, as long as you're sure."

"Absolutely." Yes, it's an experiment so secret I can't even tell my mom. Yes, Dr. Sternfield's passive-aggressive hard sell is annoying. But I sense we're on the edge of something incredible.

She pulls a clip out of her pocket and winds her hair up into a bun. "Since we still have your old blood sample, I'm already familiar with various antibodies that might've gotten in the way. You have a few odd ones, you know. Probably from your trip to Asia a few years ago. But no show stoppers, thank goodness."

Thank goodness is right. It's scary that Evie's family

bringing me along for their vacation to Indonesia when we graduated from middle school could've ruined my chances for this. I say, "The only thing luckier would be if Charisma came in a capsule instead of an injection."

She traces her lower lip line with a manicured fingernail. "Well, someday, I dream of mass producing a version that's sold over the counter—perhaps a powder you could inhale to bypass the blood-brain barrier. It could come in bright yellow packets with pink hearts stamped on them. What do you think?" She gives me a wink that makes me wonder if this last part is a joke meant to put me at ease.

My mouth can't bring itself to laugh, though. I follow Dr. Sternfield to a door that she unlocks with another code, leading to a small room. Inside, she has me take a seat while she washes and gloves up. From a small steel cabinet, she takes out a large syringe.

"I know it's intimidating, but if it makes you feel better, I've injected myself with needles even larger. Two seconds of pain for a lifetime of gain."

She wipes my upper arm with an alcohol pad and in the promised two seconds injects the treatment. With deft movements, she pops a little bandage on my arm. I could swear I feel the contents of the syringe flow up my arm. Even though I can hardly wait not to be shy, a tight panic fills my chest. Oh, wow, I've really done this.

She pulls off her gloves. "If you feel panicky, take deep breaths. And if you need to talk to someone, you've got something I only give to very few people—my personal phone number. Use it, okay? We're going to change the world, you and me."

I stare at the tiny bandage that covers so much. "I just want to change myself."

"Fair enough. Now, how about we go upstairs and see if they still have anything with truffles left?"

We don't say another word as we leave the room. I rub my arm, wondering what sizzles just below the skin, running rampant through my arteries. Could I rip off the bandage and suck it out like snake venom? How long before it starts affecting me? A day? A week? These are questions I should ask Dr. Sternfield, but now that the deed is done, I can't bring myself to speak to her, standing only a foot away in the elevator and wearing a satisfied expression.

Before hurrying off, she whispers, "Remember, not a word about the Charisma or Sammy's clinical trial to anyone, okay?"

I stammer my agreement and she's gone. A nagging in my brain says I should've demanded more details. Well, soon, hopefully, I won't be afraid to speak up ever again. My future now seems so much wider, waiting to be filled with opportunities, freedom, and maybe even Jack, if I can repair the damage of last night. I stroll to the cafeteria with a light step. But I still lack the courage to join Chloe, Shane, and the others laughing around a long table.

For what I hope is the last time, I sneak off to a corner to eat alone.

As I savor grilled salmon and asparagus, no geoducks for me, thank you, I take advantage of finally having phone reception. Evie texted again, with more detail. She and Rafe kissed "like crazy" after the party. Of course, I'm thrilled for her, but even more intrigued by the rest of her message— Jack couldn't understand why I left early. Once she told him I had, he left too.

Really? If only I hadn't jumped to conclusions and freaked out about Alexandra. Now he'll think I'm a total flake. Well, he probably already did after the beer incident. Before I can call Evie to find out more, Sally Sims announces we have two minutes to get to our next activity. Bleh. If I had the secret access codes for the lab downstairs, I'd hide out with Ruby instead.

I chomp down the rest of my lunch, make my way to the Watson and Crick conference room, and take my place in a circle of chairs. Rosa rushes in at the last minute, her face pale. How odd. I've never seen her as anything but subdued. Suspicion darts through my brain. I check her arm for a bandage, but, like me, her shirt sleeves cover any evidence.

Joe calls the meeting to order. "Excellent work on the beach, you guys! What was your favorite part?"

Hands go up to mention the water, the hunt, the sunshine, blah, blah, blah. Prerequisite icebreaker over, Joe dives into therapy territory. "Anyone have something they'd like to share since our last meeting?"

We blink at each other in uncomfortable silence until a girl named Kiera speaks up. Since our last meeting, she's dyed the bottom few inches of her red hair gold, making it look like her head's on fire. She grumbles about how her parents devote most of their attention to her brother Jacob, who has the gene for Huntington's.

This prompts Joe to ask the rest of us if we're jealous of the attention our parents shower on our siblings. I don't care that Mom dotes on Sammy. So do I.

A familiar sensation clenches my belly at the prospect of speaking in front of a group. Guess the Charisma hasn't kicked in yet. Chloe better keep her word. One kid after the next rattles on about how awful it is to be ignored by the world whenever their brothers or sisters are around. What babies.

When it's Shane's turn, he stretches his long legs out in front of him. "I don't mind when my sister gets attention."

Joe raises his bushy eyebrows. "Really? Be honest. You're among friends."

Shane smirks. "Yeah? Well, when people notice her, they also notice me helping her. You know how much action I get from girls who think I'm a saint?" The guy next to Shane gives him a high five.

Joe frowns. "So you use your sister's affliction to pick up girls?"

"Why not? Win-win." He glances my way without smiling. My eyes go to the ceiling.

Joe rubs his chin. "Well, I guess there's no reason not to find the silver lining in your situations. As long as you aren't exploiting anyone."

Shane grins. "Works great for an exit strategy too. When I get bored, I can pretend to be so concerned about my sister that I can't devote time to a *relationship*."

A couple of guys snicker along with him. The rest of us sit with our jaws hanging.

Joe glances around the group. "What do the rest of you think about that?" His gaze stops on me. "Aislyn, tell us the first thing that comes to mind."

I blurt, "Douchebag." Oh my God, did I just say that?

The group laughs, except Shane. Joe claps until we quiet down.

He says, "Well, thanks for your candor, Aislyn and Shane. Is there anyone else who'd like to share?"

Chloe raises her hand. And, true to her word, she launches

into a long-winded story about how much she loves Bailey but feels belittled when their parents devote so much energy to her. Even though I know it's a bunch of BS, I find her tale drawing me in. Every eye on the room is glued to her. She babbles on until it's time to meet in the ballroom for the next event.

Chloe skips next to me as we herd out. "That worked pretty great, huh?"

Yeah, great. But all I can think about is the treatment making its way through my system, attacking innocent cells and doing who knows what. Was my insult to Shane the first change in my personality? What if I'm unable to control future outbursts? Maybe that's all being an extrovert is, the lack of impulse control. Never thought of it that way. But if the Charisma has already caused me to act this far out of character, what else am I in for?

SIX

Back in the ballroom, Sammy's eyelids droop, but he's less flushed than earlier. "The doc put me on a nebulizer. No biggie."

Mom has an arm around his shoulder. "We should go."

Sammy doesn't argue, which is all the evidence I need to know he's feeling crummy.

We wave our good-byes to the Nova Genetics staff and other families. I search the room for Dr. Sternfield. No sign of her. Probably recruiting others into her secret mini-study. I know enough about research trials, underground or not, to realize that a sample size of one won't cut it.

We amble into a sunshiny afternoon, and protesters. They wave their signs, chanting, "Don't mess with nature!"

The extra guards ensure we can get through to our car.

But I'm annoyed Nova Genetics didn't let us use the VIP parking inside the gate. It's mostly empty, save for a dark sedan from which a man and woman in military uniforms emerge.

The protestors erupt into a frenzy of "super soldier" accusations when they spot the military folks. Mom huddles an anxious-looking Sammy as we rush on. I stare at the picketers in disgust. With all the world's desperate problems, they waste their energy working against medical advances that could help so many.

Suddenly, a wild-eyed woman steps from their midst, and points at me. "I know that one. She was here Friday."

All eyes flash my way. My shoulders tighten with a jolt of revulsion. I recognize the woman with Cleopatra hair and oniony breath. She points a phone my way.

I cringe. "What are you doing?"

She cackles and keeps the phone camera aimed at me. "Giving you a taste of your own medicine."

I tuck my head, confused until I remember how Dr. Sternfield videoed the protesters. Who would the protesters show my image to? Me, who actually *has* been genetically enhanced. Well, hopefully.

We hurry into the car and drive off. At the first light, Mom sticks one of her Pearl Jam CDs into the player and tries to lighten the mood by encouraging Sammy to sing with her about a kid who goes ballistic. And either I'm feeling a little ballistic myself or the gene therapy has already loosened a bolt in my brain, because without hesitating, I join in.

Sammy's eyes go wide and Mom shoots puzzled glances my way. She has to swerve to avoid hitting a deer.

As I sing, I text Evie, pumping her for info on Jack. He really missed me at the party? What about him laughing with Alexandra? Evie writes: HE'S INTERESTED. GOT IT? SOME OF US FIND WACKY SHY GIRLS VERY AMUSING!

Not that she, or anyone else, did last night. I ache to tell her about Dr. Sternfield's experiment, but it would freak her out, even though it was way past time I took action. Besides, I'm sworn to secrecy. Still, the desire to confide in someone pounds inside my chest. Such an overwhelming urge to spill seems new. Even though I usually tell Evie everything, it's because I want to, not because I *have* to.

We get home, worn out but content. I tiptoe upstairs imagining the Charisma flowing through my body like the scent of gardenia wafting over a tropical island, caressing everything in its wake. All my little genes getting a much-needed overhaul. Ahhh. That night, for the first time I can remember, I go to sleep excited about what the next day will bring. Maybe the drug should be called "Optimism."

Once I'm on my feet the next morning, a stabbing pain shoots through my temple. I stumble to my desk, rubbing the side of my head. As quickly as it hit, the pain disappears, thank goodness. Dr. Sternfield didn't mention side effects, so it might be from all the excitement yesterday.

Online, I click a video Chloe posted of a rave last night, after she returned from Nova Genetics. I blink, and blink again, making sure I read correctly. Where had she found the energy? On a Sunday night?

A shaky camera follows her onstage in front of a college-age crowd. The pounding techno music stops while she gives a short speech on how the people of the Puget Sound can't survive without more bike lanes. Panned shots of the crowd capture rapt expressions and cheers. Huh? Chloe's always been a drama queen, but I never realized she had such a flair for public speaking.

Sammy barges into my room and hops to the desk. "Wow, Chloe's gone all movie star."

"You got that right." I add a "Yay!" to the sixty other comments under her video, even though I haven't ridden my bike in a year.

Humming, I eat oatmeal with Sammy, get ready for work, and drive to the pool. Will the Charisma make my day tolerable or even fun? I wade through my shift waiting for the urge to do something radical such as sing in public, but as the hours pass, there are no random acts of exhibition. And the kids in swim class all want to be on the other teacher's team for games. My workday is basically a neutralized version of my shift on Saturday. Oh well, if a lack of bad stuff happening is all the Charisma ends up giving me, I'll call it a win. I leave for the day, more relieved than anything else.

After work, I pick *Flowers for Algernon* from my school's required summer reading list. Fifty pages in, I put it aside and go to the mirror to examine my face. A more extroverted me should look different, right? The same old wary gray eyes stare back. I try on a few smiles to see if they reveal anything more sociable, but I look more loony than magnetic.

The doorbell jolts me from my inspection.

Downstairs, Evie bounces inside. Her gaze darts meaningfully toward my room.

We run upstairs, out of Mom's earshot. Once on my bed, Evie examines me with a somber expression. "So, how are you doing?"

For a moment I think she's onto the Charisma, until I realize the last time she saw me I was soaked through after fleeing Drew's house like a madwoman. I wave off her scrutiny. "I'm over that. Blame it on the beer. Now tell me about Rafe."

She considers me for a moment longer, and, apparently satisfied I'm beyond any lingering hysteria, she breathlessly describes how she and Rafe got together after the party, again last night, and they'll hang out tomorrow.

My applause is sincere. "Fantastic!"

She throws herself backward, arms overhead and dangling over the side of the bed. "Feels like it's taken forever, and now boom, boom, boom, it'll be three times in five days. What if he gets tired of me?"

I kick her foot. "Oh no you don't. The more he gets to know you, the more he'll want to be with you."

She pulls her arms down to hug herself, shivering. "Senior year could be so amazing." She halts. "If only you and Jack . . ."

"Yeah, I know."

"There's still a chance, Aiz. He really, really likes you. I can tell. But you've got to let him know you feel the same. No more running. I know it isn't easy." She balls her fists and pounds the quilt at her sides. "Both of us could have the senior years we've dreamed of." As she says the words, her eyes become sad, as if she envisions a less-than-amazing senior year for me. One where she moves into more and more experiences and I'm left behind. But that might not come to pass after the huge chance I took yesterday. How can I not share news this gigantic? It's not like Evie would report me to the FDA.

But I can't.

Her sigh is long and loud. "I was so sure exposure therapy was the answer. In some patients it actually alters their brain scans."

"Hey, have you given up on me? Because I haven't."

She turns to her side and leans on her forearm. "I'd never give up on you. I just don't know what else to try." Her voice breaks.

I sit on the bed next to her. "You're creative. I'm sure you'll come up with some exposure that doesn't involve another party. Not until I'm ready, anyway. But maybe I could try something small. Teeny-tiny."

"You sure? There are lots of things lower on the inhibition hierarchy than parties, you know."

"Such as?"

She glances around my room, her gaze resting on my phone. "How about you text Jack? You guys have chatted online before."

"About stuff for *The Drizzle*. And he always initiates it."

"Exactly." She gets up to grab my phone. "Just this once, you should start things off. Get back on the horse before you feel too comfortable on the ground." She dangles the phone.

Little does she know I've saddled up a new animal altogether, even if I'm not sure how to ride it yet. "I don't know. What would I say?"

"How about 'hi'?"

My pulse quickens. "That's it? Hi? Like 'Hey, Jack, this is Aislyn stalking you'?"

She plops back onto my bed and tsks. "Don't be so negative. He'll be psyched to get your message."

"You don't know that."

She sighs dramatically. "He ran straight to you at the party, and then he left when he found out you had."

"So?"

"This doesn't take honors program smarts. Get a clue." She yanks my hand and slaps the phone into it.

She has a point, but it still doesn't make the thought of reaching out to him easier. Yet, it also doesn't seem utterly impossible. Just a text, right? One tiny text.

I gulp and type HEY. My finger hovers over the SEND button.

Evie leans in closer. "Ready, set, go!"

I take a huge breath and hit the button. Evie's eyes bug in shock. A wave of anxiety immediately rises in my chest. Oh crap, what have I just done? Jack will think I'm desperate. He'll think I'm weird. He'll think I—

HEY BACK!

I almost drop the phone. "Oh my God, he answered in ten seconds."

She bounces on the bed. "More like five. So what are you going to text back?"

"Text back?"

She speaks very slowly and clearly. "Yes, now is when

you ask him something complicated, like what he's up to. C'mon, you're doing great."

Okay, this is officially pitiful, having to get small-talk texting advice. Before I can think things through long enough to change my mind, I text him.

Seconds later: WAITING FOR ZEKE TO GO TO SKATEBOARD PARK. WHAT DID YOU DO OVER THE WEEKEND?

DUG FOR GEODUCKS YESTERDAY. Hmm, there's not sounding come-on-y and there's actively sabotaging any chance of a love life. Geoducks? Seriously?

YUM. JEALOUS. WHAT ABOUT NOW?

HANGING WITH EVIE. WISHING I HAD A BOWL OF ICE CREAM. Okay, weak, and random, but better than my last text.

HOW ABOUT TOMORROW?

Ack. My chest tightens and my brain screams, "Run!" But what I type is: I COULD EAT ICE CREAM ANY DAY.

WITH ME?

With him, on him, whatever he wants. OKAY.

GREAT!

I can't believe it. We're actually going to hang out. Evie cannot keep the smugness off her face, not that she even tries. But I forgive her. Just like I'm sure she'll forgive me for accepting the Charisma. When I tell her. Someday.

After arranging to meet Jack after work, I put down my phone and squeal.

Evie jumps from the bed. "How incredible is this?" She rubs her palms together. "Okay, time to choose the perfect outfit." She opens my closet.

I sit on the bed, stunned by what's happened. By what might occur tomorrow evening. But what if whatever made me brave enough to text him isn't powerful enough for a face-to-face encounter?

Evie holds up a pair of black cropped pants. "Purge time. Can I put these in the 'donate' pile?"

"Sure." Okay, breathe. Figure out what a normal girl would obsess on for a date. Makeup, yeah, that's it. I tiptoe over to the mirror to play around with some rarely used eye shadow while Evie hacks through my closet.

When she has a few outfit options stacked on my bed, and a larger pile of things to donate, she slides next to me so we both face our reflections. "There's something kind of different about you."

"Must be the glow of lust. Or this smoky blue shadow?"

She squints. "It's bigger than that. You seem, um, sparklier somehow. Even your voice sounds different, huskier."

I rumble two octaves below normal, "You're making me self-conscious."

She scoops up a fingertip of eye shadow and rubs some

on each lid. "Maybe the confidence you're getting from exposure therapy shows up in your looks."

Or maybe gene therapy does. I take a deep breath to stop the quivering in my belly.

We go back to sorting clothes while I think about texting Jack. Maybe it had nothing to do with Charisma. It *could* be explained by the fact that I'm really into him. Just like how Chloe glowed over her new boyfriend yesterday. Crushing on someone can change a person drastically. It's what all the songs are about.

By bedtime, Evie and I agree on every acceptable clothing ensemble for the "new me." We're debating nail polish when my phone buzzes with a broadcast text from Chloe: WATCH THE KBLB NEWS STREAM! EVEN BETTER THAN THE RAVE!

I show Evie the message. She frowns. "That's it? No clue as to what?"

I roll my eyes. "She assumes if she tells folks to watch, they will."

Evie opens a bottle of Scarlett Secrets nail polish, which she begins applying to her pinkie. "You going to check it out?"

"Nah." I point to the polish. "Um, even I know that that shade of red is only for toenails, unless you live in Jersey."

Before she can argue, my phone buzzes again. It's Chloe. YOU WON'T BE SORRY!

I laugh and turn on my computer. "Okay, now I'm curious."

Evie paints her nails while I find the site. Front and center beams a video of Chloe. I take the laptop to my bed so Evie can watch too. Chloe is the person-on-the-street interviewee for a local music festival. She delivers a breathless rundown. Afterward, the reporter asks her to come back tomorrow.

Evie blows on her nails. "How come you never told me Chloe was so photogenic?"

I examine the still-shot. "I never thought about it before."

But now I do. If I'm more sparkly, Chloe's downright blinding. And she bloomed with something extra yesterday. It could be that things with her halfback have exploded into something bigger than she let on. Well, whatever it is, it's working for her. And things are working for me too. I have plans with Jack. Plans!

So let Chloe take on the planet with her new video fame. It's all good. In fact, there isn't a thing for me to complain about, except maybe that half of my wardrobe now lies in the donate pile. And I have to wait until tomorrow to see Jack. But a little anticipation isn't the end of the world. Not by a long shot.

Beloved Docent at Local Zoo Loses Battle
with Unknown Illness

by Jenna Dawson, *The Gig Harbor Herald*

Long-time resident Stephanie "Steffie" Wong, who headed up the primate labs at Nova Genetics, died Saturday after a brief illness. In her spare time, she volunteered at local zoos, teaching children about animal habitats and conservation efforts. She was considered a world expert on primate behavior and worked with Nova Genetics to test ground-breaking work in gene therapy in the most ethical manner possible. As she frequently reminded students at her tours, "We share over ninety-nine percent of our DNA with chimpanzees. Treating other primates 'humanely' means acting toward them with compassion and dignity, the way they treat each other." As such, she was a vocal advocate in demanding that medical testing that utilizes non-animal methods always be the first choice.

Stephanie is survived by her parents and sister, and a memorial service is planned for later this week. In lieu of flowers, her family requests donations be made to the Sierra Leone Sanctuary for Chimpanzees.

SEVEN

At the pool the next morning, I greet my class of five-year-olds, which includes Molly, a chubby-cheeked girl with long black bangs, who refused to budge from the side of the pool yesterday. Her mother calls from the bench, "Get your whole body into the water, sweetie." Molly shakes her head.

Patrick, my teaching partner, and I lead the other kids through bubble-blowing and blast-offs, while Molly stares balefully. When I invite her to join in, she stiffens. "Maybe next time," I say.

I wade off to launch a game of Sharks vs. Minnows, reminding myself not to feel rejected when the kids beg to be on Patrick's team, the way they did yesterday. But a strange thing happens. One by one the kids announce they want to play on Team Aislyn. What? Even Patrick tries to hide his surprise.

We play for five minutes, and then, with two kids laughing and hanging off of my arms, I swim to Molly's side, keeping my gaze soft. "Wanna try a giant turtle ride?"

Biting her lip, she nods. Buoyed by more than the water, I coax Molly onto my back and away from the wall. It feels like she'll choke me with her death-grip.

I gasp. "Not so tight, kiddo."

She releases her grasp, but my head suddenly feels light and a shaft of pain sears behind my eyes. I should slow down a bit. Taking steady steps, I stay close to the edge of the shallow end in case I need to unload Molly quickly. But by the end of the ride, Molly wears a huge smile and my head feels fine.

The next class flows as effortlessly as the first. Again, the kids choose to be on my team. I joke with Patrick that he must've eaten garlic for breakfast. But he insists the reason for my newfound popularity is that my teaching skills have improved overnight. He can't explain how exactly, only that I'm more present somehow.

More present. Could genes have anything to do with that?

As I shift from classes to lifeguard watch, my whole body pulsates with a weird kind of energy. Maybe it's presence; maybe it's my imagination.

Five minutes into my shift, Heath, who's usually linked to one cheerleader or another, saunters next to the chair. "Hey, Aislyn, ready for senior year?"

I adjust my visor. "I guess. Going to enjoy summer first."

He slowly examines me. "You're different than I thought."

I shrug. "Less mute or less hopeless? You posting any more public humiliation photos?"

He startles and then laughs nervously. "I post crap like that all the time. None of my friends take it seriously."

"How about your enemies?"

He blinks a few times. "Wow. You don't pull your punches, girl." His eyelids lower and he clears his throat. "So, are you with anyone?"

My butt slides toward the edge of my seat. "Huh?"

"You know. Do you have a boyfriend?" Along with his casual smile is a stitch of anxiety I've never noticed before.

I shift my eyes back and forth between him and the pool. "Uh, not really." But my odds are better than they've ever been.

Heath tosses an upward gaze as well-honed as a samurai sword. "Then you wanna hang out tonight? Catch a movie?"

I almost fall off of the chair. He wants to see a movie with me? Someone he thinks of as "a waste"?

I scan the pool. "I've got plans."

"Maybe tomorrow?"

At that moment, I catch sight of a boy getting ready to hurtle down the waterslide with another kid on his shoulders. I whistle and give them a warning over the bullhorn.

Instead of ignoring me, one of them salutes and the other yells "Sorry" before they go down the slide one at a time. Wow, even my lifeguard communications are improving.

Heath taps my ankle. "Aislyn? Tomorrow?"

"Um, no thanks." This shouldn't feel as good as it does.

Disappointment in his eyes, he struts off.

I examine my torso as if that'll provide an explanation for his sudden interest. But my wardrobe makeover didn't include the pool employee orange one-piece. I put a hand to my long ponytail. Nothing special today, not even makeup, unless you count the attractive streak of zinc oxide on my nose. Have I led him on somehow? Nah, I barely glanced his way. Maybe I'm sending out anticipatory pheromones for tonight.

After my pool watch, it's time for snack-bar duty. I rub at the side of my head, which has begun to throb, and take a calming breath before sidling next to Camilla, my coworker. After a few moments, the headache subsides.

Normally, a gathering this chatty and numerous is grounds for hyperventilating, but instead I greet a boy from my swim class who'd asked if I was a mermaid. I smile as if selling Sour-Sliders and Cookie-Clusters is my land-based dream. He grins back. Soon I'm making jokes with him and his sister as well as the kids behind them. The effortless laughter continues throughout the line, taking on a comfortable rhythm, as if the give-and-take with the crowd feeds something within me.

Smiling big, I say hi to a guy named Alex from AP math. His barely whiskered jaw drops open, and for a change I'm not the one blushing.

As he hands me his money, he whispers, "Has anyone ever told you they'd like to calculate the area under your curves?"

I jolt back. Ewww, is he flirting with calculus jokes? "Uh, seriously? If you leave right now, I won't tell anyone what you just said. Here's your Praline Petticoat Parfait."

He slinks off, leering over his shoulder. Guess I'm bringing out the best and worst in people today. Still, it's a worthwhile trade, given the rest of the customers stay away from geeky come-ons.

At four p.m., I step lightly to my car, praying the easy flow of the day will continue into the evening. It's hard not to speed home.

When I get there, Mom announces she's taking Sammy to the warehouse store for a shopping trip, which always includes a belly full of high-fat samples and pizza that she hopes will stick to his bones. I make a sandwich for dinner and click through my phone. Chloe has another video clip up. Wow, that makes three. But she doesn't limit them to her own news. Apparently, a guy named Sebastian, who she met at Nova Genetics, had a successful audition today for a local dance company and advanced to the next level of the admissions process. I play the video Chloe posted.

The footage is grainy, but those leaps and pirouettes are amazing. There's even a congratulatory comment under the video from that obnoxious guy Shane. Boy, it hasn't taken him long to connect to Chloe's universe.

Curious as to whether Shane's bad-boy talk was all for show with the teen group, with an extra performance for me, I check out his page. It blasts my eyes with a flurry of Shane photos over a banner that reads: *Guess what, ladies? I'm available and accepting applications for my next girlfriends. Satisfaction guaranteed. Send photos and numbers.*

I squint. What the hell?

Even more surprising are the number of photos posted to his page as part of the "selection" process, which began the day before. He's received a dozen replies from non-crazy-looking, non-desperate-looking girls, who share shots of themselves in party dresses, bikinis, and everything in between. It's like that TV show where multiple women compete for one guy, and the winner gets to be in a failed relationship.

I shake my head in wonder and get ready to hang out with a guy way better than Shane or any TV stud.

Jack's old-school enough to pick me up, and his silver Ford arrives at six thirty exactly. Deep breaths. Charisma might make it possible for me to go on a date, but that doesn't mean it'll be easy. With wobbly knees, I open the front door.

I hold on to the frame for support when we're face-to-face. Another deep breath. "Um, c'mon in." I take a step back. Okay, so far, so good. I haven't spilled anything on him or fainted.

He steps into the foyer and peeks inside. "Doesn't your mom want to meet me or anything?"

Wow, he really is old-school. How sweet. I scoop my bag from the end table and say, "She took my brother shopping. But I've left her a note with your description, social security number, and criminal background check." Is this really me, speaking in full sentences and cracking a joke?

His eyes widen for a sec before he breaks into a grin. "Well, I hope the meth lab incident doesn't stop her from letting me take you out again."

I smile, my face tingling at the notion of "again."

On the car ride to my favorite ice-cream place, I maintain my side of the conversation without hyperventilating. Jack speaks more slowly and softly than usual, the way you'd do with a kitten, the way I had with Molly earlier. Maybe he'll offer me a giant turtle ride next. Now there's a yummy thought.

Once we've bought our cones, we find a wrought iron bench in front of a tiny fountain where kids dodge streams of water shooting from the mouths of bronze faeries. Jack licks his cone slowly, savoring it. Watching him, I understand why eating ice cream in public is banned in certain countries.

He says, "I like how you don't pretend to be on a diet the way other girls do."

"Hmm. You're not implying anything, are you?"

He looks horrified. "No, of course not! You're, uh, perfect. Anyway, I'm not for hinting at stuff when I can just say what I mean." That much seems true. His straightforward honesty is something I've always found refreshing, even when it's a critique of something I've edited for *The Drizzle*.

We perch on the bench, chatting while we enjoy the ice cream. When the cones are gone, we take advantage of the clear skies to stroll around the outdoor shopping area. Under a brightly striped awning, I point at a mannequin dressed in a safety-pinned-together jacket. "Okay, that doesn't make sense, no matter how many *Vogue* spreads Evie foists on me."

Jack's eyes twinkle. "A girl who loves dessert and hates fashion that tries too hard. Where have you been all my life?"

My breath catches in my chest. Right here, I want to say, imagining us, like this. Even though I was convinced it would never be possible.

At a park on the end of the walkway, a band has set up for a free concert. They launch into summer-happy tunes with an edge. We sway to the music and applaud some toddlers who've gone into full-on dance mode.

With a happy sigh, I allow the music to float through my body, right down to my altered DNA. Ahh. My breathing and heartbeat flow in perfect harmony with the song. And then, for a brief moment, I have the strangest sensation, as if I've somehow merged with the crowd around me. It's a warm, powerful feeling, utterly connected to the world. My eyes flash open. What's going on? I thought Charisma would be more about sizzle and confidence than all this warm, fuzzy stuff.

Taking a sharp breath, I mentally retreat to my normal wariness, with my psyche hovering just outside the group. Even so, the people around us don't seem as distant and "other" as usual. Maybe Jack's presence, not gene therapy, is having an effect on me.

At the edge of the audience, a cameraman from a local news station, who must've lost a bet, shoots video of the crowd. His camera points my way, then seems to stall. My first instinct is to hide behind a woman with big hair, but for some reason I shrug off my self-consciousness and stare straight into the lens. After a few moments, the camera seems to nod before resuming its sweep of the audience.

Jack leans toward me. "The news-guy has the hots for you."

"That's nuts."

"Uh, no, it's completely logical."

I feel my capillaries do their thing with my cheeks. Dr. Sternfield could earn a fortune if she fixed the gene for blushing. Oh well, one therapy at a time.

As the sun sets, we make our way toward Jack's car, with strains of music in the background and lingering warmth in the air. He glances my way and casually takes my hand. Every nerve ending in the skin that comes into contact with his sparks crazily. Palm to palm, elbows grazing, we stroll in unison. Me and Jack. Oh my God. It's the sweetest.

The drive home goes way too fast, and, before I know it, we're at my front porch, hands clasped and swinging between us like a rope bridge. I hate to say good-bye, yet I savor this moment. Knees shaking, I sway in front of him with a feathery quiver in my chest.

He brushes a strand of hair from my cheek. "I had a fantastic time."

"The best."

"It's like that essay you wrote for *The Drizzle* freshman year. About a perfect afternoon you remembered with your mom, dad, and brother at the beach. How everything lined up, just so, and you floated along, better than a dream."

"You remember that?"

"Of course. It reminded me of camping in the rainforest with my family, before my parents split."

I nod, knowing how it feels to have most of your best

memories on the "before" side of some awful line that started the "after" in your life. But tonight I'm part of a shimmering now, one of those precious beads I'll add to my string of exceptional moments.

Jack gazes at me and shakes his head like he's having trouble believing something. "I've always thought you were great, but I never realized just how amazing you were until tonight. It's like you glow or something."

"Okay, I know I don't have a tan, but—"

"You know what I mean."

Do I? My insides sure seem to. Warm and alive and so, so happy.

He steps toward me. I match his movement as he leans closer. And closer still. My eyes close and I lick my lips. Finally, finally...

The porch light pops on, and we both jump back. With a creak, the front door opens, and Mom peeks out.

Her eyes widen when she sees Jack. "Oh, hey, I heard something out here . . ."

I wait for Mom to get a clue and go back inside before the atmosphere shifts from awkward to unsalvageable. But she doesn't pick up on my mental messages that scream "Go away!" Hemming and hawing, she hovers until Jack holds out his hand and introduces himself.

She seems impressed by the gesture, but still doesn't retreat into the house after the handshake. Is she doing this on purpose? Just because she hasn't tried dating since Dad doesn't give her the right to mess up things between me and Jack.

The three of us fall into an uncomfortable silence for a long moment. And then Jack pulls out his car keys and announces he'll be leaving. My body deflates like a soccer ball that's been kicked too hard.

"Maybe we can go to Erin's party tomorrow night?" Jack calls over his shoulder on the way to the curb.

"Sure," I say, noticing Mom's frown.

At least there's hope for another chance with him. I follow Mom inside, fighting an urge to throw one of my carefully chosen gold flip-flops at her. That's odd. Violence isn't exactly one of my go-to traits. Maybe it comes with the glowing.

Who knew genes could be so unpredictable?

EIGHT

The next morning, I call Evie first thing to relay my perfect-until-the-last-minute evening.

She sighs loudly. "Okay, next time you'll need to make your move quicker; waiting 'til the end is too much pressure. Seriously, find a way to be *alone* alone during the first hour. Know what I mean? The rest of your time will go great after that."

It's funny listening to her give boy advice, seeing as how she's only two dates ahead of me. Being diligent students, we've spent many hours discussing hypotheticals and watching MTV. But finally having the chance to plan *in situ* experiences, well, no comparison.

She laughs. "Aislyn's got a boyfriend, Aislyn's got a—"

I hang up and waltz downstairs, where Sammy gulps the enzyme capsules he needs to take with every meal, and Mom looks up from her coffee. She says, "Sad news in Nova Genetics' family newsletter. That sweet caretaker Steffie passed away." She shakes her head. "They say she had a history of health issues, including asthma."

I sink to a chair, a lot less hungry than I was a moment ago. "Wow, I thought she just had a cold. She was always super-nice to the teen group."

I bet gene therapy could've eventually cured Steffie's asthma and whatever other problems she had. How horribly unfair to work for a company that develops medical breakthroughs, but not be helped in time herself. Hopefully, my participation in a gene therapy trial, even unapproved, will push this science forward.

After a somber breakfast, I head to work. My glumness over Steffie's death lifts when I arrive at swim class, where Molly jumps into the pool and hugs me. Patrick and I exchange raised eyebrows.

I ride the day with the same ease as yesterday. No, more than ease, liberation, as if I've been unleashed from years of wearing a chain and muzzle. My new boldness makes me curious to test how this Charisma works. I stroll through the crowd, giving one guy a smile, the next a slow blink. The first seems pleased, the second intrigued. Interesting. I spend the rest of the afternoon playing with my new personality like a gadget. The tiniest expressions prove as potent as cinnamon in your hot chocolate. I'll have to learn how to handle them with care.

Not ready to leave the pulsing energy of the crowd at the end of my shift, I find a warm deck chair and relax to the happy noise of swimmers as I pull out my phone and use the camera as a mirror. This blond-haired girl with gray eyes doesn't appear any different. But she has a date and is heading to a party, so what do I know?

I check out life in the virtual lane. On Chloe's page, a bunch of messages offer get-well wishes. What a bummer to get sick when she's so clearly in her element with the news videos. I start to add a note, but before I can, Chloe posts an update saying false alarm, she's feeling great. I let out a breath. Her news relieves me more than it should.

Chloe then posts a video from Veggiefest along with a form for viewers to denounce GMOs. Hmm. She's always spoken up for various causes, but I've never seen it go anywhere until now. The only way to describe it would be to say she's more charismatic. A nagging suspicion creeps into my thoughts. My curiosity too strong to ignore, I send a message: LOVE WHAT YOU'VE BEEN UP TO. MY LIFE HAS CHANGED FOR THE BETTER TOO. LET'S CHAT!

That's not exactly divulging any secrets, is it?

I scan the comments under Chloe's video. One from Shane says, "Following in your footsteps!"

Huh? I click to his site. More photos of himself and more photos of girls "applying" to join his harem. A mysterious "Stay tuned!" banner scrolls across.

I rub my cheek. It's awfully coincidental that both Chloe and Shane have amped up their online presence this week. But it doesn't make sense that Dr. Sternfield would've given them Charisma when they clearly didn't need to be more extroverted.

Troubled by my suspicions, I click around to as many other teen sibs pages as I can find. Most strike me as ordinary, the only possible exception being Rosa's. Her posts in English include announcements about "Having the BEST day!" and her Spanish entries are filled with exclamation marks.

A sliver of pain shoots behind my eyes. If any others have taken the gene therapy, do they have side effects? Even if I don't ask them directly, there's someone I could contact. Should've done it sooner. I pull up Dr. Sternfield's number.

She answers on the second ring. "Well, hello there, Aislyn. How's life?"

"Mostly great, actually."

She laughs. "As expected."

"There's just one thing. I've been getting these weird headaches, and sometimes I'm a little dizzy."

There's the tiniest pause before she says, "Completely

normal. Your brain is producing new proteins, and creating new neural pathways. Once things settle down, the headaches will go away."

"Are the other people you gave Charisma to having the same side effects? I heard Chloe was sick earlier."

A longer silence this time. "If I've allowed others to experience the gene therapy, it wouldn't be prudent to say anything. I don't want to influence how you perceive the changes in your life with anecdotal evidence from others. You know how research works." Her voice gets lower. "Aislyn, you've kept this under wraps, right? No blabbing?"

"Of course not," I say, thinking about how much I ache to tell Evie.

"Good girl. Since I trust your discretion, I'll let you in on some news: Sammy's in the AV719 pool. I wouldn't be surprised if he's, ahem, randomly selected."

"Wow. That's fantastic. Thanks so much."

"Remember, keep quiet until it's official, okay? We don't want to jeopardize anything."

I wave to a couple of lifeguards strolling by. "Of course."

"Now, give me the scoop on your new life."

I share a few details, including the party with Jack tonight. As I do, my cheeks grow warm. "It's like I'm the person I've always dreamed of being, you know?"

"You have no idea how thrilled this makes me, Aislyn."

And, really, the headaches are so fleeting, they aren't really an issue at all.

With my nerves calmed, we hang up. I'm lucky to be part of her secret study, like winning the lottery. Me, the girl who drew the short straw on not growing up with a father and dealing with a crippling personality disorder.

As content as a cat under a skylight, I gather my stuff and head out, exchanging hellos with half a dozen people on the way to my car.

That evening, Jack's right on time again. As I let myself out, I say, "Good thing you passed the police check."

He winks. "In this state, anyway. But if you want me to break any laws, just say the word."

"Hmm. I'll think of something."

We float into a gentle sunset.

Jack shakes his head. "I can hardly believe I'm with the same girl."

This stops me short. He is with the same girl, isn't he? I mean, I'm still me, only more willing to let others see that me. I brush my fingers against my temple even though nothing hurts. My skin prickles as if my body's trying to figure something out. Inhabiting a new personality must be like a snail making its home in a new shell, wiggling and adjusting its innards until everything fits just so.

Fortunately, my feelings of discombobulation soon dissipate as we drive along tree-shaded streets. When Jack parks the car, I find my legs aren't as wobbly as last time, and the music playing at Erin's house is more of an embrace than an assault.

Evie and Rafe have already taken up a spot in the corner. They raise red cups in salute to Jack and me. Rafe nuzzles Evie's neck, and she glances my way with a sly smile. So they've found enough *alone* alone time to get comfortable with PDA. Well, hopefully Jack and I will catch up soon. In the alone time anyway.

We join a conversation about someone's dad getting Botox and another girl's sister who got a boob job for her eighteenth birthday.

Zoe, an artsy girl who's more Evie's friend than mine, shakes her head. "I'd never want to be so fake."

The guy next to her glances at her healthy chest. "Easy for you to say."

She slaps his arm. "We should accept who we are. Anything else is phony."

The others nod.

I straighten my shoulders. "People should make their own choices. As long as they aren't going nuts with a bunch of surgeries, it's their decision. Just like dyeing your hair or going on a diet. Who are we to judge?"

Everyone stares in silence. Evie squints intensely at me.

Zoe tugs at a multi-pierced earlobe. "All those air-brushed ads make people feel horrible about themselves if they don't measure up. I refuse to buy into it."

I say, "We don't have to hold ourselves to Hollywood's impossible ideals. But most of us alter ourselves every day to be more attractive. If you wanted to be one hundred percent natural, you wouldn't wear deodorant or style your hair."

Jack's shocked expression is almost comical, but he's able to sputter, "Yeah, I don't want anyone telling me what I can and can't do. I can say no to the stupid stuff."

Evie doesn't stop staring at me.

Jack motions toward the kitchen. "You want something to drink?"

I have a quick flashback to Drew's party. "Maybe a soda?"

Jack smiles and heads off. The kids around me transition from plastic surgery gossip to a new all-ages club downtown.

The guy next to Zoe says, "They had some nasty E there last week. Tory Simmons had to get her stomach pumped."

Zoe sighs dramatically. "Damn, if people aren't re-molding themselves physically, they're doing it mentally."

I point to her cup. "Like with beer?"

Everyone laughs, even Zoe, who's smart enough not to argue the point. Persuading others to see things my way is potent, filling me with energy and giddiness.

Evie yanks my elbow. "Got a sec?"

"Sure."

She leads me into an empty garage that smells of turpentine. The door has barely closed when she whips around. "What the hell is going on?"

"What do you mean?"

She counts on her fingers. "You texted Jack. You *went out* with him. You came to a party without me begging or you puking. And now you're the center of attention. Basking in it, even. After last weekend, I can't believe this is possible."

I try to contain my grin. "You're the one who's always claimed that exposure therapy is the be-all, end-all. Maybe it finally kicked in."

"Exposure therapy gave you a major meltdown at Drew's party."

"So, what else could explain it?" I'll admit, I'm having fun with this.

She crosses her arms and paces. "I don't know. Maybe I'm just the one freaking out now because you're so not the Aislyn I'm used to." Her jaw is set tight.

It seems cruel not to let my best friend in on the news. Besides, she already knows something's up, and I'll implode if I try to keep it from her any longer.

Taking a deep breath, I lean toward her. "If I tell you something, would you promise never ever to tell anyone else?"

She rocks on the balls of her feet. "You're okay, right? This isn't going to be something horrible?"

I smile. "Not a bit. Promise not to say a word?"

"Of course. Now tell me."

I brace my shoulders and swallow. "Okay. There's a doctor at Nova Genetics who's working on a gene therapy to make people more sociable. And on Sunday I got a once-in-a-lifetime opportunity to try it." Oh, God, sharing my secret is the hugest rush.

Evie cocks her head. "How? Like Prozac? Or more like cocaine?"

I laugh, the relief of telling sending me into a light-headed state as I give her the specifics.

Her face pales and she shakes her head. "Aw, Aiz. It sounds so, so extreme. What if it doesn't work?"

"You've already seen that it does work. Amazingly. At the teen siblings meeting, I even called a guy a douchebag."

She purses her lips, staring at me with flame in her black eyes. "I don't know whether to be proud of you or smack you."

I pretend to flinch. "Maybe we should get back to the party and enjoy the new me before you decide."

With Evie sighing dramatically, we head out of the garage. This time she follows me.

Jack raises his eyebrows when we rejoin the group. I whisper, "Girl talk."

I sip the soda he brought and hand it back. He puts his lips exactly where mine were and takes a long swallow. His tan jawline glints with the hint of golden stubble to match his hair. I want so badly to drag a finger along it, slowly.

Suddenly, the room goes tilty and my head light. Whoa. I grab Jack's arm for support.

"You okay?" He wipes splashed soda from his cheek and licks it off his finger.

Rafe laughs. "Dang, someone cannot handle her alcohol."

I regain my balance. "I'm fine."

Jack nudges me toward the sofa. "C'mon, let's sit down."

Even though I feel okay, I let him lead me there. We nestle into the cushions, our bodies pressed into each other. He smells of cedar and spring rain. Maybe I should've gotten dizzy earlier.

He places the cup on an end table. "If you need to go home, let me know."

I bite my lip. "I could stay here, in this spot, all night."

He whispers in my ear, "I hear ya."

"Okay, knock it off, you two," booms Johnny Sonoma, who plays every varsity sport. He sinks next to us, and pulls Abby O'Keefe onto his lap.

Before we know it, a half-dozen kids join us, sitting on the floor around the sofa or hovering on the armrests. Jack and I soon meld into the laughter and slurred conversation of kids I barely know. How come I never noticed how friendly these guys are? It's invigorating, being the party's center of gravity. Other kids join us, watching from the sidelines and trying to get a word in. But we're at the heart of the frenzy. At one point, I catch Evie watching from across the room. She shakes her head in wonder.

She and I have a lot to discuss. I need my best friend to help me come to terms with all of this.

For now, I enjoy learning about my fellow classmates while I cuddle next to Jack. His skin is deliciously warm. At some point, the lights in the room dim and the music intensifies. Johnny and Abby get up to dance. A few others join them. Jack gives me a quizzical look.

"Sure," I say, rising with him, my head as clear and stable as a diamond.

Soon, everyone's dancing. I get that feeling I had the other night, as if I'm connected to a mass of humanity that throbs and flows. Instead of breaking off from it, this time I let myself sink into the sensation. Mentally, I'm crowd-surfing, in perfect harmony with my body, which Jack holds so tightly I feel every button on his shirt.

Within a miasma of music and laughing, Jack and I lock gazes. We bring our faces closer, ever so slowly, until our lips touch. We pull back, smiling, and then lean in for real, meeting in a kiss that's warm and pulsating. Oh, man, if holding hands is like a flame, kissing is an inferno. My body seems to know what to do better than my brain for a change. So I let it. We shift into each other for long, perfect minutes.

Someone yells at us, "Take it outside!"

I look up from my daze to find that Jack and I aren't the only ones caught up in the moment. We throw our heads back, arms overhead, and dance, not caring about anything but the music. Many songs later I notice how my dress sticks to my back and how hard I'm breathing.

Jack catches me by the elbow and escorts me to the hallway. He checks his phone. "Damn, you were supposed to be home twenty-five minutes ago."

I nuzzle into his chest. "Don't worry. My mom probably fell asleep."

Zoe and another girl slink toward us pointing cameras. "Anything you want to say to the world? Maybe a PSA for plastic surgery?"

I clear my throat. What to say to "the world"? The first thing that comes out is: "Have a blast. But if you have too much of a blast, be sure you're an organ donor."

Everyone laughs. I pretend to as well, even though I know the reason for my weird comment is the scary probability of Sammy needing a lung transplant someday.

A few minutes later, when I say good-bye to Evie, she nudges my arm. "Okay, I wanna sign up for the you-know-what too."

I glance at Rafe, who hasn't strayed from her side all night. "You're doing fine."

Jack speeds home, only to take our time parked in front of my house. Whenever his skin meets mine, I shiver. No way will I bring him to the porch, where Mom can interrupt us. At quarter after eleven, I kiss him one last time and run to my door with a smile that makes my cheeks hurt.

Opening the door quietly, I let out a huge sigh to find the living room empty. But as I tiptoe upstairs, Sammy's coughing seems to jangle the walls. I peek into his room to find Mom offering him tissues and a plastic pail.

They both turn to me with wounded eyes.

I say, "Sorry I'm late."

Mom pats Sammy's back. "You couldn't call?"

Sammy hacks another chest-rattling cough and puts his face into the pail.

"I totally lost track of the time. Really, I'm so sorry."

Sammy wipes his mouth. "Give her a break, Mom. She's never had a boyfriend before."

Mom's stern expression is more about breaking bones than granting breaks, but all she says is, "You'd better get some sleep if you want to be alert at work tomorrow."

I nod and shut the door.

But my insides tingle too much to go to bed. I savor the electric memory of my first real kiss, and my second, tenth, and twentieth. As if I could sleep after that.

I hop onto my computer, and, before I know it, post a few random thoughts about the party. A couple of other kids who were there answer with notes of their own. Soon there's a flurry of updates and connection requests. Someone posts videos of us dancing. In the midst of the activity, I notice Chloe returned my private message from earlier with: HAPPY YOUR LIFE ROCKS. MAYBE ALL THAT THEORETICAL KNOWLEDGE ABOUT GUYS WILL BECOME ACTUAL. HAHA! HAVE YOU SEEN SHANE'S PAGE TODAY?

I groan, but check out his page anyway. Apparently, he's taken his girlfriend application process to the "next level." Half expecting he means orgies, I find the next level involves a plan for local film students to follow him around and produce *The Shane Show* for the city cable channel.

Puh-leeeze. What girl would want to be part of that? I sigh. No amount of Charisma would persuade me to do that.

Unless . . .

Grinning, I get a wicked idea, and fill in the online application form. Without any bikini shots handy, I link to a dance video from the party. Someone needs to put this guy in his place.

I submit the application, and then a trickle of guilt persuades me to find ways to use my upgraded personality for something more than messing with Shane's ego. No ideas as to what this greater good might be occurs to me by the time I slip under the covers, yet I fall asleep hopeful I can make a difference in the world. My own world has already changed for the better. Miraculously. Of that, I have no doubt.

After only six hours of sleep, I awake the next morning raring to go. For sixteen point nine years, my mornings were always weighted by fears to face the day. Time to make up for that.

I grab my phone, only to feel the room sway as I find dozens of messages on Chloe's page about her passing out at a club last night. She insists it was only because things have been so crazy busy. But not too busy to invite everyone she knows to a huge solstice party on the beach tonight, which she promises will be epic.

I feel my own forehead. Normal. Still, I text Dr. Sternfield with news about Chloe, just in case.

My phone buzzes. I hope it's the doctor with some reassurances, but it's Evie. YOUR VIDEO GOT PICKED UP ON THE TEENS TALK SITE.

What video? I check out Teens Talk. That silly recording from Erin's party has over two thousand hits already, and a bunch of comments from people who've also visited the organ donation site. Really? I spin around in my chair. So this is what it feels like to have something go viral. In a good way.

Back on my page, I scroll through dozens of congratulations and more connection requests. Most of the messages are positive, but scattered here and there I find anonymous stuff such as HOW DOES IT FEEL TO GO FROM LOSER TO DIVA? and HOW LONG BEFORE YOU MAKE THE RETURN TRIP?

I pull up Evie's number on my phone. My vision blurs for a second, and the room starts a lazy spin. I close my eyes. God, I wish my synapses or whatever's crackling in my brain would behave already.

When Evie answers, I say, "I'm already getting hate mail."

"Jerks."

"But I still want to do more videos. A ton of people signed up to be organ donors. That's huge."

She pauses. "It is. Maybe your next video could be planned a little better, though? I would've helped you pick out a more flattering outfit and fixed your hair."

Is that hurt I detect in her voice? I say, "Of course you would've. But this is still great, right? And now you won't have to drag me to parties. I can be the friend you always wanted me to be."

She sighs. "You already were the friend I wanted you to be."

If I were, why did she set party quotas? But my instinct tells me to have this conversation in person. Funny, three days ago, I would've preferred difficult conversations via text. Now I want to connect, face-to-face, so there are no misunderstandings.

Evie breaks the silence. "So what's next on your plan for world domination?"

"Whatever it is, you'll be the first to know."

"That's more like it." Maybe things are fine between us after all.

I skip downstairs, confident the day will fall into place. Sammy shakes a box of Magic Munchos at me. Mom pours glasses of orange juice. I approach them with resolve in my step, wishing everyone could feel as optimistic as I do, despite the lightness in my head.

But when I open my mouth to speak, my world suddenly goes black.

Unexplained Outbreak Among Heroin Addicts
by Stephan Mott, *Portland Planet*

Portland health care workers report a bizarre and alarming trend among the city's heroin users. In the past three weeks, more than a dozen have gone into comas after bouts of manic behavior, which is in direct contrast with the typically sedative effects of opiate use. Law enforcement representatives believe a new drug may be on the street and have been questioning injection drug users in an attempt to identify its source. Anyone who believes they may have been exposed to this drug is urged to contact their physician or the Hazelwood Free Clinic immediately.

NINE

When my eyes open, I'm on the kitchen floor. "What happened?"

Mom's on her knees next to me, the phone at her ear. "She just came to."

I try to rise. The room spins.

Mom says, "Relax. Keep your head down."

An excellent idea, given the flashing spots in my vision. "How long was I out?"

"Just a minute." She feels my forehead and speaks into the phone. "Maybe a slight fever." She turns to me. "When's the last time you ate?"

"Dinner."

As she listens to the phone, her features pull tight. She clamps her hand over the mouthpiece. "Aislyn, did you ingest or inhale anything unusual at the party?"

Ingest? Inhale? Oh. "If you mean heroin or crack, no." Should I mention the gene therapy? Not yet, not yet. I needed to speak with Dr. Sternfield first.

After a few more questions, Mom hangs up. "I'm taking you to the emergency room."

I stand on my own. "But I'm okay."

Steering my elbow like a rudder, she forces me toward a chair. "Fainting is not okay. Even for only a few seconds. Let's get you some food and then we're out of here."

While Mom foists an egg and toast on me, I ask Sammy to go upstairs and grab my phone. He seems happy to be the one assisting the patient for a change.

He bows as he hands me the phone. "Anything else I can do?"

"Um, wash my car?" I gobble my breakfast, aware of Mom staring at my back, no doubt speculating upon which gateway drug I tried. "I'm feeling a lot better. Besides, neither of us can afford to miss work."

"I'll reschedule my client. You can call the pool on the way. Now, c'mon," she says in her this-isn't-a-negotiation voice.

I drag my feet to the car. The weather's shifted to gray skies and a slight chill. Typical June. On the way to Florence Bishop Children's Hospital, I call in sick to the pool and text Dr. Sternfield with the latest.

Mom scrutinizes me at every stoplight. "Your eyes are glassy."

I fake a smile. "I'm fine, probably just too much activity this week." I itch to tell her about the gene therapy. Given that Chloe's passed out too, I doubt it's a coincidence. But she insisted she was overtaxing herself, just like me. That's all it might be. Too much of a good thing. And the downside of telling is Mom might demand that Dr. Sternfield give me something to reverse this good thing. I shudder at the thought of going back to being the girl who could barely get a sentence out around Jack; the girl who was invisible to all but a few friends, except when she humiliated herself at science fairs and parties. Charisma is a miracle. My brain simply needs to get used to it.

Mom clears her throat. "Sure there isn't anything you want to tell me?" When did she get so suspicious?

"Um, like what?" And when did I get so evasive?

She frowns at the windshield, which frames a world of drizzle. "You're awfully mercurial lately, glum on Sunday morning, and then exuberant about Jack a day later."

"Hate to break it to you, but I'm a teenager. We're supposed to be unpredictable."

She sighs. "But never you."

That was the problem.

We ride the rest of the way in silence, except for my phone, which buzzes. I check for a reply from Dr. Sternfield, but it's Jack asking to hang out tonight. My head goes light again. Whatever's going on had better not interfere with Jack-time.

Under Mom's suspicious glances, I text Jack a yes. I also text Chloe to tell her I fainted too. Maybe that'll prompt her to trade notes. After a final text to Dr. Sternfield in case my first one didn't go through, I put my phone down.

At the emergency department, the nurse purses her lips. "Since there aren't acute symptoms, the wait may be a while." See, even she isn't worried.

We take our plastic seats, designed more for wiping off vomit than for comfort. We're regulars here, thanks to Sammy. Which is how I know my phone's useless in most of the building. I try to ignore the infomercial for liposuction blaring overhead while Sammy sits on a stadium cushion he brought along and pulls out his sketchpad. Why didn't I think to pack the basics, the way I've done on so many visits here?

One infomercial and two cartoons later, a medical assistant, whose piercings droop as much as his shoulders, asks me to follow him. Mom'll stay in the waiting room with Sammy unless she's needed.

We thread our way past carts of equipment to where the assistant weighs and measures me before taking my temperature and blood pressure. He types into his pad. "Well, you seem stable now. But we don't mess around with fainting."

"Yeah, my mom either."

He shrugs. "Parents do that. Enjoy it while you can." He leaves me in a room.

I change into the flimsy gown and perch on the exam table. The walls are covered in paintings of vines and monkeys to make kids forget they're stuck in a hospital. Not working. They should hire Sammy to do a mural.

A lanky woman with short grayish hair and arresting blue eyes marches in a few minutes later. "Hi Aislyn, I'm Dr. Sandra Culdicott." Her lined face looks as if it hasn't cracked a smile in a long time. Not the typical perky doctor they employ here.

She gives me a quick exam while she rattles off a long list of questions. The only thing I omit from my answers is the Charisma. Which of course is the only thing that would explain the fainting.

She pecks at her tablet. "Since you don't seem dehydrated, I won't give you a saline bolus. But I'm going to order a basic metabolic panel that you'll do at the lab. We'll also do a urinalysis and an EKG. If everything looks normal, we'll send you home and then you should see your primary care doctor in a few days to follow up. But if you faint again, come in right away."

How much would all this cost Mom? A wave of guilt sweeps over me. But if I reveal the gene therapy, who knows how many additional tests the doctor will order up? Mom'll be billed out the kazoo and I'd be kept here all day, maybe even longer.

A half hour later, after the EKG machine spits out a ribbon of results and a lab assistant collects the necessary bodily fluids to prove I'm not dying, I'm dismissed. We head back out into the drizzly day.

I check my phone. "If we hurry, I can pick up the last two hours of my shift."

Mom stops as if someone's yanked her with a lasso. "What if you faint while you're in the water? No, you're staying home. To rest."

Sammy gives me a knowing look and apologetic shrug.

At home, after Mom uselessly takes my temperature again, she leaves to drop off Sammy at a neighbor's so I'll have no excuse not to nap while she's at work. Of course, now the sun shines bright and hot, promising a spectacular late afternoon.

Not feeling a bit tired, I check my phone. Chloe hasn't responded to my message. Well, she has, but only to invite me again to her bonfire-potluck-party-you-don't-wanna-miss tonight. Sounds like something fun to do with Jack, plus a chance to see Chloe up close and figure out if she also got Charisma.

Jack's game when I text him the details. That gives me

time for a quick nap to fulfill my daughterly obligation. After all, Mom's orders were to take a nap today. She said nothing about tonight.

When Jack arrives a couple of hours later, we meet with a kiss that feels shy for only a moment before a longer one takes its place.

"Ready?" he asks.

"For anything."

His eyes widen in a most satisfying way.

We drive toward Ballard, about thirty miles northwest, through downtown Seattle, which always strikes me as the "big city," even though Tacoma's no slouch. Along the way, we pick up ears of corn for the cookout, and, with a wink, Jack buys a jar of passion fruit juice to add to our offerings. Our last purchase is a large taro bubble shake, a milky, lavender concoction of sweetness that's laced with chewy balls of tapioca, the "bubbles."

With the warm wind blowing through the car and Mumford and Sons pounding through the speakers, we ride in a delicious state of anticipation, passing the bubble shake back and forth. We have to shout over the breeze and the engine, but mostly we're laughing, until I almost choke on a tapioca bubble.

Jack slows the car. "Careful, you don't want to end up in the hospital."

"Ugh. I've been there enough for one day."

"What? Are you okay?" His shoulders turn as if he's ready to steer the car back home.

"Totally fine. It was just, uh, for my brother. He has to go a lot for his CF. But he's okay." I feel like I've poured a cup of acid into this pool of bliss. No more lies, I vow to myself.

Soon enough, Jack spurs me into laughter again, all the way to Golden Gardens Park. The rains from this morning have washed the skies clean across the water all the way to the jagged Olympic Mountains in the distance.

We stroll toward the rocky beach, where a cluster of drums beat next to the crashing surf. A few brightly dressed women sit cross-legged behind blankets loaded with crystal jewelry and large hula hoops decorated in rainbows of gaffer tape.

"Happy solstice!" a woman with long braids and a flowy dress calls to us. "Would you like your fortune read?"

Jack seems willing, but I turn her down. I don't need a fake psychic to tell me that my future has changed for the better.

Chloe swirls through dozens of folks in their teens and twenties. I recognize an African American guy with huge shoulders and dimples from Chloe's online page—her boyfriend, Jesse. If the Charisma doesn't explain her recent glow, it's clearly this hot guy sliding an arm around her waist.

Jack and I add our offerings to the food tables and grab

cups of passion fruit juice for ourselves. A grill sizzles with skewers of chicken and pineapple that lace the air with a sweet smoke. I inhale the evening, confident that the strangers happily chatting around us are opportunities to be explored rather than threats to avoid.

Before Jack and I can slide into a friendly cluster, someone grabs me from behind with a squeal. "Aislyn!"

It takes me a moment to recognize Rosa from the Nova Genetics siblings group. Her heart-shaped face is flushed and her large brown eyes are overly bright.

She meets me with open arms. Literally. Is this really Rosa? Since when does she hug? Since when do I hug back? A tiny knot twists in my stomach at the not-so-intangible changes in her personality.

Her laugh tinkles like wind chimes. "So Chloe convinced you to come too. Excellent. Such a night for it. I feel so energetic, so alive. I just tried out for next year's cheerleading squad at my school. Isn't that amazing?"

I take a step back. I'd been totally wrong about Rosa being shy speaking English.

A boy with short dark hair and intense eyebrows sidles up to her. She takes his arm and introduces him as Jonathan. The pride in her voice indicates whatever she has going with him is new. No doubt my voice sounds the same when I introduce Jack.

I try not to stare too intensely at Rosa. "It's weird seeing you outside of Nova Genetics. You seem different." It has to be Charisma, but will she admit it?

She waves off my words. "The place where I'm different is at those lame meetings. Aren't they awful?"

How to ask what I want without the boys catching on? I say, "The day wasn't a total waste, was it? Did Dr. Sternfield take you to see the chimps?"

She blinks at me for a moment and then a grin flickers. "Just Ruby. She was super-friendly."

That's an admission if I ever heard one. "Bursting with charisma?"

Rosa glances at Jonathan and says nervously, "I guess." She points to a guy playing guitar. "He's excellent, no?"

So, the vow of secrecy is still in effect.

I give up trying to get info out of Rosa for now and let myself drift into the music, the crowd, the perfect evening. The guitar player actually *is* excellent. Maybe he's been medically enhanced too. Hah.

Jack and I, always connected at some part of our bodies, meet Chloe's friends and followers: students, musicians, artists, and folks whose life mission seems to be finding the best parties. I hold my arm out to a girl who paints it with an intricate design of swirls and flourishes that remind me of the ocean. Nearby, the real ocean splashes against the rough beach. Chloe prances just outside the dark border on the sand marking where the surf reaches. I pull Jack toward her.

She holds up a cup of something in greeting. "Glad you came, Aislyn." She eyes Jack. "Bet I know who you are."

Blushing, I confirm her guess.

She makes a theatrical pout. "Shane'll be disappointed."

Jack's expression is puzzled, but he keeps smiling. "Shane?"

I groan. "A ridiculous guy who came to our family event."

Chloe grins and points. "Who also brought his own camera crew tonight."

Twenty yards away, Shane laughs with two girls wearing halter tops to show off some serious ink on their backs. A guy with a camera on his shoulder and a girl holding a boom microphone follow their every move.

Chloe hollers until she catches Shane's attention. With a wave, he saunters over.

To me, he says, "My newest applicant!"

Jack and Chloe say in unison, "Applicant?"

Oh yeah, I did, didn't I? Time to follow through on that little plan. I give a come-hither glance to the camera until it's covering me, and say to Shane, "So I made the cut?"

He eyes Jack. "If it's cool with your loverboy here, it's cool with me."

Jack looks confused, even after I give him a reassuring kiss on the cheek. I gaze into the camera lens. "Actually, none of this is cool. Any girl who thinks she has to compete to hang out with a guy who's fooling around with a dozen other girls should think again." I turn to Chloe. "Would you put up with a guy two-timing you?"

She laughs, "Hell no, not even for a hottie like Shane."

Shane pats his chest in mock horror. The tattooed girls fawn over him and give me the stink eye. The shorter one says, "You don't know what you're missing."

The three of them launch into gyrations in time to the drums. The camera guy's hips swivel vicariously. Well, I tried.

Jack and I grab spots next to the roaring bonfire. He laughs when I explain the whole business with Shane. Whew. Bringing me up close to his face, he says, "But no more applications, okay?"

I kiss him leisurely. "I'm totally, completely taken."

With tiny embers floating through the air, we enjoy the conversation, the food, the music. Rosa and Jonathan join us again. Who'd have thought I'd hang out with folks from the Nova Genetics teen group, with at least two of us acting way more extroverted than usual? And way happier.

Thank you, Charisma.

Even though Shane is the primary target of the camera, I notice it pointing toward me, Chloe, and Rosa more often than anyone else. Either Shane clued in the camera guy or we really do sparkle more.

At one point Chloe convinces Rosa and me to join her in a bizarre hula that she insists is an aphrodisiac. Jack doesn't argue when I leave his side for that. The three of us girls laugh hysterically and mug for the camera.

The scents wafting through the air now include marijuana and something flowery, as if we're on a tropical island. I close my eyes to it and savor the happy noise surrounding me. Soon I feel Jack's warm lips on mine and breathe him in.

We sway and glide alongside each other as the sun dips into the horizon. I bask in the warmth and lightness and love. In another life, I could've been a hippie, I bet. The night is ours and I never want to leave. I don't even want to open my eyes.

But a scream jolts me out of my delicious haze.

All heads snap to a huddle of lacy pink on the ground. Rosa.

TEN

Fifty cell phones whip out, whether to call for help or take video, I couldn't say.

Jonathan kneels at her side, yelling, "Rosa, wake up!"

Suddenly, Chloe pulls me to her side and rasps into my ear, "She'll come to soon. I only blacked out for a few minutes. It's normal."

"Normal for what?"

"You know what. And we shouldn't say anything."

"Even if we can help?"

"How?" Her voice sharpens. "All we'd do is cause a whole lot of unnecessary freak-out that won't help anyone."

Fortunately, there's a nurse among the beachgoers who tends to Rosa. And before the first siren arrives, Rosa's stirring. I have to admit Chloe's right. Nothing here outside of the "normal" symptoms of Charisma.

Normal or not, the medics insist on taking Rosa to the hospital, even after she begs them not to. Before they load her into the ambulance, she calls out to the crowd, "I'll be mad if you stop the party."

We wave her off with good wishes, and murmur reassurances to each other. The drums start up again, a hypnotic rumble.

I glance at the time and say to Jack, "We should get going."

On the drive to Tacoma, our tired silence is only interrupted by a message beep from my phone. It's from Dr. Sternfield: THE FAINTING IS BECAUSE YOUR BODY IS WORKING IN HYPERDRIVE. THERE'S SO MUCH TO BE EXCITED ABOUT! EAT MORE, DRINK MORE, AND SLEEP MORE. YOUR DREAMS WILL COME TRUE AS LONG AS YOU KEEP CALM AND QUIET.

I breathe a long sigh. "Rosa's going to be okay. Just too much going on."

"Sounds familiar." He taps the steering wheel in the same rhythm as the drums from the beach. "Funny how things changed so quickly for you and me."

"Way overdue."

He runs his fingers along my arm. "Tell me about it."

The heated atmosphere is spiced with anticipation. At

home, we say a luscious good-night and promise to get together the next day. Tingling from scalp to toes, I float into
the house.

Where Mom perches on the sofa, beady-eyed.

I say, "Did you get my note?"

Her voice is hard. "You were supposed to rest."

"I did. But I also had plans with Jack. I'll be fine for work
tomorrow."

She pulls the afghan tighter around her shoulders. "I
don't know what's gotten into you lately."

Well, to be fair, she doesn't. I have to remember how
bizarre my behavior must seem. "Mom, I've never been
happier. I hope you'll be glad for me."

She sighs. "Of course I want you to be happy. But Sammy
had something to be happy about tonight too, that he wanted
to celebrate with both of us. He's been accepted into the
AV719 trial."

"Oh my God, that's great!" I rush over to hug her. We owe
Dr. Sternfield and Nova Genetics so much. Someday I'd tell
Mom just how much.

Our spontaneous hug shatters the tension. We can always
agree on wanting the best for Sammy.

Mom tucks my hair behind my ear. "Now, go get some
sleep."

I skip upstairs. Really, so much good far outweighs a couple of tiny side effects. Sammy will probably have a few from the AV719. We all simply needed to acclimate.

The following morning, I get a message from someone at the Red Cross, who saw my plea for organ donors and asks if I'll make a public service announcement to encourage blood donations. I pause, my mind reeling. There's much more to Charisma than hanging out with Jack. My new abilities could make a meaningful difference.

I pore through requests from marketing organizations, one offering to pay me for every shout-out I do on their behalf, another suggesting I open my page to advertisements, promising that with my "star power" I could earn enough for college in no time. Wow. The chance to cover college would take such a load off of Mom. I've done a good, good thing by stepping up for Dr. Sternfield's treatment.

Amazed by my online opportunities, I check in on *The Shane Show*. It's full of photos and clips from last night. *Exuberant* is the only way to describe how I appear in the videos. A few messages hint that Shane's program will be picked up by TrueNufTV. The mainstream media does not waste time.

On that note, I head downstairs to congratulate Sammy on getting into the trial. But when I reach the dining room, I stop short. Mom's at the table with a pained expression. We have to stop meeting like this.

"What now?" I ask.

"You tell me."

Uh-oh. Keep calm and assess the damage. "What?"

She twists her mug back and forth on the tabletop. "I got a call from Chloe's mother. Both Rosa and Chloe have fainted in the past week. Did you know that?"

"I heard Chloe was sick, but she got better already."

"Well, just in case, I've contacted Dr. Gordon. He's arranged a meeting for the teen sibs who attended the event last Sunday so we can get to the bottom of this."

My gut twinges. Would everyone keep quiet until the side effects went away? "Mom, *this* is probably nothing."

"We're meeting in an hour at Florence Bishop. It's the closest hospital to Nova Genetics." Mom and Dr. Gordon, the power duo of efficiency.

I say, "But I have to work. I already missed yesterday. They'll fire me."

"I've called your boss. Health comes first."

No arguing with her favorite mantra. I'm finally fit to be a decent lifeguard and I'll lose my job by being absent so often. Great. Huffing, I fry myself an egg, showing Mom how healthy I feel. Because I am. Except for the anxiety that someone will spill our secret and ruin the best thing that's ever happened to me.

I eat quickly and head upstairs to call Evie with the latest.

She whistles. "So are you going to come clean?"

I whisper even though my bedroom door is shut. "I don't see any upside to doing that."

"C'mon, Aiz, even after fainting?"

"I told you there's an explanation."

"Then why didn't Dr. Sucksfield warn you beforehand?"

I huddle into myself and clutch the phone tighter. "Maybe she only realized it after the fact."

"Sounds sketchy."

I sigh. "You're still on my side, though, right?"

Longer pause than necessary. "Of course. It's just that if I can't count on you to be the sensible one, we're both in trouble." She hangs up.

She counts on me to be sensible. I count on her to give me a boost when I'm freaking out. Guess neither of us is living up to expectations.

Mom and I drop off Sammy at the neighbor's on the way into downtown Tacoma. He hauls a backpack full of art supplies and comic books, and marches toward their door like a soldier facing battle. I say a silent prayer the neighbor's sons will include Sammy in their games for a change.

At Florence Bishop, Mom and I are directed to a large room with a private buffet, where Rosa and her parents huddle with crossed arms and sullen faces.

I hurry over and give Rosa a hug. "Everything okay?"

"Much better. Too much go, go, go. Even my ears are buzzing. My body's on hyperdrive, you know?"

Hyperdrive. So she's been texting Dr. Sternfield too.

We help ourselves to meatloaf and corn, and sit at a table with Chloe and her dad. I ask Chloe how she's doing.

She loads her fork with lumpy mashed potatoes. "A little dizzy. No big thing."

Her dad, a hulking man with graying brown hair, stabs his knife in the air. "No big thing? Kids aren't supposed to faint. I've never fainted in my whole life." He points the knife toward me and Rosa. "Your parents think it's no big thing?"

I look at my plate, thankful Mom sat at a different table. "I feel fine now."

"Me too," Rosa says, rubbing her ear.

Chloe's dad shakes his head. "Kids."

As we eat, I survey the room. Mom huddles with a cluster of other parents, no doubt exchanging data. Shane jokes with the twins, their laughter ringing out every few seconds. Thankfully, the camera crew for *The Shane Show* isn't here.

The crowd quiets when Dr. Gordon enters the room along with two women in white coats. One is the tall short-haired doctor who examined me yesterday, the second one much younger with a blond ponytail and horn-rimmed glasses.

Dr. Gordon shakes a few hands and then clears his throat.

"Thank you all for coming on such short notice." He nods to the doctors. "And thank you, Drs. Culdicott and Fisk, for joining us."

He says, "So far, we know of three teens who've had fainting spells since the family gathering. Therefore, we're hunting down possibilities of a common contaminant. The more we know, the better we can help you."

Kiera, of the red hair with fiery ends, calls out, "Couldn't you have texted us?"

Dr. Gordon clasps his hands. "It's more effective to speak with everyone face-to-face and scan for physical symptoms. It's also crucial not to panic or spread stories until we know what's going on."

Kiera makes a hacking sound. "What are the symptoms exactly?"

Dr. Gordon counts off on his fingers. "Headaches, mild fevers, and fainting for short periods. We've also heard reports of personality changes."

A boy with apple cheeks shouts, "Like Dr. Jekyll and Mr. Hyde?" He wags his head back and forth, eyes goggling.

Wrinkles crease Dr. Gordon's fleshy forehead. "Nothing so sinister. It's been described as people acting in a more extroverted manner than normally."

"Like Chloe!" one of the twins shouts.

Chloe beams. "Check out the KBLB site tonight." I still

can't understand why she'd accept Charisma, but at least her feistiness gives me confidence.

My mom's voice cuts through the din. "Do the symptoms you've seen have anything in common with the illness of your staff member Steffie Wong?"

Everyone in the room goes stock-still. Why is Mom freaking everyone out? We've only been fainting, not dying.

Dr. Gordon raises his arms to calm us. "We deeply mourn the loss of Steffie. But there's nothing to indicate any connection."

Nods and murmurs ripple through the crowd. Then a few more questions that don't tread new ground. Time to get to business. Dr. Gordon and the other doctors each call out a name and three kids march to the front for an interrogation.

Chloe nudges Rosa and me. "We'll all be smart about this, right?"

Rosa and I say, "Of course."

"Good. Then let's go hang with the others." We pull up chairs to the table with the most teens.

Shane levels a hard gaze at me.

I brush a lock of hair from my face. "What?"

He leans back and crosses his arms. "Just enjoying the personality change from the girl formerly known as ice princess."

I cross my own arms. "Why does the guy-currently-known-as-a-gigolo care?"

He licks his lips and smiles. "So, how many times have you fainted?"

Rosa puts a hand on my arm. "We should save the medical talk for the doctors."

I squint at Shane. "What about you? Any fevers?"

"I always run pretty hot."

I roll my eyes.

Soon the doctors call up the next three teens, which include Chloe and one of the twins. They head off as if this is so much silliness to be endured.

Kiera sighs. "Complete waste of time. Just because a few kids got sick."

Ten minutes later, the doctors dismiss the second group and call me, Rosa, and the other twin. Hey, maybe I'll get out of here soon after all. And see Jack tonight.

Rosa takes my arm and whispers, "Don't worry. We're okay. I've never felt more alive, more connected. I really see everyone more clearly, how they feel, what excites them. It's amazing. I want to feel this way always. Don't you?"

Of course I do. Which means our secret is still safe.

I sit next to Dr. Culdicott. She asks me to retrace my steps at Nova Genetics last weekend. I do without mentioning the Charisma.

When I reach the part about visiting a chimp, the doctor

raises her eyebrows. "You didn't mention this in your initial exam."

"I didn't?" I peek at Rosa, who speaks to Dr. Gordon using exaggerated hand movements. Sweat stains bloom under her arms despite the air-conditioning, and her body seems to sway precariously on the chair.

My attention is so focused on Rosa, I miss Dr. Culdicott's question. "Excuse me?"

"I asked whether you touched the chimps at all."

"Uh, yeah, I shook Ruby's hand."

"And then you went to lunch? Did you wash your hands first?"

I feel like a naughty preschooler. "Uh, no."

"Aha." She types as if she's uncovered the Dead Sea scrolls.

My attention is drawn to Rosa, who holds her hands over her ears. Glancing around, I notice everyone in the room is fixated on her too. Uh-oh.

She slumps against Dr. Gordon, moaning. Dr. Culdicott rushes over to them, and has Rosa settle to the floor. The younger doctor with the glasses calls for assistance.

And the room falls silent.

Rosa weakly waves the doctors away. "I'm okay," she says in a raspy voice, before going silent.

I hold my breath as pressure builds in my head. Get up, Rosa, get up.

Everyone's face twitches with anxiety, yet curiosity too, and even excitement. A gangly orderly with an orange beard shouts for us to make way so he can get through with a gurney. The crowd parts, their interest and apprehension becoming more palpable when Rosa's body goes limp in Dr. Culdicott's arms. The doctor and the orderly lift her onto the gurney and roll it out, followed by Dr. Fisk.

The silent vacuum in their wake only lasts a few moments. Xavier, Dr. Sternfield's intern, rushes into the room, knocking over a chair. Wait a minute. He wasn't at the family event. He doesn't need to be here.

Although I've rarely heard him use anything but a soft-spoken voice at Nova Genetics, his words now come out like a newscaster's.

"Enough," he says, "I know what's making people sick."

ELEVEN

Everyone in the room turns his way. I inch toward the door.

Chloe's dad slams the table. "Well, tell us."

One mom, whose face has gone splotchy, tugs at Xavier's sleeve. "Before any more kids pass out." The other parents snarl and sputter as they tighten around Xavier.

Xavier pulls back his shoulders. "I think the kids who've been fainting were given a gene therapy."

There. The volcanic ash of the truth settles over the crowd.

Dr. Gordon's mouth drops along with everyone else's. Then he wags a finger at Xavier. "Now, wait a minute, wait a minute."

But no one's waiting for anything. Chloe's dad yells, "A gene therapy? What in Hades for?"

Chloe's next to me, cursing. The mass of bodies around

us heats the room to stifling. Yet I can't force these locked knees to move, and that old familiar drowning sensation squeezes my lungs.

Xavier clears his throat. "To be more outgoing, less inhibited."

The room erupts again. Dr. Gordon, who wobbles amid crazed parents, shouts, "Please, calm down. I assure you Nova Genetics isn't in the business of administering rogue gene therapy, and certainly not for inhibitions, despite what this young man asserts." He turns to Xavier. "You should be ashamed of yourself for needlessly upsetting everyone."

Xavier doesn't flinch. "You have a better explanation? Tainted geoducks, maybe?"

Dr. Gordon's face is scarlet. "The rest of you please hold on until I set this young man straight." He ushers Xavier out a side door.

The room falls silent as everyone digests what's going on, and then explodes with exclamations of disbelief. Chloe's dad grabs her by the shoulders. "You what?" he screams in her face. That's when I catch sight of Mom storming toward me, her gaze ready to ignite. I huddle behind a chair, as if that'll do any good.

Her face radiates fear and rage, to an extent I've never seen. "Did you know anything about this?" She grasps my arm. "No more lies. This is dangerous."

I put up my hands in surrender. "Can we talk later?"

The side door opens and Dr. Gordon pops his head into our room. "Chloe and Aislyn, I want you out here too."

Kiera whines, "Why didn't I get any gene therapy? No fair."

With everyone glaring daggers, Mom drags me out the door, which leads to a hallway. Chloe and her parents tumble after us.

Dr. Gordon shoots Xavier a pointed look. "Tell them what you told me."

Xavier says, "Three weeks ago, a researcher offered me an experimental gene therapy called Charisma, or CZ88. She wouldn't show me the exact combination of genes it targeted, but I trusted her work enough to say yes. The next day I felt really powerful, not afraid to ask my parents if I could enroll in an art class, which they think is a waste of time for a pre-med student. And I wasn't as hesitant about speaking with people who came in for gene sequencing."

He swallows, and the shine in his eyes dulls. "But then I started getting headaches and feeling dizzy. I fainted a week ago, and again last night."

Dr. Gordon rubs his brow. "Now, I'm going to ask you again. Which researcher did this?"

Xavier's stance falters for a second. "I'd rather speak to someone more official."

Chloe's dad's face goes dark as he closes in on Xavier. His voice drips venom. "Like a lawyer? Why? Did you do this to my daughter?"

Xavier balls his fist. "No."

Chloe's dad pokes Xavier's chest with a stubby finger. "Then stop pissing around. Who's behind this?"

Xavier glances at Chloe, then at me. I give him a nod. The secret's already out. No use getting pummeled by Chloe's dad.

Xavier takes a long breath. "Dr. Sternfield."

Dr. Gordon sputters. "Charlie? Impossible."

Xavier's posture stays ramrod straight, although I sense his insides crumbling at betraying his boss and idol. "I wish it weren't true."

Dr. Gordon turns to me. "And you, Aislyn? Did Charlie give you something?"

I swallow. "Um."

Mom glares. "The truth. Now."

I remember Rosa's limp body and say, "Yeah."

There's a chorus of gasps. Dr. Gordon addresses Chloe. "You too?"

Chloe crosses her arms. "Dr. Sternfield's a freaking genius. The drug even took my personality to a new level."

Chloe's father snaps, "That *genius* should be in jail."

Dr. Gordon loosens his tie. "Please, let's get the facts before we convict."

The door next to us opens, sending a wave of noise blasting into the hallway. Along with Shane and his dad. I shouldn't be surprised that the drug is behind Shane's girl-gathering escapades, but what was Dr. Sternfield thinking?

Shane shrugs. "The truth will set us free, right?"

His story matches ours. Dr. Sternfield gave him, Rosa, and me the CZ88 last weekend. Chloe and Sebastian received it a week earlier and Xavier a week before that. None of us know if there are others.

Mom tugs at her necklace. "We have to tell the doctors, now that we know the truth." At the last word, her gaze my way could knock a bird from the sky.

Dr. Gordon fumbles with his phone. "I should call Charlie first, see what her side of the story is." He paces away from us.

Mom yanks me away from the others. Her throat pulses and her skin is crimson. "You allowed yourself to be used as a guinea pig for a shyness drug?"

The weight of her wrath slams me. "Dr. Sternfield promised it would be safe. She's on our side. Look how she got Sammy into that trial for AV719."

Mom's breathing becomes noisy. "Unbelievable. That woman administered an untested drug? On kids?" She blows out in exasperation. "You've always been so sensible. And this is just madness."

"Is it really so crazy to want to be fixed?"

Chloe and Shane are battling the same arguments with their parents. Sweating profusely, Xavier leans against a wall looking miserable. I hope he isn't about to faint. But he, like the rest of us, stands to attention when Dr. Culdicott joins us in the hallway.

Dr. Gordon steps toward her. "How's Rosa doing?"

Gotta give him points for asking about Rosa first. Unless it's just for show.

Dr. Culdicott's face is grim. "Still unconscious." She points back toward the room. "The folks in there said something about a gene therapy?"

Dr. Gordon rubs his hands together. "I'm trying to assess that allegation."

She whips toward me and barks, "What happened?"

I clear my throat and tell her about the Charisma.

Chloe plants a hand on her hip. "The fainting and headaches are normal, just ask Dr. Sternfield."

Dr. Culdicott says, "Who?"

Now it's Dr. Gordon's turn. "My daughter, who runs a lab at Nova Genetics. However, I highly doubt she'd participate in something like this."

Dr. Culdicott pauses a moment, and then takes hold of the door behind her. "After I dismiss everyone not involved with this drug, I'm going to speak with you all. This time you're giving me the whole truth." She forges into the other room.

Chloe's mother tugs Dr. Gordon's jacket. "Dr. Sternfield never mentioned the CZ88 to you? The whole idea is crazy, right?"

He removes his glasses and wipes them with a handkerchief for the second time in five minutes. "Yes. My company targets diseases, not personality traits, which can't be ascribed to a single gene anyway. This must be an enormous misunderstanding."

Mom taps her foot. "Oh, come on, there's no misunderstanding. We need to notify the authorities." She pulls out her phone even though it's probably useless in here.

Dr. Gordon's hand rests lightly on her arm. "There doesn't seem to be cell access here. And which authorities would you notify exactly, Danielle? I'll do everything possible to figure out whether and what the kids got and how to reverse it. It's crucial we keep this under control so we can focus on a fix rather than dealing with the hysteria that's sure to burst if this goes public."

Mom stares at him, nostrils flaring. "Let's hear what Dr. Culdicott has to say."

Desperate for some peace, I slink down the hall. If I hold my phone up high, it gets a weak signal. So I type in a message for Dr. Sternfield and raise the phone overhead to press

SEND. I also text Evie with the news that all is out in the open. That should make her happy.

After fifteen minutes, the door opens again. Dr. Culdicott says, "I have some perplexing news. First, Rosa's gone into a coma."

We all inhale sharply.

The skin around Dr. Culdicott's eyes is sallow, as if she's worked too many shifts in a row. "Second, there's a young man named Jesse who's been admitted to the ED, complaining of fainting. He says he's—"

Chloe's voice falters. "My boyfriend?"

The doctor nods. "Who insists he's never been to Nova Genetics or been involved in any gene therapy."

We blink at each other as the implications of this news settles in.

Dr. Culdicott heaves a long sigh. "Whatever you got in this gene treatment may be contagious."

I swallow. "Contagious? How can that be?"

Dr. Culdicott says, "Any theories, Dr. Gordon?"

Xavier pipes up. "The altered DNA is carried by a virus. Dr. Sternfield's been trying different viral vectors to get past the blood-brain barrier yet still provide sufficient doses of multi-gene therapies. She could've made a miscalculation on whether the virus was deactivated."

Mom says, "So how contagious is this virus that carries the gene treatment?"

Dr. Gordon glares. "Hold on, hold on. Let's not get ahead of ourselves."

Dr. Culdicott glances from face to face, as if trying to ascertain the truth of what must sound insane. I can hardly believe it myself. My blood runs cold at the possibility I've infected my family and friends with CZ88. Oh my God, Jack too.

The doctors huddle, and then head off to consult with other staff. Everyone else waits in the meeting room, the parents discussing lawsuits and the teens not saying much to each other, which is weird given how sociable we're supposed to be. Shane and Chloe each take turns on the wall phone, though.

An hour later, Dr. Gordon returns. "I'm heading out to track down information about the purported gene therapy. In the meantime, I've suggested to Dr. Culdicott that you be kept here overnight for observation. Nova Genetics will cover all expenses."

I turn to Mom. "I don't need to stay over. I haven't felt headache-y all day."

Mom glares. "You'll do what the doctors suggest."

The doctors suggest we ride up to the third floor and make our way past a secure door with a camera that Dr. Culdicott waves to before we're buzzed inside. I head through, more annoyed than anything else. Only when the door clicks behind me do I wish I'd taken the time to run outside for one more breath of fresh air and a stroll through the garden.

Charisma must be making me paranoid.

Online feeds...

Posted by TheShaneShowCrew: Send your good vibes to our bro, Shane, who's stuck in Florence Bishop Children's Hospital (which for the record treats patients through age twenty-one). If you're a hot nurse on duty there, give us a shout-out!

Posted by FarrahS: Chloe and Jesse! Both of you?? What's up with that? Kisses and hugs, you guys! When's the next party?

Posted by Mia Santiago: The Ravens' cheering squad is announced! Congrats to my girl Rosa!

Posted by KieraTheRed: A crapload of kids who went to Nova Genetics last weekend took a drug to make them lovable. How pathetic is that?

Posted by JackThompson: Aislyn? Why aren't you answering your phone?

TWELVE

Dr. Fisk escorts the boys down the hall while Dr. Culdicott leads Chloe and me into a large room with three beds and faded pink curtains. She says, "A med tech may take another blood draw later, now that we know what's up." With a pointed flick of her eyes, she leaves.

Chloe claims the bed by the window and I take the one by the door. Hopefully Rosa will recover enough to take the spot between us, all slumber-party-like. After a few minutes of discussion, our parents take off to fetch us overnight items.

The second they're gone, Chloe and I dive for the corded phones on the shelves next to our beds. Of course my first call is to Evie.

She answers, crunching on something. "Aislyn! What's going on? I texted you a million times."

I try to keep my voice calm as I tell her. "I just don't understand how Chloe's boyfriend got it." That's the weirdest thing. Gene therapy is not supposed to be contagious. But creating a virus to attack specific cells and stitch DNA into just the right spot is still a radically new science.

"Does Jack know yet?"

I shiver uncontrollably. "I'm not sure what to tell him."

Her voice lacks all of its usual laughter. "I'd go with the truth."

My cord-wrapped hand blooms red. "That should go over well."

There's a knock at the door. "Gotta go. Could you please, please check and make sure Jack's not fainting or anything?"

"This is seriously—"

"You're the best." I disconnect myself from the cord with trembling fingers.

A nurse marches in followed by Xavier, Shane, Jesse, and a light-brown-skinned guy with close-cropped hair and a languorous way of moving that reminds me of a feline. He introduces himself as Sebastian. Both Chloe and Xavier met him at Nova Genetics. Apparently, he has superior dancer genes, which doesn't take genomic sequencing to figure out.

In a no-nonsense voice, the nurse says the boys will have to return to their own room next door if things get too rowdy. Before leaving, she adds, "No funny stuff."

Most of the guys grab chairs and make a semi-circle around the bedless side of the room. Chloe and Jesse nestle next to each other on what should be Rosa's spot, eyeing Chloe's bed as if they have plans for "funny stuff." Thank goodness for curtains.

I say to Sebastian, "Saw your video on Chloe's page. How'd your call-back go?"

Sebastian crosses his legs in a graceful swoop. "I did okay."

Xavier, who doesn't seem able to take his eyes off of him, says, "Bet you nailed it."

"It helps that I'm way less inhibited these days."

Shane cocks his head. "So how did you end up here if you aren't part of the siblings group?"

"Xavier and I kept in touch after he sequenced my genome." He laughs. "Sounds kind of weird when you say it that way, huh? Anyway, when I posted about feeling light-headed, he told me to get my butt here."

Xavier sighs loudly. "Still can't believe Dr. Sternfield lured you. If I'd had any idea …"

"Hey, she got to you too."

"But I needed it. You're the best dancer I've ever seen."

Sebastian pulls a leg to his chest, stretching. "With auditions, I needed an edge. Dr. Sternfield knew that."

I say, "She knew us all." I frown at Shane. "But it seems

like you'd be a better guinea pig for testing a drug that would make you less extroverted."

He grins. "Dr. Charlotte promised me something a little different."

"Really? A cure for obnoxiousness?"

His eyelids lower to half-mast. "She said it would make me irresistibly charming."

Good Lord. I pretend to study him. "Not working."

He runs a hand through his longish curls and gives me a slow once-over. "You know, I thought the cold-hottie thing was working for you. Never would've guessed you'd go for the big, scary injection. You keep surprising me, Blondie."

I channel my inner Evie to shoot him a lazy eye-roll. But for some reason, he doesn't annoy me as much today. Could be I'm building up an immunity.

Shane glances around the room. "What about the rest of you guys? What did the RILF promise you?"

"Rilf?" I ask.

"Researcher I'd like to—"

"Never mind."

Chloe tells everyone about her political ambitions. I mention the disastrous science fair. When it's his turn, Xavier squirms so much I wonder if the CZ88 worked on him as much as I thought. Finally, he says, "I wanted to express myself, especially with my family. They come from the Philippines. If I miss Mass on Sundays, they say extra novenas for my soul."

Sebastian blows out a puff of air. "That's a lot of pressure."

Xavier gives him a grateful smile. We're all quiet for a moment.

Xavier's eyes circle the room. "I don't want to scare you guys, but is anyone still feeling faint or running fevers?"

All of us claim to feel fine. Shane hasn't even fainted.

I rub my temple. "Dr. Sternfield isn't answering my calls. You sure you don't know any more about what she gave us?"

Xavier pulls a notepad from a counter that runs behind our beds. "There were so many genes and phenotypes she was investigating. Maybe if I start brainstorming, something will come to me." He scribbles furiously.

Shane snags the TV remote. He surfs through channels until he becomes transfixed on one. I gaze at the screen and squint.

Sebastian points a toe at the TV. "Isn't that Kiera?"

Shane turns up the sound. Sure enough, Kiera faces the camera, breathless and flushed. "Some of the kids took a secret drug to make themselves popular."

The overly hair-sprayed reporter asks, "Secret drug?"

Kiera flips a lock of her striped mane forward and strokes it. "Nova Genetics is always coming up with stuff for rare diseases. But who doesn't want to be popular, right? You should see this one girl, Chloe. I mean, she was already kind of a diva, but she got on the news and everything." Kiera giggles, as if self-aware that here she is on the news too. Then she attempts a pout. "Of course, it all caught up with them. They've been fainting left and right."

So much for keeping this under wraps.

The reporter faces the camera. "We don't have details yet on who provided the drug and how many people received it. Nova Genetics refuses to comment. We'll be investigating further as well as updating you on the condition of the victims."

Shane bats the remote through the air. "Victims?"

Chloe huffs. "I'm the only victim here. That bitch told the whole world I took an illegal drug."

Sebastian rises to pace, his every step like water flowing. Without any apparent effort, he spins until he ends up at the window. He frowns. "You aren't going to believe this."

We join him, everyone's eyes as big as poker chips. A swarm of news trucks tethered to reporters congregates in the edge of the parking area. Everyone will know what we've done. Even Jack.

Shane slaps Xavier's back. "This is good news, dude. The coverage will pressure Dr. Charlotte to fix us fast."

Chloe sniffs. "Or scare her into running off to a foreign country. Crap, I should be working with KBLB to do a feature on Charisma."

I cough. "I thought you were mad about Kiera outing you on TV."

She straightens her shirt. "I want to control my own publicity. This story could take us places."

Xavier says quietly, "Not if we go into comas."

Sebastian scoots closer to Xavier. "Rosa is probably the exception. Let's focus on the positive. Because so far I've gained a lot more than I've lost. I barely notice the headaches anymore. And I see people so differently. Clearer."

I stare at him. Hadn't Rosa said something similar?

A booming voice comes from the corridor. "Where are the kids?" With a whoosh of air, Dr. Gordon's in the room, greeting each of us, and then pausing for a dramatic breath. "I'm happy to see you all looking so chipper."

"What does Dr. Sternfield say about all this?" I ask.

His cheek twitches. "It totally slipped my mind that this was the weekend she took off to go camping, off the grid. In the meantime, we'll do whatever's necessary to get Rosa back to her old self, and you guys too."

Dr. Sternfield camping? She's never struck me as the outdoorsy type.

Shane's eyes narrow. "What if we don't want to go back to

our old selves? The side effects are supposedly temporary."

Xavier inhales sharply. "Temporary coma? If Dr. Sternfield miscalculated the side effects this badly, we want the CZ88 reversed as soon as possible."

Jesse punches his palm. "I need whatever the hell's in my system out before football season. If I fail the drug test because of this—"

Dr. Gordon raises his hands. "Slow down. You guys relax here tonight, and avoid the press. I've alerted the hospital operator to screen calls."

Chloe sulks. "Why? The story's already out."

He shakes his head, causing his cheeks to wobble. "*Some* of the story's out. So far we've been able to shield your identities." His face becomes somber and his voice lowers. "As you may know, there are people who don't support gene therapy, and may want to take their frustrations out on what they see as a threat."

Chloe clutches Jesse's arm. "What do you mean?"

Dr. Gordon wipes a finger under his glasses. "It's not just vicious protestors. There are businesspeople who don't want this science to develop. If gene alteration can fix diseases with one or two injections, where would that leave the makers of drugs that are routinely proscribed for years? When people stand to lose a lot of money, they can be dangerous. I suggest you keep a low profile. Okay?"

We nod blankly. Thanking us, he leaves.

As soon as the door shuts, Chloe says, "Do you believe that? He only wants to protect his butt."

I play with a loose thread on my blanket. "You ever run into those anti-gene-therapy folks up close?"

She groans. "They're just a bunch of losers with signs. Boy, Dr. Gordon totally got into your head. He's trying to scare us to protect his rotten daughter."

Shane slaps his forehead. "Oh, man. We totally missed an opportunity to blackmail him for our silence."

I sigh. "Seriously? What would you have asked him for?"

"Some entertainment, for starters. This place is hardly party central."

Sebastian rises and spins. "We can make our own entertainment. Who's got tunes?"

Xavier turns the TV to a music channel. Sebastian convinces us to get off our sorry butts so he can show us a few hip-hop moves. As promised, we're all soon dancing and laughing. His hands are on my shoulders, guiding me through a Scooby when my mom walks in.

She holds out a small overnight bag. "Perhaps it's time to calm down?"

Dr. Fisk enters the room behind Mom. "Mrs. Hollings is right. Why don't you guys return to your own room? I'll give everyone a quick look-see."

Sighing, the boys say their good-byes and head off. Dr. Fisk starts with me, rattling off questions. She types briskly. "It all sounds good." With a curt nod, she moves to Chloe's bed.

Mom sits in the chair next to mine. "You seem anxious." Actually, she's the one chewing off her nail polish. Her fear rolls off in waves.

I select a pair of sweats from the three choices she brought. "I'm only afraid of what my friends will think."

"What about what *I* think?" She leans forward. "I never believed things were so painful you'd take such drastic means to change them."

I stare at the floor. "What about losing out on that science scholarship? Or dealing with creeps at the pool? I couldn't even survive a party. There's always something to deal with, Mom, every day. I'd have tried anything to go from the way things were to what I've had in the past days. It's worth a few headaches and a fainting spell."

She takes a long breath. "You shouldn't worry about the scholarship. If I make more cold calls, take on more open houses for the other agents, I can—"

"Mom, you already work a ridiculous number of hours. And you need every bit of extra money for Sammy. It's time I carried more of the burden."

Chloe's voice rises on the other side of the room. "I'm telling you I feel good."

Dr. Fisk keeps a neutral volume. "Your fever is over a hundred and two."

"I promise I'll let you know if I feel weird."

Dr. Fisk stands. "I'll be back."

Mom asks if she can speak to the doctor in the hall. Then she gives me a quick hug good-bye. Something tells me I should hug her bony body longer. But instead I just tell her I'll see her in the morning.

She and Dr. Fisk take off together, and soon our dinner arrives. Bland chicken, steamed vegetables, and fruit from a can. We watch more TV, where the news reports spread quicker than our viral vectors. One station advertises a roundtable show tomorrow about the promise and peril of gene therapy.

After Chloe's parents stop by with her overnight things and ask us twelve times how we feel, we get ready for bed. I nestle under the covers and turn off the light.

In the dark, Chloe speaks up. "Whatever we have, I've given to Jesse. You know how much that sucks?"

If CZ88's super-contagious, wouldn't more people have caught it from us? With Jesse as the only person directly infected, I can take an educated guess as to one transmission mechanism. But could you catch it with a kiss? A wave of nausea twists through my belly. Good thing Evie's checking on Jack.

Tomorrow, when I'm home, I'll call him myself. By then, I'll have more information. We all will. We have to.

Hunt for Gene Therapy Victims Broadens

Sondra Chevez, Northwest News Central

In light of recent reports of an unregulated gene therapy administered to seven Tacoma teenagers as well as reports of additional victims in several Northwest cities, authorities are scouring local hospitals for unexplained cases of fainting and coma. The families and friends of patients who've experienced such symptoms insist their loved ones acted much more boisterously than usual before they fell ill. Representatives from the State Health Department have set up a command post in Seattle, and our sources indicate they will host a news conference soon.

How far this has spread and who's to blame are among the many critical issues we're investigating, the most important of which is determining the potential danger of CZ88, or "Charisma," to the general public.

THIRTEEN

The next morning, the news crews battle with protestors outside for sidewalk space. When the boys arrive after breakfast, we dream up disguises to get past the crazies unscathed. Except for Chloe, who can't wait to be filmed.

Sebastian insists we'll be less anxious if we get our blood pumping. Anything to release this awful jittery feeling. Even Xavier puts down his ever-present notepad to join us, laughing and flailing until he announces he needs to take a break. The sheen of sweat on his brow and the grayish edge to his complexion have Sebastian and me exchanging pointed glances.

Xavier's appearance only worsens when his parents arrive. His dad, who has the same buzz cut as his son, glares at us. He and his wife huff over to Xavier to each take an arm. Xavier's feet drag beneath a woeful gaze as they head out the door.

Two minutes later, an older male doctor summons the rest of the boys to their ward for a checkup. Dr. Culdicott arrives for Chloe and me. When the doctor pulls out a stethoscope, my new, sociable self asks, "Do you normally work in the ER or up here?"

She raises an eyebrow. "Up here, but after twenty years as an army doc, they welcome me in the ED too."

Her take-no-prisoners demeanor makes a lot more sense. I ask, "How's Rosa?"

She slides the stethoscope around my back. "The same, I'm afraid."

I try not to imagine the foreign DNA chomping through my system as the doctor checks my lymph nodes. Her expression remains neutral.

I say, "Dr. Sternfield mentioned I was exposed to some weird antibodies, probably when I visited Indonesia. Is that why I'm not fainting anymore or in a coma?"

"Possibly. It would be easier to answer if we could locate Dr. Sternfield."

I clear my throat. "Could I have spread this to my family or boyfriend?" How bittersweet that this is the first time I've actually used the term *boyfriend*.

"Too soon to say. Have you and your boyfriend been intimate?"

Heat rises in my cheeks. "All we've done is kiss."

"Then tell him to be alert for any symptoms. That's the same instruction we're giving all family members and anyone else who's had contact with you guys."

I feel like a typhoid carrier.

Dr. Culdicott heads toward Chloe, who still has a fever. Without an answer on what time we can check out, Dr. Culdicott takes off.

Minutes later, the boys return. Except for Xavier, who's been taken for further testing. We go around the room assuring each other in hollow voices that the rest of us feel okay. Even Chloe, who clearly does not. The laughter of earlier has been replaced by protestors changing and cars honking outside.

Shane digs his hands in his pockets. "It's like that old horror movie, where everyone's trapped on an island while an insane person slaughters them one by one."

Chloe's eyes widen in horror. If Jesse weren't busy comforting her, I'm sure Shane would be the next one slaughtered on this island.

I snap, "Aren't you the guy who said the groupies were worth a few headaches?"

His expression loses its typical edge. "Xave didn't look so hot. And I don't think it's because he and Sebastian stayed up half the night whispering to each other."

On the chance he's really concerned, I say, "Xavier should

get better soon. Whatever we have is probably not transmitted very easily, so as long as we're careful, they should let us go."

That brings a grin flickering back onto Shane's mouth. "Define *careful*."

I don't bother answering. Sebastian switches on the TV to a local news channel.

Two stories in, we find Dr. Gordon, flanked by a team of white jackets in the Nova Genetics auditorium. He announces, "We're vigorously investigating reports of an unsanctioned treatment allegedly administered by a researcher here. I want to emphasize that such behavior would be in gross violation of our strict standards. My staff is working with the authorities in their investigation and I'm directing our full efforts toward mitigating the situation." He ends the conference and heads out of the room without answering any questions.

Chloe presses her palms to her face and moans. "Why are my ears ringing so loudly? Why can't I—" She slumps forward.

Jesse clutches her shoulders. "Chloe!"

I punch the call button. Within moments a nurse bursts into the room. After a quick check, she barks into a handset.

Dr. Culdicott rushes inside, followed by two aids rolling in a gurney. Jesse holds on to Chloe's hand as the orderlies move her off the bed.

Dr. Culdicott, grim-faced, marches next to the gurney. "You have to stay here."

Jesse won't let go of Chloe's hand. "She needs someone who loves her nearby."

The doctor uses a voice that's clearly given orders before. "Let her go. Now."

Jesse's hand remains outstretched in the air for a few seconds after he releases Chloe's. Then, groaning, he plunks down at the foot of my bed.

I scoot next to him. "She's gotten better after fainting before, she can do it again."

We sit silently, lost in thought. This is all so surreal. Why did Dr. Sternfield choose us in particular? Were we just the easiest marks, or did each of us offer some scientific reason for inclusion in her perverse experiment? I don't know whether being chosen randomly or deliberately would make me feel worse.

Sebastian rocks his chair back and forth, rubbing a hand over his hair. "Did you know Xavier started college a year early on a full scholarship? His family's so proud, but after he graduates they expect him to join his dad's practice. And marry a Filipino girl."

I hand Sebastian a tissue. "What does he want?"

His smile is rueful. "To do medical research. And fall in

love with whoever he wants." He sniffs. "I wish we'd had a chance to hang out before now."

I launch myself from the bed. "I'm calling Dr. Gordon. He needs to hunt down his daughter, even if they have to send out the Forest Rangers."

Jesse punches his palm. "That crackpot research company should be burned to the ground." His face glistens with what I pray isn't a fever.

Shane says, "What we really should—"

A voice from the corridor sounds like it's coming through a bullhorn. "All of you, put a mask on now. They're on the bedside tables."

"What's going on?" Jesse yells.

"We'll update you once you've complied."

Since the only way to get information is to "comply," we grab masks and call back to the person outside when our noses and mouths are covered.

Dr. Culdicott enters in what looks like a spacesuit. Her eyes flash wary behind the clear face shield. "We're going to maintain stricter infection control, and move you to a negative pressure room."

Another masked person comes in to fiddle with the ventilation system. Or maybe he's cutting off our air, because suddenly I'm struggling to breathe.

Shane sinks into a chair, stretching his legs out the way he did in the Nova Genetics teen group meeting. "We've already got whatever it is Dr. Charlotte gave us. Why the wartime measures?"

Despite Shane's casual attitude, my muscles pull in tighter and tighter. And Dr. Culdicott crosses her arms around herself solemnly. There's something bad coming. Really bad.

Finally, with a sigh, Dr. Culdicott says, "I'm very sorry to tell you that your friend Rosa has passed away."

FOURTEEN

My body freezes. It doesn't seem possible that Rosa's gone. Forever. And for what? Because she wanted to talk to the boy she liked, and was desperate enough to be seduced by Dr. Sternfield, who is now a murderer.

Dr. Culdicott gazes over our heads out the window for a moment, and then snaps to attention. She clears her throat. "Our PCR tests have identified the same virus in all of your blood samples, probably the vector used by Dr. Sternfield to deliver the altered DNA. Normally, gene therapists remove the infectious aspects of these viral vectors, but perhaps in her eagerness, something went wrong."

Sebastian says, "But can you cure it?"

"Identification is the first step. We're starting all of you on a regimen of interferon, which is effective against a number of other viruses. But even if we halt CZ88's vector, your symptoms are likely the result of the altered DNA it carried, which could remain in your cells after the virus stops spreading. It's complicated."

Of course. Complicated. Which means they'll never figure it out in time. Instead of a fever, I feel cold, so cold.

Even Shane looks like the sass has been knocked out of him. He rocks his chair back on two legs and then lets it fall forward with a *thunk*, over and over.

Dr. Culdicott says, "We've notified your parents, who won't be allowed to visit for now." She takes a long breath. "I'm sorry about Rosa. Losing someone so young is always a damn shame."

She asks the boys to gather their belongings from the other room. Jesse stays behind to collect Chloe's things, and I grab my stuff as well as the little notepad Xavier left behind. I flip through pages, which list dozens of possible genes along with scribbled notes. It's enough to get my hopes up until the last page, where he scrawled *JUNK* in huge letters, as if he decided that all his speculation didn't amount to anything.

A masked nurse escorts us to an airlock chamber that seems to suck us into the room. The scared eyes of the boys blink over their masks. We claim beds half-heartedly.

The brightly lit space has no windows and is lined in

plastic sheeting, floor to ceiling. A steady hum of something draws our possibly diseased breaths through filters for scrubbing. The nurse only stays a few minutes before excusing herself. Once the door shuts, we rip off our masks. To hell with them. CZ88 is already running through all of us.

Sebastian's eyelashes glisten, and for once his body is still. "Poor Rosa. Do you think she got any enjoyment from the Charisma before, you know?"

I grab a tissue. "She was hopping with excitement because she finally got together with the boy she crushed on." I share tidbits about Rosa, as if that will acknowledge her life. That's what prompted all of us to accept the Charisma in the first place, right? To be seen, to be known, to connect. How dare Dr. Sternfield exploit us for that?

Shane sighs. "I say we demand Dr. Gordon figure out how we can see our families, or at least make good-bye videos for them, just in case."

I expect Sebastian to scold him for being so morbid but instead he jumps off the bed. "Every second is precious. Video me. In honor of Rosa."

I snatch my phone and point the camera at Sebastian, who's already begun to spin and stretch and leap as if crazed. Even when sweat beads down his neck, he keeps at it, pirouetting once, twice, five times in a row. He doesn't stop until his legs give out. Kneeling on the floor, he sobs.

Shane and I run over and grab his shoulders. Although I hate to ask, I have to. "Are you sick, Sebastian? We'll buzz the doctor."

Sebastian rises. "No! It's not like they can do anything anyway. Frustration and hopelessness are stamped on their faces." He gazes at Shane and me. "Just like it is on yours. You can't hide your feelings from me, not since I got the Charisma."

Shane and I exchange quizzical glances. Is the gene alteration causing Sebastian to become delusional?

Swaying, Sebastian stumbles. "Gonna lie down."

Shane steadies him by the elbow. "Fantastic idea."

I cross my arms and pace, cursing at myself for being so gullible. When I see Dr. Sternfield, I'm going to take advantage of this voice I'm no longer afraid to use. Maybe these fists too. I say to Jesse, "You're the only one who's truly innocent in all this."

He's next to the door, tossing a cup, catching it in one hand and then the other. "I don't know how you guys could've been so clueless."

I stare at the floor. "It must be hard for someone like you to understand why anyone would be so desperate to change."

He catches the cup with a hollow smacking sound. "What do you mean, someone like me?"

"Someone who has it all: good-looking, confident, athletic. I'll bet you've always gotten loads of attention, the star football player."

He twists his face. "I'm not a star. Not that I haven't been tempted to do something radical to become one."

"Steroids?"

"That's what the real stars on our team do. Everyone knows it. Sometimes, I've come so close to joining them, just to shine. But that wouldn't really be me. It's cheating."

"You think the CZ88 was our way of cheating?"

He steadies his gaze. "Don't you?"

The phone by my bed rings. We all glance at each other. It rings again. Shane seems glued to Sebastian, and Jesse won't stop with the stupid cup. I snatch up the handset.

"Aislyn?"

My heart skips. "Jack? How did you find me?"

"Well, your mom acted weird when I called your house and Evie's been texting me all kinds of bizarre health questions. So when I saw those news stories, it didn't take honors math to make the connection."

I clear my throat. "I've been meaning to tell you, but I'm so embarrassed."

"This Charisma drug is why you stopped running away from me?"

I bite at my lip. "I never wanted to run, but it was so hard to talk to you."

"Why? I was always into you. You're the prettiest, smartest girl I've ever met."

"I didn't feel that way. Look how nervous I was at Drew's party. And at the science contest, oh my God."

"You would've warmed up to me eventually, on your own."

"Well, now we'll never know."

There's a long enough silence for trembling to take root in my legs. Finally, he says, "As long as you're okay and can get out of there soon, it doesn't matter."

I turn my back to the guys and cup a hand near my mouth. "You might not think so after I tell you the rest. One of the girls here gave what we have to her boyfriend. They've been, um, very physical, I think, but the doctors moved all of us into a pressure-controlled room now that someone died."

There's a catch to his voice. "Someone died?"

I tell him about Rosa.

His breathing is audible and rapid. "Should I get tested too?"

"Call Dr. Culdicott here at the hospital. Have you been feeling different? Like more outgoing? Or getting headaches? Or light-headed?"

"Nothing like that." Another pause. "I'll call that doctor. Aislyn, this is crazy."

"I'm so, so sorry. Tell me what happens with the doctor. Please."

"Of course."

And he will, unlike me, who couldn't find the guts to call him first. When I hang up I have a headache. A sign of impending coma? I slip under my covers and pull them over my head. But squeezing my eyes shut against the world doesn't help any. Even when I fall asleep. My dreams are dark and furious.

In the middle of the night, the door suctions open and two orderlies wheel an unconscious Sebastian to ICU. A moan erupts from my throat and I feel so, so heavy. In my half-asleep state, I promise myself that as soon as I'm able, I'll post his dance video online. Let the world get to know him in a way we'll never get to know Rosa.

The next morning, a new doctor delivers the news that all the other teens who accepted CZ88 are comatose. There are also a number of patients at Seattle General with similar symptoms.

My breathing becomes shallow. "So why haven't we gotten sick yet?"

The doctor says, "Even when plagues killed off millions, there were plenty who survived. Maybe you're the lucky ones."

I fall backward on my bed.

Jesse grunts. "Great. We've got the plague. I feel so lucky."

The doctor fidgets, his protective clothing making a chafing sound. "Every person is different, with different immunities."

Jesse starts with the cup tossing again, missing the doctor's mask by inches. "Or maybe the virus is taking its time, like AIDS."

"You three are stable at this point."

Jesse laughs. "At this point. Chloe seemed fine after she stopped fainting. And then, boom!" The cup lands on the floor with a large *crack*.

The doctor takes a long breath. "I know it must be frustrating."

Jesse growls and claws at the bedcover. His eyes are wet and red. "It's been over a day since I fainted. The calm before the storm, right? How long do you think I have?"

The doctor tries to reassure him. But what can he say? And I've been symptom-free longer than Jesse, so if there's a storm coming, it'll hit me first.

I get up to pull the curtain around my bed. "You can do my exam."

Without commenting much, the doctor lumbers to each bed and performs our examinations. Except for some ringing in Jesse's ears, we're all stable. For. Now.

The doctor waddles out.

Shane grabs the phone next to his bed and dials. "Hello,

Dr. Gordon. This is Shane again. We need something better than these ancient phones to communicate with our family and friends while it's still possible. Otherwise, I'll see if a news station can provide us with something in exchange for an interview about your daughter." He slams the receiver.

Jesse perks up enough to give him an air high five. "Serves the bastard right."

My phone rings. I jump to get it.

Mom says, "Oh, sweetie! How are you?"

"Okay. Just sad about Rosa, and worried about the others." As well as myself.

"Honey—" A small sob comes through, which sends ice to my core. Mom never cries. She's always so, so busy on our behalf.

Somehow she regains her composure enough to say, "Dr. Gordon is confident they'll figure something out. They're digging into the DNA component of the virus they found in you kids. You just have to hang tough, the way I know you can, okay?"

I swallow. "I'll try."

Sammy's raspy voice joins her on the other extension. "Get home soon, Aislyn." He coughs.

My voice breaks. "I'm so sorry about all this, you guys."

When we finally hang up, I can hardly breathe. Shane, who's also just finished a call, looks as green as I feel. He pounds a fist on his bed. "Have the docs interrogated you about, uh, contacts?"

"I guess." Suddenly, understanding dawns. "Is one of your girlfriends sick?"

He rubs his eyes. "The two girls I hung out with on my show are saying stuff. I mean, there was a little kissy-face for the camera, but we were saving something for the next episodes, you know? Anyway, one of their families is threatening a bogus lawsuit."

I cross my arms. "You mean to tell me that the great player Shane hasn't had any hookups since he got the Charisma?"

He squirms. "I just met them. I'm not that much of a dog."

Jesse harrumphs from his bed on the other side of Shane's.

I rub my lips, remembering Jack's warm touch. Oh, God, I hope I haven't given him whatever I've got. If only Mom had interrupted all of our dates.

A bubble of despair rises in my throat. Not wanting to break down in front of these guys, I hustle into the room's adjoining bathroom. Under a hot shower, I let myself cry and pound the tile. When my hands are bruised and my skin pruned, I shuffle back to the room.

A masked person in a biohazard suit works on an outlet. He rears back from me and says, "You need to put on a mask right now."

I quickly grab one. There's a laptop at the foot of my bed.

Shane clicks away at another one on his tray table. Twenty minutes later, the technician rises and gathers his things. "I don't know who you guys bribed, but you've now got your own Internet connection." He bolts toward the door.

I log on. My page explodes with posts, many congratulating me for changing myself for the better, many more hoping I don't drop dead in the process. Kiera must've outed the rest of us. Surprisingly, a handful of people ask how they can score some Charisma too. And a message from a woman in Los Angeles asks how to deal with the "slutty" side effects. Okay, that has to be a joke.

I thrash through Nova Genetics' site in search of a picture of Dr. Sternfield we can use for an online search party. Camping trip, my ass. Squinting, I examine the staff page once, then again.

"It's like she never existed," I say, a chill slithering through my body.

"Huh?" Shane asks.

"Dr. Sternfield isn't mentioned at all on the Nova Genetics website. I want to broadcast her picture. Hunt her down."

He types. "She can't hide from all the search engines." He clicks a bit. "Hmmm, nothing since med school. It's like she knew she'd have to go into hiding one day."

And she recruited us anyway. The iciness in my veins turns to heat.

Seething, I broadcast the med school photo along with a plea for anyone with info to contact the hospital. My legs bounce relentlessly. Actively hunting the doctor gives me unexpected energy.

But throughout the day I only get a bunch of messages from people who sound more and more unhinged. I go to sleep that night without any progress.

In the morning, I awake to Shane saying loudly, "Jesse, you okay?"

Jesse lies on his bed with a dazed expression and his hands to his ears. "I'm fine," he mumbles, looking anything but.

"You better tell us if you're not, dude." Shane grabs the remote.

On TV, a flurry of experts speculate upon the extent of the outbreak and whether this is the result of terrorism or a mad scientist. I ask Shane to turn it off, but an anchorwoman's porcelain features come to life with the announcement of "news just in."

Despite the terror in my gut that we'll learn of more victims, more deaths, I lean toward the TV. A picture of Dr. Sternfield snaps up. Somewhat blurry, but more recent than the one I posted. The anchorwoman says, "In a bizarre twist, the Nova Genetics researcher who allegedly provided an unsanctioned, lethal gene treatment to at least two dozen people across the

Northwest, has been discovered in a disturbing video sent to our station. We warn you that the following images may not be suitable for young viewers."

What on earth? Has someone tracked down the doctor?

A solemn-faced Dr. Sternfield stares into the camera, her eyes and lips set in hard lines. Wind whips her auburn hair against a grainy, gray sky.

She says in a shaky voice, "I'm sorry. For everything." The camera shot pulls back a few feet to reveal her hovering atop the side rail of a bridge.

My blood, or what's left of it, drains to my feet. I will her to get down from the rail, to come back from wherever she is and develop a cure for us.

One bed over, Shane growls. "Do not do this. Do not do this."

Time seems to stop as the camera wavers. Dr. Sternfield looks to the sky as if seeking an answer. The she squares her shoulders and nods.

I pull the quilt to my chin, praying she'll come to her senses.

Dr. Sternfield takes a deep breath. Then, with a kiss on her fingers and a wave, she turns away and jumps.

FIFTEEN

No.

No.

No.

I lurch forward as if to dive into the TV after her. The camera follows the doctor's descent to the water far below, which she hits with a soundless splash that swallows her whole. For a long moment, the water remains unchanged, and then the video cuts out.

Shane and I turn toward each other. His features are rigid with shock.

The newscaster returns. "Our sources are trying to identify where this bridge is, but the video appears genuine. We're working to uncover whoever sent it."

Shane explodes. "That's bullshit!"

I can't stop holding my stomach. "Why would she do this? It doesn't make sense."

Shane aims the remote, firing up one station after the next. He throws the remote onto his bed. "If she isn't dead, I'll kill the bitch."

I stare numbly at the TV. Rosa's death killed my joy. Dr. Sternfield's death has killed my hope.

I scan the room. Jesse's awfully still. I stumble over to nudge his shoulder. His breathing is so shallow, and he won't respond when I tug at his arm. "Wake up!"

Shane buzzes a nurse and puts on a mask. Within minutes a medical team arrives in a flurry of activity along with another gurney. Two large women load Jesse on and roll him out. Just like that.

And now there are two of us left. With no researcher who'll swoop in and announce she's developed a cure.

Shane's face is pale. "Damn. This is scary."

I clamp my eyes shut, trying desperately to keep the tears at bay. I'm not even seventeen. This can't be it. I should be home, with Mom and Sammy, doing normal stuff, working at the pool, hanging out with Evie, telling my family how much I love them. I can't let them not know that.

I wipe my cheeks. "Maybe we should do those good-bye videos you talked about."

Shane breathes deeply. "You want me to go into the bathroom so you can have some privacy?" Oh, God, if Shane's respecting boundaries, our hours are truly numbered.

I take deep breaths to fight off the panic. "I don't know what to say."

He sits next to me on my bed. To think that at home, no guy my age has ever been inside my room. When Shane takes my hand, it's comforting, not like he's hitting on me. "You tell each person how much they mean to you. Maybe talk about your best times together. And what you wish for them in the future."

His suggestions sound so final. Yet that's what these videos might be, dammit.

My words come out in hiccups. "I don't want Mom and Sammy to see me crying."

His voice is gentle. "Then you stop the video, wash your face, and try again."

I nod.

"I'll leave now, but if you want me to come back, just holler." He takes his laptop into the bathroom and I stare at mine, planning to do the video for Mom first. I inhale deeply. And then again.

Sniffling, I press RECORD. Then I tell Mom how sorry I am, and that she's the best parent anyone could hope for. I love how special she makes Sammy and me feel. The video takes several do-overs, but finally I get it all out in one take.

Then I do one for Evie. What do you say to your best friend in the universe? I try my hardest, which just starts me crying again, but I don't stop the video. I recount how at the beginning of every school year, we'd draw a map to maximize the number of times we'd run into each other between classes. Each time we did, I'd experience a moment of calm amid the chaos of the school day. She's always been my touchstone. I end her video with, "Cap'n Crunch, Cap'n Crunch, Cap'n Crunch."

If only escape were that easy.

I blow my nose and take a few more breaths before I do Jack's. It's mostly about would'ves and should'ves. I finish his video overwhelmed by the feeling of being cheated out of something that hadn't truly been mine yet.

That leaves the most difficult video. But what to tell Sammy?

I click the RECORD button and clear my throat. "Hey buddy. Here I am in the boring hospital. Thought I'd send you a little video in case . . ." In case of what? No, I couldn't say that.

I erase the clip and start again.

And again.

Hell is trying to tell your little brother that things will be okay, when you know he'll be devastated. No way do I want Sammy's last impression of me to be as a liar.

Finally, I go with my heart. "Hey, Sammy. If you're seeing this, it means things didn't go so well. I know you're sad. I want you to know I love being your sister. You're the strongest person I know. And even if they didn't find a cure for me in time, I know they'll find one for you. They have to."

I stop the video to wipe my eyes, then continue. "Anyway, now it's your job to keep Mom out of trouble. Don't let her play grunge songs too loud. And when she comes home really tired from work, let her take a nap. You can create a whole new cast of manga characters or a mural while you wait. I love you, Sammy."

Click.

It's only then that I realize something about my brother. All these years, I've assumed his passion for art was a fun way to pass the time, maybe even an escape from his daily hassles. But now I understand that isn't the full story. Sammy wants to make a mark, to create something lasting during whatever lifespan he's been given. How could I not have seen that sooner?

Blinking rapidly, I save the videos in a folder named IN CASE OF EMERGENCY.

I hunker into my blanket and watch a show about global warming until Shane returns from the bathroom, his eyes puffy. Without asking, he tosses his laptop onto his bed and plops next to me so we sit shoulder to shoulder facing the

TV. That's how we remain until Dr. Culdicott comes in, her own eyes full of confusion.

Shane grasps my hand tightly. "Tell us."

She folds her arms and draws a long breath into her space suit. "There may be over a hundred victims across the West Coast. Apparently, Dr. Sternfield tapped into a network of people who make a living volunteering for clinical trials. Furthermore, Xavier's situation has become very tenuous. He had to be resuscitated twice in the past few hours."

A sob flares up from my chest. That sweet guy, who deserves so much more time. With Sebastian.

Shane says, "Our odds pretty much suck, don't they?"

Dr. Culdicott shakes her head. "As soon as we figure anything out, we'll tell you. In the meantime . . ."

Shane's pulse is fast. "We've already made our good-bye videos."

Dr. Culdicott's head jerks. But instead of scolding us for giving up, she nods. "The boys serving in Afghanistan would do that too."

The next days are a fuzzy, frantic haze. I spend as much time as possible video-chatting, saying what needs to be said, even if it comes through tears. The doctors inject us with interferon, but our viral load doesn't budge.

A week into our stay, on the Fourth of July, Sammy waves

a flag during our morning video chat. "Mom's taking me to see the fireworks and—" His plans are interrupted by fierce hacking from his chest.

Instinctively, I lunge for a tissue box. "Your AV719 trial can't start soon enough. Next week, right?"

His eyes are full of tears as he chokes out, "No trial."

"They're not doing the trial?" Nova Genetics isn't even the lead researcher on it.

Sammy shakes his head. "They're still doing the trial, just not with me."

I can barely breathe. Did they kick him out because of me? "I can fix this, Sammy. Let me call Dr. Gordon and he can call the university."

Sammy stares into the camera, breathing heavily. "It wasn't their decision. Mom doesn't want to risk it, not after what happened to you."

I scream, scaring the hell out of Sammy, and Shane, who runs over to me. I shake him off and yell into the screen, "That's insane. Put Mom on."

Sammy shakes his head. "Gene therapy isn't a miracle. You should know that."

"This is totally different. I can't believe you guys didn't tell me. Put Mom on now!" When she shows up, I yell, "How could you take Sammy out of the trial?"

"Calm down. You're scaring him."

My voice goes shriller. "Scaring him? What about curing him? You've seen the data on AV719. He needs it."

"Not now, Aislyn. When you pull yourself together, we can discuss this like adults." She cuts off our chat.

Oh, God, what have I done? Now my decision to accept CZ88 has life-and-death consequences for Sammy too. I rock on my bed, sobbing.

Shane pats my back and makes soothing sounds, but I ask him to leave me alone. I have to fix this, to make sure Sammy gets his chance. Jumping up, I grab the phone.

When Dr. Gordon answers, I try to control myself, but my words still blast out like an air horn. "How could you let my mom take Sammy out of the AV719 trial?"

His voice is subdued, reminding me he's still in mourning for his daughter. "Believe me, I tried to convince her other- wise. Give her time."

I want to throw the phone against the wall. "Time? If we wait too long, Sammy's lung capacity might be too low to qualify for anything but a transplant."

"She's had a bad scare, Aislyn."

"Then you need to find a cure for me fast, and get her unscared."

He sighs the sigh of someone who's suffered through many dark hours. "I'm trying."

"Not hard enough. People are dying."

Now his voice cracks. "I know, Aislyn, I know."

After the call, I can't stop pacing. If I weren't stuck in here, I could convince Mom, face-to-face. I almost barrel into Dr. Culdicott when she arrives. "When my brother has his inpatient visits, there's a checklist of criteria he has to pass before they'll discharge him. What's the list for Shane and me? You can't keep us in here forever."

She blinks rapidly and seems to catch her breath. "Your isolation has more to do with the possibility of infecting others than your symptoms at this point."

Symptoms that they can't treat anyway. "But all the evidence shows this isn't airborne; we'd have to purposely transmit it."

She shakes her head. "There's still so much that's unknown about gene therapy. And plenty of people are fighting against your release."

I force myself to calm down and appear matter-of-fact. "How about if we're symptom-free for a certain number of days? And Shane signs an oath not to hook up with any girls?"

Dr. Culdicott's facemask seems to crease down the middle along with her forehead. "It's as much a political decision as a health one. The governor would have to sign off."

I say, "Every day you keep us here is a day away from our families."

She sighs. "I'll discuss it with the epidemiologists."

As she leaves, I shout, "Happy Independence Day!"

That night, hours after the fireworks, I wake up in the dark, with Shane thrashing five feet away, and footsteps overhead from the night shift. A rising terror eats at me. All I can imagine is closing my eyes and succumbing to a void that never lets me wake up. Or worse, waking up to the awareness of being in a coma, my body a tomb encasing my mind.

I second-guess every conversation I've had recently. I should've convinced Mom to take more time for herself. I have to make Evie realize she has the courage I've always dreamed of. Sammy needs to understand he's already made an indelible mark, way beyond his artwork. Does Jack know how much I appreciate him looking past the incredibly awkward girl I'd been and wanting to hang out anyway? I mentally list the things I'll say tomorrow, which could be the last time I speak to the people I love if the CZ88 is lying in wait. It's an unnerving way to live. Or die.

But I wake up the next morning. Dr. Culdicott doesn't yield on the symptom-free threshold, but she doesn't deny it either. I chat with Sammy and Mom, who cuts me off whenever I mention the AV719 trial. The third time I bring it up, Sammy asks to chat with Shane. Fine. As long as Shane doesn't try to give him dating advice.

Speaking of dating, this is my chance for pseudo-privacy. I open a chat with Jack.

He greets me with pool-reddened eyes from his morning swim. I can almost smell the chlorine on him. God, I yearn to be close enough to smell him, period. And touch him. My skin tingles with the hope of feeling his fingers run along it again someday.

I twist the cover sheet into a rope as I update him. "Everyone we so much as sneezed on hasn't shown the virus in their bloodstream. As long as we don't share needles or anything, no one else will get this." Saying the words, I wonder if he speculates upon the "or anything" part as much as I do.

His face gets closer, as if he can read my desire. "An ACLU lawyer talked about you guys on the radio's interview show yesterday. There are laws on your side. And this sounds like it might be a similar transmission to HIV."

I hold my breath. "Does that scare you?"

He swallows, glances away and then back at me. "I just want to be with you, Aislyn. We can wait for, uh, things until you're cured."

I run a finger along the edge of the computer. "Dr. Gordon keeps warning us we're safer here than out there." I sigh. "Got the contact info for that ACLU lawyer?"

He sends it after our chat and Shane and I call her immediately to present our situation. She accepts our case on the spot, pro bono.

Afterward, Shane and I plop side by side on the middle

bed, our hangout, and he picks up the TV remote. We limit our news consumption so we can sleep at night, but it's impossible to avoid the CZ88 death tolls and coma counts that bombard us.

He clicks around the stations, unable to resist pausing when he runs across another story on Nova Genetics, this time featuring a middle-aged woman who looks a lot like Dr. Sternfield. It's her mother, Sheyla Sternfield. Apparently Dr. Sternfield was given, or chose to take, her mother's name.

Sheyla Sternfield addresses the camera with a hard, clear gaze. "My daughter never would have committed such a desperate act if she hadn't been hounded. I hope you'll at least leave her memory in peace."

Something about her demeanor seems off, something I can't place. Maybe I expect more signs of grief. My eyes tear up at the prospect of my own mom having to mourn.

"Want me to switch the channel?" Shane asks.

"No. Something about her expression doesn't seem right."

He nods. "Yeah, I see a certain something too. God, if we ever get out of here, think of the party tricks we could do."

It's not like we can read minds; it's more a matter of being really, really perceptive to people's expressions, which is probably part of what being sociable entails. Thank you, dearly departed Dr. Sternfield.

I say, "Think her mom's coldness turned Dr. Sternfield into a mad scientist?"

He grunts. "It would take more than that. Besides, Dr. Gordon seems decent. Both parents make their dent on the kids."

I chew my lip, not sure how to reply.

His eyes show sudden awareness. "Oh, sorry." He lays his hands flat on his thighs. "Not trying to be nosy, but what happened to your dad, anyway?"

"Short story, a diving accident." I glance at him.

Shane squeezes my fingers. "I'm sorry."

I nod, taking deep breaths that don't get me as much air as I need.

The next morning, Dr. Culdicott tells us that in her conference calls with the powers that be, no doubt egged on by a certain ACLU lawyer, the consensus was to make a list of criteria to release us.

"Like what?" Shane asks.

She counts off on her fingers. "Of course, your vitals must remain stable. And no other symptoms, such as fainting or ears ringing. It would be helpful to have a reliable test for CZ88 that's more economical that what we've been doing. There'll also be a psych eval to assess whether you would behave responsibly once you got out."

We nod. Shane better not mess things up for us.

"Then, maybe, just maybe we'll get the governor to lift the isolation order." Before she leaves, Dr. Culdicott adds, "By the way, have you been in touch with other CZ88 patients? We're trying to locate a young lady named Sophia Washington who's gone missing from Seattle General."

I say, "She didn't wait for the isolation restrictions to be lifted?" Maybe I should break out of here and holler at Mom until she changes her mind about Sammy's trial.

Dr. Culdicott's eyes wrinkle behind her ever-present plastic shield. "Either that, or someone might have forced her to leave. There have been questionable folks loitering at hospitals with CZ88 patients."

An unsettling chill slides down my back. "Yeah, we read about those weirdoes who wanted to do an exorcism on the patients in LA. You think they went to Seattle?"

"That's what we're trying to figure out. But no cause for alarm; we run a tight ship. No one gets in or out without permission."

So much for my escape plans.

The next morning, I hear Shane talking to himself in the bathroom, which I tease him about when he gets out.

"Just practicing for my interview. Gotta be believable."

I drop my breakfast fork. "You don't have any symptoms, do you?"

"No. But they might think we're lying just to get out."

"Hmm. If we can convince each other of our truthfulness, we can pass the test with anyone."

We sit on my bed cross-legged, knee to knee, and stare into each other's faces.

Shane grins. "You first."

"Fine." I close my eyes for a moment to cleanse my facial expressions. When I'm ready, I say, "I'm feeling absolutely no symptoms of CZ88 today."

He stares at me intently. "You're telling the truth. Now, tell me a lie so I can calibrate."

"Wouldn't it be a better test if I didn't tell you up front whether I was lying?"

"Fine."

I take another face-neutralizing breath and say, "When I first met you, I thought you were the biggest jackass."

He nods. "Easy. Truth."

"Now you seem halfway decent."

He squints. "I detect teeny-tiny twitching. You don't think I'm halfway decent?"

I glance downward, away from his hurt. "Okay, full disclosure. I think you're more than halfway decent."

His smile brings out dimples. "Ah, there we go. Very truthful."

"Your turn."

He wipes his face. "When I first met you, I thought you had issues."

"I could've told you that without our face-reading abilities. Both that I had issues and that you thought so."

"Now I know you're full of yourself."

I slap his arm. "Hah! Lie, lie, lie."

"Okay, how about this? I think you're hot and sweet and I wish Jack loverboy were out of the picture so I could take his place."

I catch my breath. Everything on his face says he's telling the truth, but I say, "Mostly lies."

Now his face reads embarrassment as he looks away. "Busted."

After an uncomfortable silence, we rehearse until we're ready for the toughest cross-examination.

That takes place the next day, with physicians, researchers, and psychologists. Afterward, Shane grumbles. "We should sue. They don't make AIDS patients go through this crap before leaving a hospital."

"They understand exactly how AIDS is transmitted. For us, there's still not enough data."

He raises his eyebrows. "We could provide them with some."

"Uh, not with each other, since we both already have it."

He runs a hand through his curls. "It sucks. This gene transfer has done the exact opposite of what Dr. Charlotte promised."

"Well, you're nicer at least."

"Some good that'll do me." He slaps his bed. "Look, I know you're all about loverboy. But there's going to come a time when you both get frustrated by not being able to do anything about it." He smiles. "So, you know what they say about being the last guy on earth?"

I rest my hands on my lap and sigh. "Usually, it's a hypothetical, as in, 'I wouldn't hook up with you *even* if you were the last guy on earth.'"

"Yeah, well, reality might be different, just keep that in mind. I'm not half as bad as you thought. You said so."

I shrug. "Maybe impending death has a way of making us overlook obnoxious behavior."

He leans closer and lowers his voice. "What if this is our last chance?"

I stare at his chiseled jaw, his glinting eyes, those white-white teeth. Everything about his demeanor reads as sincerity, not mocking. If I didn't like Jack, would I go for Shane, now that I've seen his sweet side?

I exhale. "Let's hope for a cure soon, okay? After twelve full days of living with each other, hooking up with me would be like hooking up with your sister."

He whips a pillow at me. "Did you have to say that?"

That launches us into pillow fight number two hundred and three.

Dr. Culdicott arrives in her usual drill-sergeant fashion, shoulders back, chin up. However, for the first time since Rosa's death, she isn't wearing the gas mask and spacesuit. It's weird to see another human face uncovered besides Shane's. She isn't smiling exactly, but she doesn't have the lined forehead I've become used to.

She clears her throat. "We're letting you go."

Oh my God, if I race, I could take Sammy to wherever the AV719 trial's taking place. It starts today.

She continues, "Tomorrow."

All my jubilation explodes. "Oh, please make it today. My brother has to get into a clinical trial and I'm the only one willing to fight for it. Please, Dr. Culdicott."

"I'm sorry, Aislyn. Multiple state health departments are coordinating on a press release to deal with the hysteria that's bound to arise from some factions. This is as fast as it goes."

"Can't you make an exception?"

"None of us can. Tomorrow it is. Besides, if your mother wanted your brother in a research trial, he'd be there." Her gaze is stony.

After she leaves, I'm as downtrodden as if she'd told us we couldn't leave. My mood only darkens when Mom calls that evening and tries to make nice. "Even if you hadn't accepted the CZ88, others would've and my decision would be the same. I'm not signing up my kid for something with so many unknowns."

"But the prelim study had amazing results. You'd have to be crazy not to jump on this."

"No. Crazy would be taking . . . Look, we should be celebrating your release, not fighting."

"I just don't understand why you're giving up on Sammy."

She shrieks, "Giving up? How can you say that? How?"

"You know what I mean."

"No, I don't. I don't have any idea what's going through your mind, if I ever did."

I sigh. "I'll see you tomorrow, Mom." I hang up, exhausted.

Shane plops next to me. "She's been through a lot."

"So have we." I lean my head on his shoulder for a long time.

Then I get up to call Dr. Gordon and try to convince him to let me know where exactly the trial is taking place. But he's as stubborn as Mom.

The next day, Dr. Culdicott's parting words to Shane and me are: "Should you feel light-headed or feverish, experience ringing in the ears, or any other CZ88 symptoms, you'll need to come back immediately."

Shane and I blink at each other. It's really happening. A

day late, but happening. And maybe when I'm home and Mom sees how good I feel, she'll change her mind about Sammy. Then we can convince the researchers to let Sammy join the trial late. Getting out of here means getting back into the world, fighting for what I want.

Dr. Culdicott shakes our hands. "Your families will be here soon. Then it's time to get back to normal."

Normal. I sigh. Nothing ever sounded so extraordinary.

And They're Out!
by Lulu Lakes for *In the Know*

Despite the outcry from panicked citizens, six hospitals in Washington State and California released eleven patients who contracted the CZ88 virus, either directly as part of an illegal gene treatment or by being infected by someone who was. This release occurs despite the seventeen patients who've died and 112 who remain in comas. State health departments in the three other states with CZ88 patients have refused to lift their isolation orders as yet.

Dr. Dean Presley of California Medical Center states, "In those cases where we've been able to identify person-to-person transmission, it was caused by either shared needles or unprotected sexual contact. There is no reason for alarm if risky behavior is avoided."

The *In the Know* website (www.NowYouKnow Too.com) will be continuously updated with health alerts and pinpoint maps of the areas affected by CZ88.

SIXTEEN

Of course, normal is relative. How could my life be routine when Rosa and sixteen others are gone forever, and my own health could go down the sewer at any moment, thanks to an evil doctor I hope is writhing in the afterlife?

So, normal is in the realm of a fantasy.

Mom and Sammy race in to hug me tightly. We stay that way for a long time.

Finally, when we break away, Mom says in my ear, "We will not discuss the AV719 trial. Period." Sammy bounces and chatters with such glee that I go along with Mom's terms. For now.

We sneak past reams of reporters as we drive away from the hospital. At home, where the reporters haven't converged yet, Mom claws toward the fantasy of normal with freshly baked cookies and a cookout planned for tonight. Outside, the weather is as perfectly summery as Tacoma gets, as if Mom special-ordered that as well.

I park myself next to an open window in the living room, unwilling to be by myself yet, and lean into sofa cushions that smell faintly of Mom's Moroccan oil. Every piece of furniture, every knickknack, every aroma I haven't noticed for years now strikes me as reassuring, embracing me back into a reality I thought I'd lost. A reality I still could lose.

As much as I hate to sour the moment, I say, "Mom, we have to talk about the AV719 trial before it's too late."

Her eyes glint and she takes a stance between me and Sammy. "You will not convince me to submit my son to a drug that hasn't been thoroughly vetted. So stop it, Aislyn. Stop it." Her whole body trembles and her eyes are red.

Sammy hugs her from behind. "It's okay, Mom. I'm not doing it."

I feel like an intruder. Even though I know I'm right, it's obvious Mom's hanging on by threads. But I can't look at her without wanting to scream about AV719.

I say, "Think I'll go for a swim before the cookout."

Mom sighs. "Aislyn, slow down. Take some time to reacclimate."

Doesn't she realize that waiting is a luxury for people with time? Trying to swallow my frustration, I say, "I need to talk to Janie about getting back to work. I want to be able to help out around here." Before anyone can argue me out of it, I run upstairs for my swimsuit and convince Sammy to do the same.

Minutes later, we're back downstairs. Mom stands there, bewildered and a touch angry. Boy, this face-reading ability is even more effective in person. I say, "You want to come with us?"

That softens her some. "No, thanks. Just don't be gone too long."

"Just a quick dip and then we'll help you prep for the cookout. See you in an hour." When I start bringing home a paycheck, I'm sure her mood will brighten. With my improved people skills, maybe Janie'll give me extra shifts.

The wind whips through Sammy's and my hair as I drive. Sammy warns me to slow down.

"I'm not even five miles over the limit, buddy."

"Not all of us are risk takers, I guess." There's an edge to his voice.

I tap the brake. "Sorry." I try to read him further, but he turns toward the window. "You know I argued with Mom on the phone about letting you into the AV719 trial. And I'm not going to give up. We should coordinate our attack."

"It's too late. They've already started. Anyway, Mom said no, remember?"

"But—"

"Shut it, Aislyn. Seriously."

I freeze. He's never spoken to me that way before. "If that's what you want." It can't be, really. Mom must've scared him good.

After a silent ride to the pool, my legs itch to run to the gate, but within a minute Sammy's huffing. I slow down and say, "You know, we can go right back home after I talk to Janie, if you want."

His shoulders straighten. "Are you kidding? I haven't been to the pool all summer."

Poor kid's been cooped up as much as I have. We'll have to fix that.

I wave to Heath, who's on gate duty. His eyes widen. In what, shock or fear?

"Is Janie around?" I ask.

He backs away. "Uh, yeah. Over there." His voice is funny, as if he's holding his breath. He must be reading too many of those trash blogs that paint CZ88 victims as something between zombies and vampires.

I spot Janie at the picnic tables chewing out a kid for feeding crows. When she sees me, she startles. Her too? I think I preferred being invisible to scaring folks.

She leads me to an empty patch of grass. "I'm glad to see you up and about."

"I'm feeling great. As soon as you put me on the schedule, I'll come back to work."

She appears unsure of what to say, totally unlike her. "Uh, Aislyn, we hired someone else."

Of course, life moved on without me. "Well, I can fill in when anyone's sick, just like they filled in for me."

She shakes her head. "Do you know how many parents called, in tears because you worked here before you went to the hospital? No, we just can't risk it."

"Are you serious? If what I have were transmitted that easily, someone else would've gotten sick already." No need to tell her I kissed Jack and he's fine.

Her neck tightens. "People are cautious, especially when it comes to their kids. So, until further notice, you and your family can't come to the pool."

"Wait, my whole family's banned?"

She glances Sammy's way as she crosses her leathery arms. "I'm sorry, but unless a doctor can assure us it's one hundred percent safe and sign a liability waiver, that's how it has to be."

Fat chance any doctor is going to do that. I remember little Molly, so scared of the water. And now, even more scared of me, the pariah. I grab Sammy's elbow. "Sorry, buddy. You heard her."

We march out. Sammy tries to play it down on the way

home, but there's resentment again in his face.

When we explain the situation to Mom, she sighs. "Just give them a chance to get used to things." She abruptly hugs me, doing a noble job of pretending not to be afraid of my germs.

I swallow. "But there has to be a way I can help out. You know, before I went to the hospital, a few advertisers offered to pay me for promos on my web page. I'm not sure they'd still want me and it doesn't seem right to profit from CZ88, but . . ."

She shakes her head sharply despite the desperation steaming off her skin. My coming home shouldn't strain her so much. I stifle a frustrated scream.

The house phone rings. Sammy grabs it. "She's not talking to reporters." He hangs up and disconnects the phone from the outlet. "Time to change the number again."

Great, more hassle for my family. For the thousandth time, I say, "Sorry, guys."

"Don't be. That reminds me." Mom strolls toward the kitchen and returns, holding out my phone. "Freshly charged."

I text Jack and Evie, reminding them I'm home, even while part of me fears what I'll see on their faces, assuming they come here.

Jack responds, HEADING OVER.

My breath catches. He still wants to be with me, in person.

Yes, yes, yes. I should've counted on him being too smart to listen to all the fear-mongers.

My skin tingles with the thought of being with him so soon. I run upstairs to freshen up. After almost two weeks in sweats, I dig through my dresser for a fitted shirt and shorts.

When the bell rings, I hurry down and call out, "I'll get it." I take a deep breath and whip open the door.

And there's Jack, my delicious golden guy.

My body feels floaty. "Hey."

Yet there's a hesitation before we hug. I try to assure myself it's to be expected. My eyes prickling, I inhale his scent— beach and sunshine. Oh man, he feels so warm and alive. I could stay like this until my insides melt.

And then I hear clicking.

Peering over Jack's shoulder, I spot two guys with cameras. I pull Jack inside and slam the door.

Mom frowns as I turn the dead bolt and hiss, "Reporters."

She rushes to the window and peers through the blinds. "They're not on our property, so there's not much we can do." She strides from window to window shutting the blinds. Jack and I help her.

I crave privacy, but I'm not letting those jerks trap me inside. "We're going out back."

Mom's face gets pinched. "They'll come around and spot you over the hedges."

I move toward the kitchen to pour a couple glasses of grape juice. "Hopefully not right away."

Jack and I head out back, craning our necks to make sure no cameras lurk beyond the shrubbery. Satisfied the coast is clear, we settle onto the swing.

He sets his glass on the ground. "Try not to spill anything on me, okay?" Was it only three weeks since we sat on another patio at that disastrous end-of-school-year party?

I laugh. "I'm not the same Aislyn who did that."

We both stop short. It's true in a way. I can't be the same. Not with all this weird DNA in my system.

He grabs my hand. "You're the same in ways it counts."

I'd love to know which ways those are, exactly. But I simply thank him and push my foot against the ground to start up the swing.

We sit turned in toward each other. Even though it feels a bit like cheating, I try to read his expressions with my new extra-observant abilities. At the same time, I appreciate his strong cheekbones and jaw, and how his skin's tanned golden brown. Only then do I notice the anxiety and concern in those endlessly blue eyes.

He lays his arm along the seat's back. Taking a chance, I lay mine along his, warm skin against warm skin. His flinch is almost imperceptible. Almost. But he keeps his arm next to mine.

"Still no leads on a cure?" he asks.

"They're pretty sure about the virus, the same one they tested you for. And the altered genes the virus carried. Now they've got to figure out how to halt the virus and reverse the gene modifications."

His voice is soft. "You sure you're still contagious?"

"I promised a lot of people I wouldn't take chances."

He grabs my hand and leans so close I can feel the heat coming off of him, then he pulls me forward so my face rests on his chest. I could cry at how right it feels to let myself nestle against this welcoming body, molded perfectly against mine. He kisses my hair, which sends tingles from my scalp on downward. My insides can't decide between melting and combusting when he rests a hand on my bare thigh. Oh, if the CZ88 doesn't kill me, this "only friends" stuff will.

But the thought of the danger I could put him into if we go any further causes me to pull back with a start. "We shouldn't even tempt ourselves."

His eyes are glazed. "You want me to leave?"

I play with the neckline of my shirt. "Of course not. Just try not to be so, um, irresistible."

He laughs. "Then stop tugging at your shirt."

I do, and halt the swing with a heel to the ground. "This whole thing is so crazy."

He only bites his lip in response. Too sweet to state the obvious. Of course it's crazy, and it's all my fault.

Clicking sounds come from over the hedge. Hell. The reporters have found us.

One yells, "Aislyn, does your boyfriend have it too? Did you give it to him?"

Jack and I rush inside, leaving behind our juice glasses.

Mom's in the kitchen washing vegetables. In the background, she has the TV tuned to a program about a good scientist gone bad: Dr. Charlotte Sternfield.

Mom grabs a towel. "Sorry. I'll change it."

I hold her arm. "No, I want to see this."

The footage pans across photos of a little girl with a shy smile. Her gap-toothed school pictures juxtapose with statements from teachers and professors who'd been awed by this science prodigy. The video clips of praise are replaced with condemnation by protesters who accuse her of playing God, or worse, Satan. Are these the so-called persecutors who pressured her into doing the unthinkable?

The show moves to an interview with Dr. Sternfield's mother. What is this, posthumous spin control? I stare into the cold, flat eyes of Sheyla Sternfield, trying to figure out whether they scarred her daughter enough to pursue her ambitions at all costs.

Mrs. Sternfield berates the media once again, claiming her Charlotte had been a "good girl." I study the woman's facial expressions, once again struck by how odd they are. It's then I realize the head-shaking and fidgeting aren't because she's distracted or doesn't care. That isn't it at all. Rather, she speaks well-rehearsed lines that ring completely false.

I step forward, mesmerized. Oh my God. The floor seems to buckle at my feet.

My pulse hammers. "She's lying."

Jack squints. "Lying? About what?"

An excellent question. "I don't know. But it's something important." Something I need to know. I feel it to my marrow.

I say, "See how she keeps touching her nose and mouth? She's not telling the truth, and I'll bet anything it has to do with the reason for Dr. Sternfield's death."

Mom puts down the towel. "Honey, I know the doctor's death was very upsetting. But we can't dwell on it. And no one should evaluate a grieving mother's words."

Well, I will. Because I know those words are BS. But I can't admit that because I haven't disclosed my newfound face-reading talent to anyone but Shane. Why freak out the people we love with one more thing, or, worse, make them feel self-conscious around us? I wring my hands. "I just want to make sure no one overlooks anything."

Mom says, "We all want that, sweetie. The researchers at Nova Genetics and the CDC are working tirelessly on a cure. That's where we have to put our faith."

I pick up on Mom's emotions. She's desperate to believe in the science that might cure me. And she needs to deal with the rage she feels against Dr. Sternfield.

For Mom's sake, I say, "Okay."

But my rage has only been relit. As I hack apart the bell peppers, I'm surer than anything I need to talk to Dr. Sternfield's mother, and uncover whatever she hiding. Is it possible Dr. Sternfield left behind crucial data that her mother's sitting on to prevent further trashing of her daughter's memory? Or maybe it's data that's being secretly auctioned to the highest bidder, like a news organization or pharmaceutical company. Okay, this is far-fetched, but finding out any detail I can about the woman who ruined so many lives is a mystery that must be solved.

There's no time to do anything about this now. Mom's admitted that she asked Evie to bring "guests." Jack, Sammy, and I set out plates, cups, and napkins as the doorbell rings.

Mom lets in Abby and a few girls from swim team. Evie's right behind them with Rafe. It's far fewer than were invited, yet far more than I expected. My guests bring flowers, food, and faces that twitch with anxiety.

I don't want to test their friendship by trying to hug them, the only exception being Evie, who hugs me first, while the others watch bug-eyed. Thank God for Evie.

We cluster in my living room, soon chatting and joking as if I didn't have a potentially fatal disease. In fact, they have a million questions about my stay in the hospital and the other kids who've been profiled on the news, especially Shane. Yeah, everyone stays two arm-lengths away, but they're drawn to what I have to say. It's bizarre. Well, bizarre is an appropriate way to describe my life these days.

I settle into my sofa like a queen, telling my story. They hang on to my every word. That part's still a rush at least.

Mom makes herself busy in the kitchen, waving off anyone who tries to help her. "You kids just have fun." Every time I glance her way, she's smiling big. Sadly, I realize this is the type of event she always hoped to host for me, under much different circumstances. And there's a pulling at her eyes that tells me her worries over my health are simmering nonstop. I want to kick myself for giving her another kid with a life-threatening condition.

The doorbell rings again. I jump to answer it before Mom. On the porch hovers a skinny guy wearing a black hoodie with a skeleton on the sleeve. He smiles crookedly. "We heard this is where the fun is." Unlike my friends, he leans in like he wants to get up close and personal.

I wedge my body behind the door. "Actually, it's private."

He grins in a way that makes me want to shower, and holds up a six-pack of beer. "We brought provisions."

"Maybe some other time?" Some other lifetime.

He winks. "I'll hold you to that, precious."

I slam the door and bolt it. Eww, weird.

"Hey, let's go out back," Abby hollers.

Fresh air sounds great even if it comes with reporters. Well, maybe if we show them that life goes on as usual, they'll get bored and leave me alone. Maybe.

We gather on the patio and try to ignore the cameras and faces that immediately pop over the shrubbery. Since I live on the corner, the reporters have an expanded view.

Evie's unfazed. She takes off her shirt to reveal a cherry-red bikini top. "You all brought swimsuits, like I told you to, right? Time for Sammy's super slide."

Sammy, who's still in his swim trunks from our failed pool attempt, hoots as he unrolls a huge plastic mat and hooks it up to the hose. Well, if the pool won't let us in, it doesn't mean we can't have fun in the water. More evidence for the reporters of Aislyn living normally.

Within minutes, everyone's ready to slide, but they seem to be waiting for me to go first. Starting at the far end of the yard, I jog and, with a prayer to the water-toy gods, plop onto the mat in a sideways slide. Whooshing to the end, I get up, laughing.

I stand there waiting for the next person to go, but no one makes a move. Are they afraid I contaminated the slide somehow? A sinking feeling fills my gut.

Sammy yells, "Chickens!" He dives onto the slide and whips across.

That seems to loosen something, because Evie and Jack follow him, and then the other kids do too. We take turns trying out every position and war call we can dream up. Yeah, I'll be bruised tomorrow, but there are worse ways to get hurt.

I let a burst of warmth flow through me, thankful to enjoy the sun again. If only Chloe and the others in the hospital could wake up and join us.

We slide until our sunscreen is gone, and then slide some more. Every time Jack gets near enough to slip past me, his skin feels hotter and slicker. Oh, man.

Just when I fear I'll pass out from the pheromone rush, Mom hollers that the burgers are ready. We towel dry and grab plates of food. Mom's outdone herself. I try not to dwell on how much this cost and how many real estate opportunities she missed while I was in the hospital.

When the sun sinks to the horizon, my friends begin to leave, as if this were a normal cookout on a normal day with a normal girl. Except for the reporters questioning each partygoer on the way out. The kids smile and chat into the microphones, hopefully sticking up for me on camera.

Evie hugs me on her way out the door. She raises an eyebrow in Jack's direction. "Don't keep him up too late."

I slap her arm. "If only."

Giggling, she leaves with Rafe.

Jack and I help Mom clean up and then we say good night to a coughing Sammy before Mom urges him upstairs. Finally, we settle onto the sofa. As much as I ache to be with Jack, it's unbearable watching his lips as he smiles, knowing I can't kiss them. I cross and re-cross my legs until I'm sure they'll chafe.

I try to think of an unromantic topic to decrease the frustration. "You know that interview we saw of Dr. Sternfield's mom, where she was lying?"

He thumps my knee with his. "Where you think she was lying, you mean?"

"No, I know she was. Her emotions were totally clear."

"Really?" He leans back and folds his arms behind his head. "Can you tell me what I'm thinking now?"

"Probably the same frustrating thoughts I've been thinking for the past few hours." All I want to do is launch myself onto him.

"Okay, too easy. But even if that woman was lying, so what?"

"So, I need to find out why. It could be important."

He takes my hand. "You just got out. Let's spend our time

being happy, not chasing down a woman who can't help you."

"You don't know that. Maybe we could find out her address and visit if she's in the area?"

He gives me a puzzled look tinged with pity. "I have a better idea. After I get off work tomorrow, let's hang out, maybe see a movie, something to take your mind off of all the crazy."

I swallow. "I just want to do something useful, not feel so helpless."

"You're doing something every day, by staying healthy. So keep doing that. Got it?" He takes me into his arms.

"I'll try."

He whispers into my ear, "I wish . . ." He sighs. "Well, you know what I wish."

"Yeah, me too." This sucks, sucks, sucks.

Minutes later, Mom comes back downstairs on the pretext of getting a glass of water, which is a comic tragedy given that the CZ88 is a far stricter hookup deterrent than she could ever be. Still, Jack rises to leave.

His skin feels cool and dry as we hug and agree to get together tomorrow evening. I shut the door and take a long breath. With a hand to my forehead, I assure myself I'm okay. I'm okay.

But that could change in an instant. I run upstairs to get busy. With a FindAnyone app to the rescue, I locate an address and phone number for Sheyla Sternfield in Cle Elum, a rural town in the middle of the Cascades, a couple hours east of here. Hmm, no way Mom will let me head there so soon after she got me home.

Yet Mrs. Sternfield might be the only one who could give me answers. Answers that'll prove to everyone I'm right about her. Besides, it's not as if driving out there would be any more dangerous than sitting around and waiting for the gene therapy's side effects to take over. In the long run, interviewing Mrs. Sternfield would do more good than harm. I know it.

If only Jack didn't have to work tomorrow. We could drive out together like some kind of detective duo. I'd show him that my intuition about Mrs. Sternfield isn't wrong. But I can't wait until he has a free day, which won't be until the weekend at least, assuming I could convince him.

I stew over my dilemma as I get ready for bed. Settled on my bed with my phone, I hit Shane's number.

"Hey, Blondie. Enjoying your newfound freedom with loverboy?"

"If only I could."

I feel his smirk over the phone. "Told you it would be frustrating."

"How are you dealing with it?"

He howls with laughter. "Do you really want to know?"

"Um, no thanks."

I quickly change the subject to my conviction that Mrs. Sternfield's mom is lying about something. Unlike everyone else, he believes me immediately.

I ask, "So you want to come with me tomorrow and talk to her?"

"Aw, here I thought you called because you miss me so much."

I sigh. "You helping me or not?"

"Count me in."

Yes. I've got my freedom. And I've got a plan. Now, if I can just keep my health.

Local CZ88 Patient Missing from Hospital
Found in Coma

by Ruthie Mansfield, *The Sound Sentinel*

Sophia Washington, who was infected with an illegal gene therapy and went missing a week ago from Seattle General, was found late yesterday, alive but in a coma, on the beach at Carkeek Park. Ms. Washington and one hundred thirty-nine others contracted a dangerous virus as a result of a clandestine trial of a DNA-altering treatment. In most cases, the treatment has resulted in a coma, and twenty-five victims have died so far.

Ms. Washington does not appear to have been seriously harmed; however, extensive bruising on her arms and blood loss have the authorities investigating the possibility of foul play. Had she not been found before the tide came in, she almost certainly would have drowned. Anyone with information on her disappearance is asked to contact the Seattle Police Department immediately.

SEVENTEEN

In the morning, I take a deep breath and head downstairs. The wary, fragile look from Mom warns me we still can't have a reasonable discussion about Sammy's trial, so I launch into my other plan.

"I'm hanging out at Evie's today." It's like swallowing acid to lie to Mom, but I know in my heart I have to track down Dr. Sternfield's mother.

Mom wrinkles her brow. "I thought Evie mentioned having to work in her parents' shop this week."

"She got out of it so we could catch up." Another lie, another gulp of bile.

Mom seems to calculate as she sips her coffee. "I suppose Sammy can tag along with me on my appointments, or spend the day at Aunt Emily's."

Aunt Emily's family lives an hour away. But since the neighbors refuse to take care of Sammy anymore, thanks to me, the boy-sitting options are limited. It's almost enough to make me abandon my plan.

Self-doubt weighing every step, I sneak upstairs to make arrangements with Shane. I also text Evie to cover for me.

She responds: YOUR MOM DESERVES A HELL OF A LOT BETTER.

Tell me about it. But it's not fair for Evie to scold me when she still gets to live a normal life, with a boy she can kiss. I type: I NEED TO KNOW THE TRUTH. HOPE YOU CAN UNDERSTAND SOMEDAY.

YEAH, ME TOO.

I'll just have to show her along with everyone else. A few minutes after Mom and Sammy leave, I head out the door.

The first reporter yells, "Aislyn! You're allowed out in public? Where are you going?"

Of course, I don't comment.

Another reporter holds out a microphone as I rush past. "What do you think about the Charisma victims in LA who were beaten up when they went to a club last night?"

I halt. "What?"

"They're calling it a hate crime. You sure you want to go out alone, without protection?"

I fumble with the keys as I unlock my car. "This isn't LA.

But thanks for the warning." Inside my car, I chew my lip, and would love to take a moment, but the reporters hover outside my window. Thankfully, no one follows me when I drive off.

Shane lives on the west end of Tacoma, near the water. The sunshine's brought out the locals and the traffic. But it's a day for open windows and loud car songs, so I try to enjoy it. I pull up to a yellow bungalow-style cottage with only a couple of reporters milling around. I smile, ignoring their questions about my lacking love life.

Shane answers the door, waving at the guys behind me. "Want the tour?"

I know exactly where the tour would end up. "We've got a long way to go and I have to be home by five for Jack."

His eyelid tremors. "Aw, the lovebirds are intent on death by frustration." He points to a black compact on the street. "My car's over there."

Wanting to make sure things go according to plan, my plan, I say, "I'll drive."

He drops his keys into his pocket. "I like a girl who takes control."

Good Lord, being released from captivity hasn't calmed him down a bit. Well, maybe that's a healthy sign. Ignoring the reporters calling our names, we head off. Unfortunately, this time one of the guys hops into his car and trails us.

Gritting my teeth, I speed through a yellow light, but the reporter sails behind me even after the light's already turned. We play a game of chase through the traffic while Shane keeps an eye out the back window. In the frenzy, I accidentally end up on a two-lane street that slows us both down. To make things worse, a garbage truck approaches, taking up most of both lanes. Great. But then I realize what looks like a delay is actually an opportunity.

"Hold on," I say.

With a foot to the gas, I swerve around the truck, causing it to honk, but I lose the reporter's SUV in the process.

Shane laughs. "Damn."

At least someone appreciates risk-taking. I drive east. The green of Tacoma grows greener as we travel toward the mountains. We spend the drive in cozy conversation, skimming past trees and hills, the stuff of life, which has never seemed more amazing. What I'd give for Chloe, Sebastian, and the others to get another chance at this. Mrs. Sternfield has to hold a clue. Her daughter could've left behind a treasure trove of research, or confided in her mother what she'd been up to. Anything's possible. I have to figure out what's behind the lie in Mrs. Sternfield's face.

Two hours later, we pull up to the secluded cul-de-sac where Mrs. Sternfield lives, not far from a resort that advertises a golf course and cross-country skiing.

I slap my forehead. "Oh, crap. What if this is just her vacation home?"

Shane blows pretend smoke from his finger-gun and drawls, "There's no way to know until we ring the bell, partner."

I park on a gravel strip that fronts a yard bursting with flowers. They surround a tidy white house with frilly lavender curtains. Not what I expected, given the severe impression I've formed of Mrs. Sternfield. Was my reading of her emotions off too?

After a few deep breaths, I get out and march with Shane to the door. He grins and rings the bell. No sound of a dog barking or hurried footsteps. I peek into the large window to our right. No movement.

I raise my hand to give the bell one more try, when the door briskly opens. The lady whose face filled my TV with her chilly personality stands before us. Instead of a golf vest or preppy greens and pinks, she's dressed in jeans and hiking boots, and says, "You're a long way from home, aren't you, Miss Hollings and Mr. Elliott?" Although her voice is stern, her eyes flicker with fear.

I hiccup. "You know who we are?"

"I can't escape the news, no matter how I try. Now, what can I do for you?" Her furrowed brow emits a faint curiosity, but fear is the overriding vibe I pick up.

Shane's chest is wide, his hand relaxed on his hip like a sheriff. "First off, we're sorry about your daughter." When did he become such a diplomat?

Mrs. Sternfield's eyelids flutter. "Thank you."

As gently as possible, I say, "Your daughter kind of connects us all, don't you think?"

She raises an eyebrow.

Shane leans forward and places a hand to his heart. "We know this isn't the best timing, but it might be our only chance to speak with someone who was closer to Dr. Sternfield than anyone else. Could you tell us a little about her? Anything that might help us figure out what she gave us and why?"

Mrs. Sternfield's shoulders stiffen, and her squint becomes more pronounced. I expect sadness at the mention of her daughter. But there's only wariness. How odd. What is there left to be afraid of, her daughter's legacy? Too late.

With what seems like effort, she loosens her stance and her stare. "Charlotte could be obsessive about her work. I know she didn't mean to cause you and the others any harm. When she realized how much injury her research caused, and how the press would hound her forever, it became more than she could bear." She wipes a dry cheek and lowers her gaze, breaking eye contact. "You know the rest. Now, I hope you will let me grieve in peace."

I examine her. Everything about this speech seems too

prepared. The emotions I read are anxiety and dishonesty, not sadness. And why hasn't she invited us in, the way a normal person would under such circumstances?

Although it feels intrusive, I step closer. "Maybe you could work through your grieving process by helping undo what she did."

She crosses her arms. "I'm not a geneticist. I taught literature."

"We just want to know if she left notes or a computer, anything that might provide info on a cure."

Mrs. Sternfield shakes her head. "There's nothing I haven't already given to my ex-husband. I'm sorry."

Sorry, my butt. And her features tightened when she referred to Dr. Gordon.

Shane and I use whatever charm we supposedly have to persuade her to say more, but she insists she has other commitments. When she closes the door, I hover next to Shane, unsure of what to try next.

I whisper, "You see her expression when she talked about Dr. Sternfield? I'm not imagining there's something off, am I?"

He nudges me toward the car. "No, there's something weird with her."

"She's hiding something. What if Dr. Sternfield left a lab behind, complete with chimps?"

"Somehow I doubt her mom would take care of monkeys. Maybe she's hiding something totally unrelated, like a moonshine still. She was dressed for backpacking."

I yank open my door. "Moonshine? Really?"

Shane shrugs. "Why not? People'll surprise you all the time. No one would've guessed you'd agree to CZ88. Or spend the day with me."

We get into the car, but instead of starting the engine, I stare at the gabled house. "Think she'd notice if we sprinted around and peeked in the windows?"

Shane hoots. "Hell yeah, she'd notice. And what would you expect to find?"

"I don't know, I just don't want to give up this easily."

"I get that, Wondergirl, but we should leave, before she calls the police."

Reluctantly, I start the engine and drive out of the cul-de-sac. But I don't go far.

A half mile down the road, I take an unpaved turn-off for a trailhead. Shielded from the street by a cluster of trees, the tiny parking lot holds a few cars, mostly Subarus bearing bike racks that scream *Outdoorsy Northwesterner*. I pull into a spot and shut off the engine.

Shane grins. "Okay, Detective Hollings, what's your next move? Or did you bring me here for nefarious purposes?" He leans his seat back a few inches.

"We should wait until she leaves and then get into her house somehow."

He turns to me, suddenly serious. "Blondie. I came to keep you company, but I doubt Dr. Charlotte left behind a cure. If she had, there'd be no reason for her mom not to share it and make her daughter a hero."

"Then what's she lying about?"

"I don't know. But I don't think it's worth us spending more time on. Not when we might not have much time left."

We stare at each other for a bleak moment.

I hug myself. "So, what should we spend our time on? Making more When-I'm-Gone videos? I want to help find a cure."

"I do too. That means giving Nova Genetics all the info we can. It might also mean giving info to other researchers who could help us."

"Like who?"

He stretches an arm out his window. A tiny moth lands on it. "Someone from VidaLexor contacted me."

"VidaLexor? But they're against gene therapy."

"They're against *irresponsible* gene therapy. They want to work with us to reverse the CZ88. Everything on the up-and-up."

"Why?"

He twists his arm, but the moth stays on it. "To be the

good guys? Great PR for them to save the day."

"I'm not interested in making them the hero."

"Yeah. *You* want to be the hero."

I rear back. "That's not fair." Okay, maybe a small part of me wants to send a message to folks like Heath Roberts or those science fair judges who humiliated me, but my quest is mostly about surviving.

"You should at least talk to the guy. I'm meeting him at five."

"That's when I'm meeting Jack."

He rolls his eyes. "Seriously? Isn't the possibility of finding a cure more important than clawing the upholstery with loverboy?"

I peer between the trees and down toward Mrs. Sternfield's cul-de-sac. How hard would it be to break in? This feels an awful lot like a crime show, but that's pretty much what my life has morphed into.

Shane caresses the spot on his arm from where the moth finally took flight. "Blondie, we are not going to break and enter. Not before we've tried something that makes sense. Come with me later. We can use our super senses to see if the guy's legit. You've got to admit, it's worth a shot."

It's hard to argue with his logic, especially when I picture Chloe lying so still with all those tubes in her, or, worse, Rosa. "Fine."

My stomach rumbles, reminding me it's past lunchtime. We cruise into the nearest small town and park in front of a café that sells breakfast all day. Over a heaping plate of French toast covered in maple-bacon syrup, I text Jack about getting together a bit later, explaining I have to meet with a doctor.

Shane offers to drive to VidaLexor. The drowsiness brought on by too many carbs convinces me to accept his offer. I lean the car seat all the way back, ignore the comment it prompts from Shane, and curl up into a sleep that hits a minute after we get onto the freeway.

When I wake up, it's to the sensation of a car no longer running. Shane leans against the driver's-side window softly snoring. I check my phone. Five ten.

I hit his arm. "We're late for your appointment."

He mumbles and rubs his eyes. "Damn, that lunch did me in."

I rummage through my purse for mints and dole out a couple. We're in a mainly residential neighborhood, parked in front of a four-story beige building with signage for various medical specialties. I say, "I thought VidaLexor had a fancy building up in Seattle."

Shane runs a hand through his curls. "Don't want stray reporters making us the poster kids for VidaLexor before they earn it."

His new, sensible attitude wins me over. I follow him up a

stairwell to a door marked VL, INC. With a chime announcing our arrival, we enter a small waiting room that smells of air freshener. A tall man with silvery black hair and a boater's tan hurries from the back.

He puts out his hand. "I'm Dr. Pete Dulcet. So glad you could both make it. Why don't we go to the meeting room, where it's more comfortable?"

I eye the dim hallway. "Out here is fine." I sit in one of the pastel-upholstered chairs.

Shane's glare goes for a knockout punch, but he takes a seat.

Dr. Dulcet does too. "How are you kids feeling? Hell of a thing you've gone through."

"We're not through it yet," I say.

Dr. Dulcet rests his forearms on his thighs. "Yes, yes. Well, I should cut to the chase, shouldn't I?" He clasps his hands together. "VidaLexor is well equipped to help you. Please let us."

I examine Dr. Dulcet's expression. So far, he comes across as genuine, but leery, guarded. "You guys aren't known as gene therapy supporters."

His eyes widen and he sits upright. "On the contrary. We've been conducting studies for years and are on the cusp of a couple of breakthrough therapies. We only challenge Nova Genetics when we have safer, more effective options available. If you keep an open mind, I believe we could help you." Nothing about him indicates dishonesty, more like determination.

Shane says, "Why don't you team up with the folks at Nova Genetics or the hospital?"

Dr. Dulcet exhales loudly. "We've tried. However, the hospital will not share patient data due to confidentiality requirements and Nova Genetics won't share data for proprietary reasons. In their case it's very much a business decision, assuming they can stay in business after this. The only thing keeping them open is the government's hope they'll find a cure for what Dr. Sternfield concocted."

Shane asks, "So what would you need in order to work on your own cure?"

Eagerness bubbles from Dr. Dulcet. "Your consent and a blood draw, which we'd sequence. We have a number of ideas on where to look."

I cross my legs. "Nova's been searching for weeks and hasn't turned up much."

"Our researchers are quite extraordinary."

I harrumph. "So are theirs. Or at least one of them. Was."

"Yes. She was brilliant. Maybe too much for her own good. But now we need to focus on your own good. What do you have to lose, besides a little blood?"

Do I want to be a guinea pig again? With some guy in a

sketchy office? No way am I going to be tricked into something.

I say, "I'm not quite seventeen, so my mom would have to sign off before I decide anything." If only I'd worried about such legalities when the CZ88 was offered. "And that doesn't mean I'm saying yes. I need to think about this."

Shane flexes his elbow opened and closed. "What's to think about? I'm eighteen and can give my own consent."

I place my hand on his other arm. "Maybe we should run it by Dr. Culdicott first?"

"It's just a blood draw. And the sooner they have it, the sooner they get to work. You're not the only one who's tired of feeling hopeless." He turns to Dr. Dulcet. "Ready when you are."

Dr. Dulcet nods. "Follow me."

Shane says over his shoulder, "You can thank me later."

He and Dr. Dulcet glide down the hall. I slouch into the seat and take out my phone. No texts from Jack yet, so I call.

"Hey," he answers. "Where are you?"

"Um, at that doctor's appointment. Well, actually the doctor works for VidaLexor. They think they can help."

"Really? That's great."

I twirl a lock of hair around my finger. "I don't know. Something seems shady. What if they just want to show the world how evil Nova Genetics is?"

He laughs. "Sounds like a BS theory Shane would dream up."

"Actually, he's letting the doctor take his blood right now."

Jack's breath comes out with a hiss. "You guys are there together?"

"Um, yeah, why wouldn't we be? But hopefully we'll get out of here soon."

"Why don't you just leave now?"

"I have to give Shane a ride home."

He pauses. "Was his place on the way?"

"Well, um, he helped me with another project beforehand, so it was just more convenient."

"What project?"

Shane approaches from the hallway with a satisfied grin.

I speak quietly into the phone. "I'll tell you later. He and the doctor just finished."

"Yeah, we should talk."

We end the call on that awkward note.

Dr. Dulcet hands me a business card. "If you change your mind after clearing things with your parents and doctors, please give me a buzz."

Well, at least he's acting on the up-and-up. I take his card and say I'll let him know.

On the way to Shane's house, he rocks along to a heavy metal radio station. "Just watch. Throwing a little competition at Nova Genetics will fire up their asses. It's game on."

"It's not a game. And if you piss off Dr. Gordon, what if he gives up? Then we're all dead. Literally."

He stops drumming on my dashboard. "Do not go there."

I grip the steering wheel. "You're right. Positive thinking. So, when should we try breaking into Mrs. Sternfield's house?"

He laughs. "Ah, my hot partner in crime isn't giving up, huh?"

"Just say you'll think about it."

"Just say you'll think about working with VidaLexor."

I park in front of his house and put out my hand. "Deal."

We shake. He leaves the car, his body still swaying to some imaginary beat. I smile to myself, thankful the Charisma has at least given me this new friend, whose obnoxiousness has morphed into something endearing. Not that Jack has anything to worry about.

As I drive away, I switch off Shane's hard-core music. For a moment, I think I hear the echo of the last song reverberating through the car. But the echo doesn't stop. Then I realize with a ripping sensation through my chest that the noise isn't an echo at all.

My ears are ringing.

CZ88 Virus Keeps Spreading

by Josephine Bailey for *USA Now*

Despite assurances from the medical community that CZ88, nicknamed Charisma, is only spread via sexual contact and needles, the number of victims continues to rise. Many have gone into comas before they were diagnosed, making it difficult to determine exactly how they were infected. Citizen groups are demanding that the patients who remain conscious and were recently released from hospitals be returned to isolation immediately.

Charisma Victim Counts

From www.NowYouKnowToo.com

Total cases: 169

Conscious: 17

In comas: 123

Died: 29

EIGHTEEN

I pull to the side of the road and clamp my hands to my head in horror, which only makes the high-pitched whistle more noticeable. My mouth goes dry. Ringing in the ears was what Chloe and Jesse complained of before they went into comas, palms against their heads the way mine are now. Wasn't my last vision of Rosa clutching her ears? I can't be succumbing to this, I can't. Not when I've finally gotten out of the hospital. Not when I have Jack back in my life. No.

I open the mirror on the visor to hunt for signs of an oncoming coma, as if it'll arrive with an announcement stamped on my forehead. My face looks normal, if you ignore the panic. Deep breaths. I feel fine. Fine. And, really, the sound seems less intense than a minute ago. Maybe just a false alarm brought on by Shane's music.

It takes another ten minutes to stop shaking enough to drive. Part of me wants to race home and hide in my room. But as long as I'm conscious, I am not going to miss out on my life. Whatever time I have left is time I'm living to the fullest.

On autopilot, I park, greet Mom and Sammy in a shaky voice, and head upstairs. I try jumping jacks and a headstand against the wall to see if I'll jiggle whatever's broken in my head. Nothing works and I have to take long breaths to keep from sobbing. The whistling continues to rise and fall as I get ready. At the sound of the doorbell, I somehow paste on a smile and make my way down holding tightly to the banister.

I expect Jack to still be upset about my day with Shane, but his face is like sunshine when he comes in. "So what are you in the mood for?"

I swallow. There are too many ways to answer that. I'm in the mood to enjoy a night where I'm not freaking out from noises in my head. I want to kiss my boyfriend. I want my friends to wake from their comas. I want a cure for Sammy, and for my mom to let him accept that cure.

All I say is, "Um."

He flashes his phone display, filled with a movie list. I scan, dismissing the one about a virus that kills half the planet, and any flick with the hint of romance. "Space alien invasion?"

Jack grins. "Perfect."

I avoid Mom's and Sammy's eyes as we leave. They hoped I'd stay home tonight, but I need to keep moving. And I don't want to fight with Mom. Outside, a couple of paparazzi pop to attention. They point their cameras and yell questions about our relationship status. To Jack, I whisper, "Sure you want to go through with this?"

He puts an arm around my shoulders. "Treat these guys like bees. If you don't bother them, they shouldn't bother you."

I don't remind him that some people die from bee stings.

We drive off into what could be a perfect summer night if it weren't for the whistling in my ears. I welcome the cranked-up car music that masks the noise.

Jack grabs my hand and plays with my fingers, as if everything were normal, which makes me want to cry. "So tell me what you and Shane were up to." Nervousness and a touch of anger creep into his face.

"Just keep an open mind, okay?" Blinking away the dampness in my eyes, I give him the short version of driving out to Mrs. Sternfield's house. As I do, his grip on my fingers loosens.

He shakes his head and exhales loudly. "Can't believe I'm going to agree with Shane on something, but your plan to break and enter is completely insane."

I cringe at the edge to his voice. He's supposed to be on my side. "It might be the only chance I have for learning what Dr. Sternfield knew before her death."

The car picks up speed. "What do you think you're going to find? The doctor was seriously messed up. Even if she left any info behind, it's probably messed up too."

My seat belt presses tight against my chest. "I've got to try something. Not just wait for whatever."

His tone softens. "Could you intern or something at Nova Genetics? It might inspire the researchers."

"If they're not inspired after twenty-nine deaths, I don't know what I could do. I really wish I could convince Dr. Gordon to work with VidaLexor."

"I think you could convince anyone to do anything these days." His nostrils flare.

I heave a breath. "Anyone except Mrs. Sternfield."

Jack's mouth strains for a moment with annoyance. He parks, and we stroll through the parking lot. Without the music to mask it, the faint humming in my head makes itself known again. My gut twists. Jack eyes me with concern, until I give him a bright smile. Thank goodness he can't read faces like I can.

I keep my head down and don't make eye contact with those we pass, even if a part of me yearns to connect with them. Despite my attempt to remain incognito, a handful of people tentatively approach to ask about my "condition." Jack nods indulgently, at first. But his jaw tightens every time someone pushes him to the side to get to me. I try to be polite as I say my hellos and inch back toward Jack, who always seems just out of reach. We make it into the theater after the previews start.

He leans into me. "That must drive you crazy."

"Most of them mean well. Better than them running in fear of me."

He pulls back to stare at my face, his features flickering dark and light in the reflection of the screen. "Wow, you really *have* changed."

For some reason, his words rankle. "Only my behaviors, not what I'm really about," I say.

He bites his lip. "What exactly is the difference?"

A woman in the row behind shushes us.

I turn around. "Sorry."

She startles. "Oh, you're *that girl*."

Jack throws me a knowing a look but doesn't add anything then or when the woman and her friend move a couple of rows back. At first I'm grateful they've given us space, and then I realize they're probably afraid of breathing the same air as me.

One screaming preview after the next assaults us before the movie finally begins. I try to lose myself in spaceships and heroic countermeasures, but it's impossible. All I can think of is that I'm "that girl," whoever she is. And plenty of people are afraid of her.

After the film, we stop for ice cream, but it feels as if we're following a script. With minimal dialog. This has the added effect of increasing the noticeability of the ringing in my ears, causing my heart to race and my focus to turn inward. Jack isn't helping any, examining me with a slight tilt to his head as if he's solving a complex equation. My own brain is a jumble. Every time I open my mouth, I can't help but wonder if the words that come out are from the "real" me or the "fake" me. And if that me, real or fake, will plunge into unconsciousness at any moment.

As much as I ache to confide in Jack, and bring back that closeness I've come to adore, I know it would only upset him to hear I'm having symptoms. Really, the best thing is to call it a night, especially when folks at the next table start to whisper and point. Jack doesn't argue when I suggest going home.

On my porch, we say good-bye with a quick hug. His gaze is more quizzical than lingering, as if he's trying to assess who I really am. Here I thought he knew.

As I unlock my door, his phone buzzes. When he glances at it, I see the texter is Alexandra. My instinct is to confront him, but the night already feels awful enough. Besides, given the way things are, I can't exactly blame him for considering a Plan B.

I hurry inside, my shoulders folded inward, my heart heavy. Mom glances up from her computer with raised eyebrows.

I say, "He needs to get up extra early for work tomorrow." There I go, back to lying.

"Probably wouldn't hurt for you to get some rest too. You've been out all day."

"Tomorrow I'll be here for Sammy. Promise. I've already told him I'll chauffeur him anywhere he wants." I roll back and forth on the balls of my feet. "Hey, if you aren't busy, how about we all have lunch together?"

The gratitude pouring from her almost knocks me over. "I'll make that happen."

Buoyed, I say, "A Dr. Dulcet from VidaLexor contacted Shane and me today. He wants to help find a cure."

Her eyes narrow. "He contacted you, a minor, directly instead of going through the hospital or me?"

"Well, he contacted Shane. I told him I'd check with you and Dr. Culdicott before jumping into his research. I'll give you his business card."

Another burst of gratitude. "I'm so glad you didn't rush into anything."

Her appreciativeness almost convinces me to admit I approached Mrs. Sternfield, but I know she wouldn't understand, and worse, try to prevent me from driving back out to Cle Elum. No, there's being forthcoming and there's being stupid.

I hoof upstairs and log online.

Big mistake.

All I see are haters, who claim I did everything necessary to get my hands on a "designer" drug. What happened as a result was my fault, so no one should waste an ounce of sympathy. Someone's even posted a death toll on my page with a message reading: "Who will you infect next?"

I bite my knuckle, tears welling in my eyes. Shane and I fought awfully hard to be released into a world that despises us. The only ones who seem to want me around are a group whose messages repel me even more than the haters. A private note from "StarBound" reads: *You know what it's like to be so scared that you practically pee your pants whenever you have to meet a new person? Put me out of my misery. I'll meet you anytime, anywhere for what you've got.*

Holy crap. A wave of revulsion reverberates through my body. I slam the computer closed, panting.

Fighting the urge to sob, I throw myself onto my bed. First, this buzzing in my head, then Jack giving me the stink eye, possibly even cheating with Alexandra, and now more haters and weirdoes. I pull a pillow over my head and moan into it. Damn, damn, damn. But covering my head only increases the screech in my ears.

I whip off the pillow and pace around my room, pulling at my lobes. Dr. Culdicott said to return to the hospital at the first sign of symptoms. But why? They'll lock me up in isolation and wait for the worst. If I have hours left, I don't want to spend them alone.

I tiptoe downstairs, only to find Mom dozed off on the sofa with her laptop. No way will I wake her. The silence of the house turns the buzzing in my ears into a roar. As desperately as I yearn to fly out the door and run down the street wailing, I trudge back to my bedroom instead.

I pace again, letting the sobs flow freely. What a crappy way to spend my final hours of consciousness. If only it were possible to achieve one more thing, one astounding, beautiful accomplishment. "Make some memories," as Evie would say. But I've got nothing. Just like the old Aislyn.

I put on my pajamas, grab a pillow, and creep over to Sammy's room. He sleeps restlessly but with a tiny smile on his lips. For a change, he isn't coughing. Thank you, God. Grabbing the extra blanket folded on his rocking chair, I spread it on the floor next to his bed and curl up there, comforted by the sound of his breathing and the familiar paintings on his walls. As if sensing me, Sammy's arm drops to the side. I reach up and hold his hand, anchoring our forearms on the ridge where box spring meets mattress, the way I do when he has a tough night. How many hours have I spent on this floor?

Clasping my brother's hand for comfort, the way he's always hung on to me, I tremble as the night settles in around us. I stare at the ceiling for long minutes, maybe hours, sometimes losing track of the ear-ringing, only to hear it again the moment I think about it. The notion of ever experiencing silence and true peace again seems far out of reach.

Yet somehow I sleep.

When I awake in the morning, my head's groggy. But I'm conscious. Amazing. Within the fuzziness of my brain, the ringing doesn't seem as loud. I stick my fingers into my ears just to be sure. It really seems lighter. Maybe I have another day to live. Another day to fight back.

Sammy's left his bed, probably wondering what brought me to his floor. Clutching my aching back, I shuffle to my room and sink onto my own bed.

Only to be roused a minute later by a knocking at my door. When I answer, Sammy peeks in. "You okay?"

"Yeah, just had a scary night, you know?"

He nods, and starts coughing. Of course he knows.

I sit up. "So, where shall we go first?" As I say the words, I once again feel a profound gratitude we have a day to plan for. It bursts through my chest with warmth and energy, and, for a moment, happiness so sharp it prickles my eyes.

"The Comix Dungeon." His coughing turns into hacking.

I rush over with tissues as he clears his lungs. "Oh, Sammy, we have to get you into the AV719 trial. If you beg Mom, she can't refuse."

He glowers and when he finally catches his breath, he says, "No way. Mom went nuts while you were in the hospital. I'm not getting into an experiment she's totally against. It's not like she's got any more backup kids."

The wind is knocked out of me. "That's how you've thought of me all these years, as Mom's backup kid?"

"No, her guarantee. And now she doesn't have one."

I have to make this right. Mom needs us. Both of us. And Sammy shouldn't have to wait one day longer than necessary to breathe, to have hope for a disease-free future.

He twists out of my grasp and escapes to his room. I stomp around my own, pounding the bed and the walls. I will not be the one responsible for destroying my brother's life, or anyone else's. Sammy and Mom need to understand that gene therapy is still a promise worth keeping. The world needs to give them that message, loud and clear. What can I do? What can I do?

I get an idea.

Throwing on clothes and brushing out my hair, I prepare to face the public. Downstairs, I step into the Tacoma morning, overcast but warm. A female reporter with pixie-cut black hair and a thousand-dollar suit runs in high heels up the front path with the others following in her wake. I shuffle in place on the porch as they gather around below me, but no one gets closer than five feet. Contagion has its uses, after all.

Shivering, I say, "I'll give a statement when you're ready." Glancing behind myself, I see Sammy poke his head out of the door, his eyes wary.

Once the cameras are in place, I clear my throat. "I want to make it absolutely clear that Dr. Sternfield acted alone. Alone. I'm confident that Nova Genetics' other researchers are qualified to develop a cure for what she did." I pause for a breath. "But they aren't the only ones who can. I hope that many geneticists tackle this problem and save a whole lot of lives. For that reason, I'm allowing any research organization that my doctors at Florence Bishop Children's deem worthy to obtain a copy of my genome sequence."

There's a gasp among the reporters, even the scruffiest guys. But the most important part of my statement is still to come.

I motion toward Sammy and continue. "My brother has cystic fibrosis, which could someday be cured by gene therapy. I'm thrilled there are clinical trials moving forward and I have faith they'll do so in a safe, responsible manner. It would be a tragedy to prevent kids from promising therapies because of one bad researcher."

There, that should put some pressure on Mom to do the right thing with AV719 and maybe get the researchers to let Sammy start the trial late. I open my arms, palms up. "If you have questions, I'll try to answer them. Just keep in mind I'm a high-schooler, not a scientist."

They fake-laugh at that, and then hurl their questions.

The pixie-haired woman thrusts a microphone my way. "Are you aware that by publicizing your genomic sequence, you'll be losing a great degree of privacy. Not only will researchers be able to search for the genes manipulated by the Charisma, but they'll be able to see whether you're susceptible to a host of other conditions."

"That's why the hospital will help identify trustworthy researchers. As for other conditions, if no one figures out how to counteract the CZ88, I may not be around long enough for those to be an issue."

A red-haired man holding a handkerchief to his mouth calls out, "Are you sure you aren't contagious? There have been cases reported thousands of miles away."

I raise my eyebrows. "Have any of those cases been spread by casual contact?"

Sammy steps forward and takes my hand. "The docs tested my mom and me multiple times. Nothing."

The man narrows his eyes. "What about dating, Aislyn? We've seen you out and about with your boyfriend."

I say, "For now, no serious relationships."

The pixie-haired woman purses her lips. "Define *serious*."

I give her a pointed look. "I think you can fill in the blanks."

She blinks rapidly. "That must be devastating for a teen girl. What does the other victim, Shane, think about that?"

I stifle a groan. "Ask him. As for devastating, I'd save that word for those who're in a coma or have died."

"So far," mutters the whiskeriest guy in the bunch.

I swallow.

I bat questions until the whiskered guy asks Sammy about his own prognosis. Sammy's breathing is rough. Time to end this.

I pull Sammy toward the door. "Sorry, he's only eleven."

When we get inside, I ride my momentum and call Dr. Gordon from my room. If Shane's right, what I've done should force Nova Genetics to work harder. After I tell Dr. Gordon I've drummed up the competition, he says, "I suppose I can't blame you."

"Also, there's something I need to know about your ex-wife."

"Sheyla? What on earth do you want to know about her?"

"Okay, this will sound crazy, but ever since I got the

CZ88, I've been able to read social cues and expressions much more clearly."

"That stands to reason."

So I'm not delusional. "It's obvious to me your ex is lying about something regarding your daughter. I'm really sorry if this is painful, but I wonder if it's possible Dr. Sternfield told her anything about what she'd done or why she was going to, um, do what she did on that bridge."

There's a long moment of silence, finally interrupted by throat clearing. "Ah, Aislyn, I know how desperate you are to find answers, but there isn't anything useful Sheyla will be able to convey. She and Charlie were close, but I highly doubt they discussed technical issues."

"Are you sure?"

His voice is that of a much older man as he says, "Sometimes there's no answer for why someone chooses to do what they do. I have to take some of the blame for always encouraging Charlie to push the bounds of knowledge." He takes a loud breath that might be mixed with a sob.

"There's got to be something we're overlooking, something I can do."

He says, "You're frustrated, of course. So am I. But maybe there is a way you could help. We're hosting a gathering this evening for potential investors to fund our efforts to find a cure for CZ88. Perhaps you could attend, and inspire supporters for the fight ahead."

"So you aren't being closed down?"

"Only because we offer the best possibility for curing you and the others, but the government has us on a short leash."

So Dr. Dulcet told the truth about that. I clutch the phone with a white-knuckled grip. "Okay, I'll try to 'inspire' your investors, but you need to talk with Dr. Dulcet at VidaLexor about working together."

"Those kinds of partnerships often cause more delay than efficiency."

"Those kinds of partnerships could save my life."

"I'll consider it, Aislyn. We're all in this together."

I hope he means that.

"A car will pick you up at seven p.m. Be prepared to deliver a few remarks to the group." He hangs up.

I stare at my phone. What have I agreed to? A speech? In front of a large crowd of strangers? Somehow that seems scarier than batting questions with a handful of reporters on my front porch. Maybe it would be better to focus upon the logistical details such as what to wear. I laugh at myself. Hard to believe a time existed when the decision of what to wear was actually important.

What does matter is keeping my promises to Sammy. Every one of them. I find him down in the kitchen, his face red from his latest coughing fit. "Okay, bro, ready for a trip to the Comix Dungeon?"

A *thunk* from the front entryway startles us. Oh, man, is one of the reporters trying to break in? I sprint to the door.

But it's only today's mail, which lies scattered on the floor beneath the mail slot. I scoop it up and place it on the entry table. One letter is addressed "To the parents of Aislyn Hollings" with the school district's return address. I rip it open.

As I read, a hard knot forms in my stomach. I kidded myself about thinking that life outside the hospital would be so great. The real world could be a bitch and a half.

Tacoma Teen Finds Time to Frolic Despite Lethal Condition

by Serena Wagner, *Tacoma Times*

Aislyn Hollings, 16, who participated in the illegal trial of a gene therapy and is one of only a handful of such patients across the US to have avoided dire consequences, returned home this week to great fanfare. Living up to the gene treatment's promise of increased sociability, the first item of business for Miss Hollings was to throw a party. This, despite evidence that the treatment she received is contagious, usually leading to coma and possibly death. One source who attended Miss Hollings's party claimed, "Aislyn acted like she was in a bikini video. And she and her boyfriend, Jack, were all over each other."

Residents of North Tacoma have lodged a number of complaints with the police and the mayor's department, demanding that an isolation order be restored. However, Liam Guthrie, a spokesperson from the Washington State Department of Health, stated, "Unless Miss Hollings or Mr. Elliott displays intent to infect others through a known transmission mechanism, we're prevented from enforcing any further restrictive measures on their behavior."

NINETEEN

The school district's letter reads: *After extensive discussions with health officials, we've decided it's in the best interest of our school population for Aislyn not to attend classes this fall.*

They are "certain" my mother will understand.

Here I've already completed the required reading list for incoming seniors, including that stupid novel *Flowers for Algernon*, which had me sobbing. Throwing the letter on the end table, I grab my phone to call Shane.

"You too, huh?" is his response.

I pace back and forth through the living room. "It's crazy."

"No crazier than you wanting to break into someone's home."

"About that, I have Sammy today, how about tomorrow?"

"Not gonna help you get arrested, but I'll see you at the big-wig party tonight. Sally Sims just called to say you'll be my date."

"Really? She must've meant that you'll be *my* escort."

"Whatever you wanna call it, Blondie. See you then."

I launch my computer to find some talking points for tonight. First thing I see is a message from a girl named Mercedes, whose avatar is all pink cheeks and lip gloss, but whose words are razor blades. *You'd better watch your back! Freaks like you are an abomination of nature and should be treated like vermin.*

My heart thrashes. Treated like vermin? As in, avoided or exterminated?

Better to focus on my speech. I find reams of articles on civil liberty, and moving accounts of a boy named Ryan White, who'd been a teenager with AIDS before I was born. The stories of how he was forced to use a separate restroom and disposable utensils at school, and even how his grave was vandalized after his death, have me grinding my teeth. But he endured the harassment with dignity and an inspiring personality that hadn't come from any drug.

I've typed a page of notes when Evie texts about hanging out today. Oh yeah, I was supposed to drive Sammy around. What a crappy sister I am.

Evie and I make hurried plans, and a half hour later, we

scurry with Sammy past reporters. Fortunately, no one follows us when we drive off, or if they do, they're sneaky about it.

We head to the outskirts of downtown Tacoma, and park in a shabby neighborhood that hasn't been overhauled with condos and overpriced bakeries. Most of the shops have faded awnings and are staffed by folks with lots of piercings.

Even though I'm wearing sunglasses and a Mariners cap, several people stop me between the car and the Comix Dungeon. For some reason, I feel obligated to answer as many of their questions as I can, probably to prove I'm not a contagious monster. It takes fifteen minutes to get inside a dimly lit store that smells of dust and old paper.

Sammy, hauling his ever-present backpack, rushes to the clerk to ask about latest issues. Evie suggests we head to the nearby coffee shop while Sammy discusses the nuances of visual story telling. We stroll off to buy iced lattes and grab a crumb-flecked table in the corner of the café.

She brushes a lock of shiny black hair out of her face. "There's a boatload of pix online of you and Shane. Anything you wanna tell me?"

Some of my drink goes down the wrong way and I cough. "Nothing." Taking deep breaths, I tell her about the crime-free mission with Shane and the bodily-fluid-free date with Jack, including the text from Alexandra.

Her straw takes on a berry-colored lipstick kiss as she

slurps at her iced latte. "I'm sure Jack's not doing anything with Alexandra, yet. But it's time for you to get practical. If you can't get together with Jack, why let someone as totally hot as Shane go to waste? Or yourself?"

"Um, because I've crushed on Jack forever? And, if he's willing to wait, assuming he is, so am I."

She sighs long and loud. No need to hunt for micro facial cues. "But you're missing out on so much, Aiz."

It's then I realize she's been uncommonly stingy with the details of her own love life lately. And her averted eyes tell me she's hiding something.

I run a finger up and down my plastic cup, streaking the condensation. "Has anything, um, significant happened between you and Rafe? You'd tell me, right? Don't hide stuff because you think I'll feel bad about what Jack and I can't have."

Her cheeks turn the prettiest shade of pink.

My breathing stops. "Oh my God. When? How could you not have told me?"

Her face crumples. "Two days ago. It's just that with your situation, it seemed totally hurtful to talk about—"

"Evie!" I lower my voice when a couple of people turn toward us. "You're supposed to tell me the important things. No matter what."

"I—oh, it's been driving me crazy not sharing this with you."

I crunch my empty cup. "Do not let this gene thing take

away my best friend on top of everything else, okay?"

"I'm so sorry. If anything else significant happens, you'll be the first to know. I promise."

My eyes sting but I nod, wondering if I'll be around when the next significant thing happens in her life. Clearing the roughness in my throat, I say, "Let's get out of here."

We head back into the comics shop. The sudden shift from blaring sun to the darkness within is temporarily blinding. But when my vision settles, I don't see Sammy.

I hunt through the cramped aisles. "Sammy?"

A couple of boys glower like I've violated some code of conduct. I pick up my pace, calling louder. Evie searches from the other side of the store until we meet up in the middle. No Sammy.

I rush to the counter and ask the clerk, "Have you seen a skinny blond boy, about this high?"

He talks around a lump of something nestled inside his cheek. "Yeah, he bought the latest issue of *Alakazomb* and showed me his portfolio. The kid's frickin' amazing."

"I know. But where did he go?"

The guy shrugs. "Probably to read or draw." His face lights up. "Hey, I recognize you. Have you seen the latest issue of *Virality?* It's about a genetic love potion—"

Evie and I frown at each other and jog outside. My heart

skydives to my gut as I whip my head around. Sammy's nowhere in sight.

Evie says, "Stay calm. He probably went to look for us."

We head down the street in the opposite direction of where we stopped for lattes. I peek into a tattoo parlor, a book store, and a thrift shop, yelling, "Sammy!"

When we reach a cross-street, I spot a blond kid down the road wearing the same bright yellow T-shirt Sammy had on. He's laughing next to a woman with purple hair. I sprint their way, relieved to find that the kid is my brother.

I grab his shoulders. "Sammy, what the hell?"

He startles. "I thought you headed this direction. Sorry."

The woman leans toward me on six-inch stilettos. "Aislyn Hollings? I've been looking for you."

I step back. "Really? How did you know I was here?"

She gives a cynical laugh. "Oh, honey, you're easier to track than a GPS signal."

A guy with biceps as big as cantaloupes steps out from a shadowed doorway. He keeps a few feet away, but gives the woman a slow nod that makes my skin feel as if it's covered in bugs.

The woman bats her eyelashes. "I wanted to personally invite you to an exclusive party. Zeke Takahashi, who got the Charisma without the bad side effects, just like you, will be there, and it would be great if you hung out with us tomorrow night too."

I cross my arms. "I doubt there's a version of CZ88 without bad effects. And why hasn't this Zeke come out sooner?"

She pulls a thick envelope from her purse and fans herself with it. "Maybe no one's made him the right offer. Easy ten grand."

"Ten thousand? For a party?"

"Lots of people want to meet you. Face-to-face."

My pulse picks up speed. "What's the catch?" Deep down I already know. Only one group of weirdoes is that eager to see me without a gas mask.

The big guy edges nearer, hands in pockets.

Purple-haired woman says, "No catch at all." She licks her lips. "You could have a lot of fun, maybe find ways to earn an even bigger paycheck. I know a few guys with deeper pockets than you could imagine." She smiles, with a sharpness to her eyes that brings jackals to mind.

I pull Sammy and Evie by the arms. "Home. Now."

Neither of them argues. As we hurry away, I peek backward to see the lady and her friend staring at us. Nothing in their expressions radiates empathy or kindness. The fact that they remain in place, satisfied I'm so trackable, sends a surge through my belly.

The guy blows me a kiss.

Did She or Didn't She?

by Lulu Lakes for *In the Know*

The latest question that has celeb-watchers speculating madly doesn't involve Botox or nip-tucks. Rather, we're trying to determine who's upped their Celebrity Index Rating via a top-shelf public relations rep and who's done so via a trip to the geneticist. If this sounds like the stuff of science fiction, think again. After two hundred thirty-seven people were injected or infected with an unregu-lated gene therapy called Charisma, their personal-ities went from meh to magnetic. These cases came with potentially lethal consequences, and forty-one deaths so far; however, there are rumors of a new, improved version of Charisma being developed via underground channels. What price celebrity? Well, readers, it appears nothing is out of the question, even if it means swapping out our DNA.

TWENTY

The entire drive home has me checking the mirrors. When I tell Sammy we're skipping the rest of the shops on his list, he shrugs as if he's used to me letting him down.

I take a circuitous route to ensure we aren't followed, and pull in front of my house forty minutes later. We study our surroundings closely before getting out and wading through a pack of reporters. Even though I should be used to them by now, their barked-out questions strike me like gunfire. "No comment," I say, urging Sammy forward.

Evie gives me an extra-tight hug at the door. "Don't let the crazies or haters get you down. They're way outnumbered. Starting with me."

"I'm sorry for before. You're the best, Evie."

"That I am. Just keep your head down, okay?" She prances

away, but her positive attitude comes off forced.

Inside, Mom sits alone at the dining room table. "We were supposed to have lunch together, weren't we?"

I slap my forehead. "Oh, yeah, of course. Sorry. We got a late start." She'll find out I've offered my genome sequence up for grabs soon enough.

She's brought home chicken coconut curry soup, infused with a tangy lemon-grass that makes my mouth pucker. Sammy and I join her at the table.

I examine her for signs of volatility and figure she's as calm as I've seen her since I've been home. "Um, Mom, could we please talk about letting Sammy into the AV719 trial?"

She clanks the ladle against the edge of the pot. Her face swims with a mixture of fear, guilt, and anger. "No one's giving my kids anything else that could hurt them. End of discussion."

"But the preliminary—"

"Aislyn, stop it. You may be able to use your new persuasion skills against the rest of the world, but I'm not gambling with my kids' lives."

"Everything in life is about taking chances, playing the odds."

"No, it's not. I thought you'd learned that the hard way." Now her expression radiates full-on terror and rage. I swear she has more gray hair now than she did a month ago.

Okay, time for another approach. I casually mention the Nova Genetics event. Maybe if I shine extra bright tonight, I'll prove that a lot of people still have faith in gene therapy.

Her eyes are wary but relieved I've changed the subject. "Sure you're up for that?"

"I have to be. Besides, these folks could invest in research that will not only cure CZ88 but other genetic problems, like CF. One way or another, I want my life to mean more than a bogus experiment."

A few drops of soup splash from her spoon to the table. She grabs a napkin to wipe them. "Your life means a great deal, especially to those of us who love you. We'll get through this."

That's more like the positive mom I'm used to. I try to remind her of the responsible daughter she was used to by washing the dishes after lunch so she can rush off to meet the client she rescheduled.

Maybe I can do another good turn and take Sammy to a few more stores. But a quick peek out the window at the huge crowd of reporters changes my mind. Besides, Sammy coughed through most of lunch.

My phone buzzes. A text from Jack. I FEEL BAD ABOUT YESTERDAY.

I type: ME TOO.

CAN WE MAKE IT UP TONIGHT?

My mood brightens for a fraction of a moment, until I realize I can't see him. I HAVE TO GO TO AN EVENT AT NOVA GENETICS. TOMORROW?

SURE. WHAT'S THE EVENT?

THEY'RE TRYING TO GET INVESTORS TO FUND RESEARCH TOWARD A CURE. I'M EXHIBIT A.

WILL SHANE BE THERE?

Aw, man, just when I think things might be okay again. YEAH. THE MORE EXHIBITS, THE BETTER.

I SEE.

I type as fast as I can. IT'S NOT MY CHOICE.

OKAY. WELL, HAVE FUN. GOTTA GET BACK TO WORK.

YOU UNDERSTAND, RIGHT? THIS IS ABOUT RAISING MONEY. THAT'S IT.

OF COURSE. WE'LL TALK TOMORROW.

Oh, hell. He can't believe there's anything going on with Shane. We spent twelve days in the hospital together and nothing happened. Why would it now?

Sammy's slung on the couch in front of the TV watching a shoot-'em-up Western and hacking into a tissue. I sink next to him. "Somehow, someway, I'm going to get you the AV719."

He keeps his eyes on the screen. "What makes you so sure I want it? That last drug made me barf all the time."

"I know, bud, but we've gotta keep trying, right?"

He gives me a long, somber gaze and then turns back to the TV.

My brain races with how I might get the truth out of Mrs. Sternfield, and whether anyone can encourage more researchers into combating the CZ88. If I'm cured, Mom'll open up to Sammy being helped.

I get sucked into Sammy's movie and completely lose track of time, which forces me to rush upstairs for a quick shower and makeup. My knee-length dress doesn't "pop" the way it would've if Evie had chosen my accessories, but it'll have to do. Besides, it's my personality I'm counting on. I wear my hair down and hook a pair of simple silver hoops through my ears.

I sashay downstairs twenty-nine minutes later.

Mom's jaw goes slack. "Oh sweetie, you look lovely, and so, so . . ."

"Understated?" I ask.

"I was going to say 'mature.'"

I have to admit I enjoy the admiration in hers and Sammy's eyes. If only I could go out with Jack tonight and get him to look at me in that way he does. Did.

But the next gawker is Shane. When he arrives, I think he's swallowed his tongue. All he can say is "Wow."

Only a few days out of the hospital, his summer tan glows

against the pale blue collar of his shirt. His black curls have been trimmed to chin length and he's shaved his crisp jawline. This is the reason all those girls still apply for *The Shane Show*. The guy they want, here, in the flesh.

He tugs at his collar and wipes his glistening brow. "This suit is killing me."

Thankfully, Mom doesn't insist on taking pseudo-prom photos in front of the rhododendrons. Funny how before I never expected to go to prom because I was too shy. Now I might never go because, well, because. The periodic headaches and now the low but constant ear-ringing won't let me forget what's probably in store.

But for now I'm alive. Outside, the night is clear and warm. As Shane escorts me to the sleek town car Nova Genetics sent for us, the reporters shove the snouts of their cameras into our path.

The pixie-haired woman from a couple of days ago fluffs her bangs. "You make a cute couple. What happened to Jack?"

I pull my arm from Shane's. "Nothing. Shane and I are going to a business event together because it's convenient. Now, if you'll please let us through."

Ignoring the flashes, a blond driver with green aviator glasses introduces himself as Baxter as he opens the car door for us. Fresh from the purple-haired lady incident, I won't get in until he shows me ID, which he does with a grin.

Shane whispers, "Paranoid." He takes off his suit jacket before sliding next to me. As soon as the driver pulls forward, air-conditioning from the rear vents blasts us.

Shane leans into the chill. "So, I'm convenient?"

I smooth my dress along my thighs so it won't wrinkle. "Things are challenging enough without fake relationship rumors."

He eyes the closed partition between the rear and front seats. "So how's life in the celibate lane going? Ready to use me yet?"

"Dream on, Mr. Last Guy on Earth." Evie's silly comment about not letting him, or myself, go to waste pops through my head.

He says, "Someday soon, you're not going to be able to resist these dimples." He's joking, of course, but there's honest-to-goodness hope in his eyes.

I shiver, and reach for the AC control. "Mind if I turn this down a bit?"

He tugs at his shirt, flapping it against his chest. "Not too much, okay? It's so sticky out."

I take in the sheen of sweat on his temple. "Are you feeling okay?"

"Just a little headache, and the heat."

My throat tightens. "Headache? Do you have a fever? Dizziness?"

"Whoa, Blondie. Just been pushing this rock star thing too hard and feel totally wiped. Lame, huh?"

Despite his nonchalance, a chill runs up my back. "Have you fainted? Is there ringing in your ears?"

"Do you think I'd be going to Dr. Gordon's fundraiser if I were about to drop? It's just too many all-nighters. Maybe beer and Charisma don't mix so well." His voice fades.

I clutch at my seat buckle. "You can go back to all-nighters after they cure us, okay?"

"You sound like you really care. I'm touched."

I hit his arm.

But I do care. Enough to pretend to watch the scenery out my side so he can't read my face. Baxter smoothly takes the road's curves, making the trip feel like riding in a sleek living room.

Shane rustles. "Got some cool footage for the new *Shane Show* today. Crazy-ass chick offered me five thousand to attend a party this weekend."

"Purple hair? Creepy guy as her wingman? She offered me double that."

The car swerves slightly. Maybe the partition between us and the front seat isn't soundproof after all.

Shane frowns. "Hell. I've been robbed."

"You agreed to go?"

He startles. "You turned her down?"

"I don't believe it," we say in unison.

We argue for the rest of the ride over the pros and cons of attending parties with insane people, not reaching any agreement by the time we reach the Nova Genetics campus. But our disagreement pales against the hordes of protesters stomping next to the gate. Most wear surgical masks.

Baxter slides down the partition. "Don't worry. I'm taking you guys inside to the VIP lot tonight."

That's more like it. We roll up behind a Mercedes and BMW. The protestors swarm alongside, shrieking their slogans of hate. A wiry guy with pale eyes catches sight of Shane and me. His gaze widens and he points us out to his friends. They mash their bodies toward the car, faces filling our windows as they yell, "Freaks! Freaks!"

I double-check that my door's locked. Shane waves and says, "Boy, I wish my camera guy were here." He points his phone at the crowd, which only amplifies their shouting.

The guards shoo the protesters with bullhorns and threats while Baxter gives our names to a woman wearing a holster. She waves us through.

We park in the oasis of the VIP parking lot. Two brawny guys in dark suits usher us toward the main door, where Sally Sims holds court wearing a shimmering black cocktail dress.

She gives us stiff hugs that are captured by an event photographer. "I'm relieved you're both doing so well, dealing with such a challenge. If there's anything I can do for you, please let me know."

I wait for Shane to ask for a doctor, but he just wants to know where the beverages are. Sally leads us to the main dining room, decorated in draped gauze and huge vases of peonies that send out sweet aroma. We stroll through a crowd of silk suits and elegant dresses.

I elbow Shane. "Why didn't you tell Sally you were running a fever?" I don't feel totally hypocritical asking, since the din of conversation covers my own ear-ringing for now.

"What good would it do? Besides, I feel great."

"Maybe they've got something preliminary they can test out on us. We should ask Dr. Gordon." As I say this, I try to detect any unwanted noises in my inner ear, but with all that surrounds us, I can't tell.

A team of waiters roam the room with trays of toast points loaded with caviar, chicken satays dipped in peanut sauce, and other delicacies. I'm tempted to grab a glass of champagne, but think better of it when I spot another photographer. Becoming the poster girl for underage drinking would not help our cause. Besides, I don't need a crutch for courage. Not anymore.

Dr. Gordon beckons us over and introduces Colonel Collins, a military researcher who doesn't smile, and Mr. Chong, who owns a pharmaceutical company in South Korea. The men ask their fill of questions, mostly addressed to Shane.

I turn to the colonel. "Why is the army interested in gene therapy?"

His stony expression reflects a moment of annoyance. "For the sake of our vets, miss. If there's some way to predict who's genetically predisposed to PTSD, perhaps we can provide the right psychotropic drugs or training to prevent it."

His face seems like it believes what his mouth is saying. But I've read too many of Sammy's comics not to know that almost every superhero has a basis in genetic enhancement or mutation. Before I can ask about super-soldiers, a Nova Genetics VP whisks him and Mr. Chong away to tour the labs.

Dr. Gordon says to me, "You look lovely, dear." There's a melancholy tone to his words, as if he's remembering a time his daughter dressed up for an event. Or maybe Shane's and my presence reminds him of the damage she caused.

Shane hands his jacket to a valet who seems to materialize out of nowhere. Then he undoes a button of his shirt.

Dr. Gordon examines him. "Are you feeling well?"

Shane grins. "Just warm." He waves down a passing waiter and snags a prawn that he dips in chili sauce and pops into his mouth.

Dr. Gordon looks at me. "You'll keep an eye on him?"

"Of course." I'm surprised Dr. Gordon doesn't send Shane straight home, but maybe a dramatic fainting episode would spur donors.

Shane laughs. "Now we should go forth and inspire, right?"

Dr. Gordon leads us around the room, introducing us to Dr. This and CEO That, all with manicured hands and perfectly groomed hair, not a synthetic fiber in sight. When Dr. Gordon finally dismisses Shane and me, we load our plates with seafood and find our assigned seats at a table on an outside terrace overlooking the Hood Canal. Gentle notes of music drift along the sultry summer air. A well-dressed couple take their places across from us.

Shane seems to rise three inches off his seat. "You're Carlos Zahn, right?"

The man smiles and introduces himself and his wife. Shane informs me this is Seattle's star soccer player.

Carlos's expression is sympathetic. "So sorry you both have experienced such madness."

I shrug it off, grateful he didn't point out that the madness was self-inflicted. "You must be used to dealing with reporters and crazies. How do you still have a life?"

He glances at his wife, Anna. "Having someone on my side helps."

Anna lifts her chin. "Focus your attention on the positive.

The more good you can offer, the more you'll receive. We're very interested in the promise of gene therapy, especially for children like our son, who has cystic fibrosis."

Sally Sims must've seated us together on purpose. Anna and I launch into a discussion of AV719. It turns out her son is in the trial. I learn where it's taking place, but also that the security is unusually high. As I pump her for info, Dr. Gordon joins us. He peeks warily at Shane, whose face is flushed, and then turns to me. "Ready to say a few words to the guests, Aislyn?"

My throat goes dry. But Shane's in no condition to get in front of a crowd. I follow the doctor to the podium. My knees wobble slightly as I step up to the small stage. There must be over two hundred investors surrounding me. Most smile expectantly as Dr. Gordon tells them how someone like me, desperate for the benefits of gene therapy, risked participating in a "premature" experiment. No mention of his daughter's involvement, which shouldn't be a surprise; powerful people operate by different rules.

After enthusiastic applause, I clear my throat and peek at the faces. A twenty-something guy with pale skin and black hair stands near the edge of the crowd, grimacing. His heavy glare causes my chest to constrict, but I manage to get my words out.

"Hello, everybody. I'm the girl you never would've noticed before. Being invisible isn't something I'd recommend. What was unbearable, though, was not having a voice, not because folks wouldn't listen, but because I could not bring myself to speak."

A few people nod; many simply cock their heads, waiting for more. The scowling guy steps forward, standing only ten feet away, hands in his pockets. When he catches my nervous glance, he inches closer, menace oozing from his eyes. Who is he? I glance around, but don't spot any burly guards among the silk and jewels.

I take a breath. "I couldn't stand up for myself, but what slayed me was that I couldn't stand up for my brother, Sammy, who has CF, which he says feels like drowning from the inside out. Whether or not you think gene therapy is worthwhile for debilitating personality traits, it's a game changer for life-threatening conditions like Sammy's. Scientists are testing gene treatments against AIDS, cancer, and a whole bunch of other diseases." I gaze at Anna and Carlos Zahn, who smile in return.

As I tell stories of hope, I'm wary of the action in front of me. A woman in a blue blazer now hovers alongside the mean-faced guy and whispers to him. Are they working together or have I become completely paranoid? The grimacing guy snaps something at the woman, and, for a second, I'm afraid it'll come to blows. But then they make their way toward a door, almost as if the woman is shoving the guy. I breathe easier. This must be how security is handled at fancy parties.

Pasting on a smile, I conclude my speech to great applause. Still, as I make my way through hand-shakes and chit-chat with potential donors, I keep an eye out for eerie lurkers.

I'm sucked into a vortex of introductions to politicians and scientists, early retirees and media personalities. Cameras flash and toothy smiles beam. Bright-eyed guests toast to the prospect of gene therapy. A tiny spark of hope ignites—maybe someone will figure out a cure without taking back all of the good stuff Charisma has given me. Soon I'm surfing on their waves of excitement.

Until I reach Shane.

His skin has gone ashy and he wipes at sweat on his temples. He laughs with a female in a low-cut dress, but he shifts from one leg to the other as if he's trying to keep his balance.

I introduce myself to the woman and say to Shane, "We should leave soon."

He puts a steaming arm around my shoulders and leans heavily onto me. "But the party's in full swing."

"I think Dr. Gordon wants to chat about the latest research." I excuse us from the woman and lead Shane out of the dining hall. In a harsh whisper, I say, "I don't care if you think your symptoms are from partying. You need to see someone now."

In the foyer, where fewer people mill around, I grab Shane around his torso. His body burns.

I jolt backward. "You're so hot."

He winks. "You finally noticed?"

I punch his arm.

He laughs. "All I really need is some fresh air. If that doesn't work, we'll talk to Dr. Gordon. Deal?"

"Fine." I turn back toward the dining hall and spot the scary guy staring at us as he types on his phone. Guess it takes all kinds of people to fund research. I hurry Shane out a side door.

Under the early evening sky, Shane immediately perks up. Maybe fresh air really is all he needs. I start toward the water, drawn to the rhythmic waves.

We amble along the shore. The sun is almost to the horizon, but the air is still warm, more like the tropics than Seattle.

Shane points. "You know where I want to go? The clam spit. You and I could've made a kick-ass geoduck-harvesting team."

I take off my shoes and carry them by the straps. "We would've made a terrible team. I thought Chloe dared you to harass me." At the mention of Chloe's name, I feel a pull at my chest.

He grabs my hand. "Chloe's strong. They all are. It's been weeks and they're still stable. And either Nova or Vida will come up with a cure soon." He stops and hugs me, more like a brother than any of his often tasteless comments would suggest. I bury my head into his chest, so comforting and warm. Too warm. "You really do have a fever, Shane. We should go inside."

"I feel way better out here. A few more minutes, okay?"

We part, but he doesn't let go of my hand as we resume our trek along the water. It's comforting and reminds me how lucky I am to have him at my side through this.

A guard stands sentry at the fence where the institute's grounds end. Fortunately, the protesters haven't traveled this far down. We check in with the guard and promise to return in a few minutes.

On the clam spit, only a couple of beach-goers huddle on a massive driftwood log. Shane rolls up his pant legs so we can wade into lapping waves that scold us, slap, slap, slap. Or maybe that's just what I think I deserve.

I say, "Okay, don't freak, but I've had ear-ringing the past couple of days."

He jolts. "Why didn't you say anything?"

"Why do you think?"

He shakes his head and glares at the sky. I pull him back toward the beach. The couple on the log stare our way, one of them tapping on a phone. When I gaze back, they turn toward each other.

"The sun'll set soon," I say.

"Let's enjoy this for a while longer." He doesn't have to add that with both of us experiencing symptoms, we should enjoy everything we can.

We alternate between hunting for skipping stones and hurling them into the waves. The couple rises from their log and faces the forested area nearby. One of them excitedly points to something in the greenery. I stretch my neck, trying to figure out what's there.

As if reading my mind, the shorter of the two turns to us and calls out in a girl's voice, "Eagles nesting!"

Shane increases his pace, heading their way. "I saw an eagle here last time. Let's check it out."

Of course, he'll run after any adventure, even one as small as sighting an eagle in the wild. Every moment is so unbearably precious. Laughing quietly, we follow the couple into the trees, where the evening sun barely reaches. In the brush, more voices rustle.

"I hope they don't scare off the birds," I whisper.

We tiptoe on bare feet along the path. We'll have to wash off before putting our shoes back on. But, really, who cares about dirty feet?

Shane pushes ahead through the ferns, probably ready to

tell the others a thing or two about eagle watching. Twenty yards in, though, he halts abruptly. "What the—?"

I hop around him for a look. At first, I don't believe what I see. In a small clearing under a darkening sky, a handful of people hover, all wearing hoodies and masks that cover most of their faces. Predatory eyes fix in on us.

My insides go cold. This is no birding convention. More like a cult. The kind that sacrifices eagles instead of viewing them.

The tallest member of the group steps forward and holds out his arms wide, as if about to take flight. "Glad you could join us, Aislyn and Shane."

TWENTY-ONE

I pull at Shane. "Run!"

He and I crash through foliage, but there's no chance. Two massive bodies spring from the trees and block us. Before I can scream, we're bound, gagged, and blindfolded. Rough hands yank my arms and push me forward. When I resist, someone hoists my legs and another person seizes me from under my armpits. They carry me through scratchy brush and then dump me onto a carpeted floor that rumbles with a running engine. There's another body next to mine, so warm it has to be Shane.

The van's doors slam and we take off on a bumpy road, Shane and I jostling into each other. I twist at the ties on my wrists, but can't loosen them. When I kick my legs at the door, someone grabs them and binds my ankles with prickly rope that digs into my skin. Oh God, are these protesters who've lain in wait for an "abomination" to destroy? I thrash like a bull, but can't loosen my bindings.

We ride for what seems like hours, toward who knows what. Bound and blindfolded, I fall into a consuming terror, far worse than any panic attack.

I scream against my gag, which only chokes me. Maybe if I calm down, whoever's taken us will say something. The van rumbles on and on, no way to calculate where we are. Or what these people want. With a renewed flash of horror I remember the messages I received to "share what I had" or how I should be treated like "vermin." Oh God, oh God, oh God.

Waves of chill and heat wash over my body again and again. It takes all I have to control my gasps and avoid choking on the gag.

Finally, the car slows to a crawl and eventually stops. The screaming in my brain widens into a dark, hopeless canyon. Will this be how things end for us? Somewhere in a desolate ditch?

Every muscle in my body clenches when someone yanks my arms and cuts the tie binding my wrists. I flail but am clutched between vise-like, hairy arms that wrap around me from behind. Beery breath hot on my cheek has me cringing. The owner of the breath says, "The more you wiggle, the better I like it."

I go still, waiting, pulse hammering.

There's grunting and thrashing nearby, before a few loud cracks lead to silence on the opposite side of the van. My heart lurches toward Shane and whatever they've done to him.

The floor vibrates as if someone else has climbed aboard. A voice with the smooth tone of the tall, skinny guy we saw in the woods says, "Hopefully, your visit with us will be brief. That all depends on you, of course."

Brief, as in they'll kill us soon? My bones go to jelly.

Now the voice is in my face, cooing. "So, Aislyn, would you like to share what you have the boring way or the fun way?"

I shake my head violently, struggling against the massive body clenching me.

The voice says, "Aw, I was hoping for more cooperation. Oh, well."

There's the sound of something snapping like a balloon. Then rubbery, gloved hands clamp my left arm, pulling skin as they straighten out my elbow. When I resist, there's a sharp slap to my cheek that has me seeing stars. I whimper through the gag.

A cold wash runs across my inner elbow. The smell of alcohol wafts over the musky smell of the thug behind me.

Something sharp pierces the inside of my elbow. I flinch. The needle pops out and stabs in again. And then again.

The voice growls, "This will be a lot easier if you stay still."

I don't have much choice, since the large, sticky person clamps my arms and someone sits on my legs. But even with my body cemented in place, the needle pierces me a couple more times.

Finally, it remains within my flesh. The voice says, "Mmm. Looks like I found the sweet spot, precious."

Precious? Who else called me that recently? A memory hovers at the edge of my brain. As my blood flows out over long minutes, my head becomes light and my thoughts fuzzy.

The voice hums. "You bleed so pretty. Only a few more vials to go."

How much have they taken? My life is draining away. A life that has taken such unforeseen turns. All because of a stupid decision. Hot tears tumble onto my cheeks as I think of Jack, my friends, my mom, and Sammy. If only I'd understood the consequences of allowing Dr. Sternfield to do what she did. If only any of us had.

If only, if only, if only.

My hearing becomes fainter. Little flashes of light spark inside my eyelids. My brain fights to remain conscious, but my thoughts flutter off one by one into nothingness. Until all that's left is a sigh.

TWENTY-TWO

I regain consciousness splayed on rough, cold ground. It's dark out except for the moon and stars. My head is light and the crook of my left elbow, cracking with dried blood, throbs like crazy.

My vision slowly adjusts. A few feet away lies a large, motionless body on its side. With branches and rocks scraping my knees, I crawl over and shake its shoulder. "Shane!"

In the gloom, he moans and clutches his belly. Thank God, he's conscious. But when I touch his forehead, it flames.

He shivers. "Where the hell are we?"

I look around. "On a patch of weeds, near a road. Somewhere in the boonies, I think. Can't see much."

His breath rasps and he tries to sit up. As soon as he

does, he pulls up his legs to his chest and lays his head on his knees, groaning.

I stroke his arm. "I'm going to look down the road, see what I can."

I get up, shake out my ruined dress, and tiptoe through pokey weeds on bare feet. Under the starlight, the road disappears into blackness in one direction. In the other, there may be the faintest glow of something man-made, but no telling how far away.

I return to Shane's side and report what I saw. He puts his hands to his ears and shakes his head.

That causes me to remember the whistling in my own. "Are your ears ringing?"

"More like buzzing," he says. "But that doesn't mean I'm dropping into a coma any second. You haven't."

Small comfort. The night air chills me through this spaghetti-strap dress. When Shane notices my trembling, he takes me into his feverish arms.

"At least they didn't kill us," I say. "Did they take blood from you too?"

He straightens an arm. "I'm guessing yeah, but I don't remember. My head's banging inside."

I hug him tighter. "Think you can walk? If we head toward what I think are lights, we have a better chance of finding help." Not that the idea of catching a ride from a stranger on a desolate road is all that enticing.

He tries to stand, but even with my help, he quickly slumps back to the ground. "Sorry, Blondie. Not going anywhere. Morning'll bring out the traffic." The moonlight reveals a sheen of sweat on his forehead; his torso quivers against me. Morning won't arrive soon enough.

I steady his shoulder until it stops trembling. "I'll go down the road a bit, see if I can spot something more."

"No, stay with me. There's nothing anyone can do for us, really."

My own vision is still fuzzy and a powerful nausea tugs at my belly. "Maybe they can't do anything for the CZ88, but who knows how much blood those crazies took. An IV could do you a world of good."

"I doubt it." He makes as if to rise, but instead settles his body down into a fetal position I sit there, cradled in the curve at his stomach so I'm facing his head.

"Think it's after midnight?" he asks.

The randomness of his question has me wondering if he's going delusional. Gently, I say, "I'm sure it's way after midnight. So you only have to stay awake a little while longer until the sun comes up and someone drives by."

He smiles. "Happy birthday, Blondie."

I catch my breath. Have I actually made it to seventeen? "Oh my God. How did you know?"

"Your loverboy's been planning a big shindig. Even invited me. Some girl named Alexandra is my biggest fan."

"What?" I thought Jack was too annoyed to even speak to me. Which he still might be, even if he planned a party. I'm supposed to be so great at reading people, yet completely underestimated him.

Shane grimaces. "Guess I can kind of understand why you're so hung up on the dude instead of on me. I was such an asshole when we met."

I grab his hand and squeeze until he grunts. "Actually, I think the term is *douchebag*."

We laugh for a moment. I feel the prickle of tears in my eyes.

I say, "When we met, I'm sure I came off as stuck-up or something."

"Nah. I knew you were shy. Getting under people's skin was just my way of getting noticed. It was stupid. I'm sorry."

I run my palm over his arm. "You're nowhere as bad as you think you are. Pretty great, in fact. And always noticeable, trust me."

"Oh, hell, the CZ88 must be about to kill me if you're singing my praises."

"Shut up."

"That's better."

I start rolling up the torn sleeves of his shirt. "Maybe your fever isn't from the CZ88. We've been going full speed all week. Your immunity is probably compromised. It could be the flu. Or a bad cold, or—"

"No, Aislyn. This sucks too much for the flu."

I stifle a sob, gazing at this boy who's been through so much with me. Who won me over in spite of himself. If I lose him too . . . No, that couldn't happen.

I grab a handful of his shirt. "Listen, Shane, you and I are the lucky ones. Our bodies can fight off the CZ88 for some obscure genetic reason. Believe it."

"I believe in your bad-assedness."

"Who do you think I learned bad-assedness from?"

He chuckles and sings, "Happy birthday, dear badass..."

I think he'll continue, but his cheek drops to the ground.

"Shane?"

No answer.

I call his name ten more times as a huge lump grows in my throat. Shaking his shoulder, I yell, "Wake up!" I pound the hard-packed dirt. "You big, obnoxious, crazy jerk!" But he doesn't stir. As if he knows there's no hope for us. Maybe there never has been.

I need to find help. Someone can still fix this. Shane and I are different from the others. We have to be. I just need to get him to a hospital. Now.

I kiss his cheek. "We'll survive this. You'll see." If he were conscious, he'd call me out for the doubt in my voice.

With unsteady legs, I rise. Back on my feet, I find a large branch and drag it to the middle of the road to mark where Shane lies. It's not like I'll recognize the spot or he'll be hollering for help.

I fight against wooziness that begs me to just lie down and wait. To fall asleep next to Shane until it's all okay. But I know better than to expect a miraculous rescue.

The road is rough on my bare feet. I try jogging but stumble after only a few steps. Fine, I'll walk.

My feet chafe against the pavement as I trudge ahead. No telling what time it is or which direction I'm heading. Should've studied astronomy. I march on, praying for Shane, for Sebastian, Chloe, Jesse, Xavier, and everyone else who risked their lives for the chance to change themselves or were infected by someone who had.

I'm so focused on the road and trying to determine if those specks ahead are lights that I don't notice the rumble from behind until it's almost upon me. Terrified it's the same people who kidnapped us, I sprint from the road just as the edge of the high beams reach me. I crouch into the foliage, brambles scratching my arms and legs.

The car screeches to a halt. Thankfully, it isn't a van. Could it be a normal, good Samaritan who will help? I'm about to emerge from the leaves, but something stops me, probably paranoia from what I've just been through.

A male voice calls out, "Miss? Are you okay?"

He sounds ordinary, nice, if you can tell from four words. But as much as I need to get help for Shane, and myself, I hesitate.

He calls out again, "I saw you run into the trees. It's not safe out here by yourself. Are you by yourself?"

His voice squeaks reedy on that last word, causing my belly to tense. I ache to trust him, to let myself be helped. The old me would've jumped up in impatience to let someone else fix everything, but the new me waits a moment longer.

The car door clicks open and the overhead light illuminates the man's face. He's maybe thirty or so, short hair and soft cheeks. His face moves up into darkness as he steps out of the car, but before it does, I catch a certain something in his eyes. Something hard that chills me and keeps me from accepting what could be the only chance at a ride to safety on this God-forsaken road.

He calls out a few more times and then swears to himself before getting back into the car and racing off. Tears roll over my cheeks as I watch the car lights disappear far down the road.

I wait a few more minutes before resuming my hike. This time I keep to the side of the road instead of marching down the middle. And I keep an ear open for the sound of an engine.

My eyes become more accustomed to the dark. If only I could see like nocturnal animals. One day, with genetic engineering, that's a real possibility. Because as much as people try to resist the technology, there will be those, like Dr. Sternfield, who can't resist the temptation to enhance. And once they do, someone will go even further by modifying germ line cells that propagate to the next generation and beyond. Then our species really will have the potential to differentiate, the way the protestors fear. I sigh. But the solution isn't to avoid genetic modification altogether. Too many people can be helped.

It might be an hour or three when the specks of light I've been chasing are close enough to determine they're attached to lampposts that line the road. Beneath the closest one is a small, squared-off structure that I realize is a mailbox. I almost cry. A gravel driveway leads to a home tucked within the trees. But a wire fence with a BEWARE OF DOG sign stops me from running to the door.

And then I have the horrifying realization that the flinty-eyed man who stopped for me might live here. Or someone worse. How can I decide whether to take a chance on whoever lives here if I can't read their face?

I peer down the road. Every few hundred yards is another mailbox and I assume another home. Well, even if I can't gauge the probability than an individual house doesn't hold a monster, I have to gamble that not all of them do.

So I find a spot between two houses, take a deep breath, and scream. And keep screaming as if I'll never stop, like a dam has burst and my whole body is a whitewater river of endless wailing.

Somewhere, there's barking and eventually a porch light. I keep screaming. Moments later, a lady comes out carrying a rifle.

TWENTY-THREE

Yelling and crying, I tell the woman I was kidnapped and that my friend is unconscious, down the road. Then I sink to the ground. She'll either shoot me or fetch help.

Thankfully, she scurries back inside and soon a siren wails in the distance. I say a prayer of thanks as the dog keeps barking.

Medics load me into an ambulance even though I insist I can walk. "I need to be with Shane." My throat burns from screaming.

One of the medics places something cold onto my sore arm. "We'll take care of it, Miss Tough Guy."

No, I'm Miss Badass. Just ask Shane.

Another siren travels on to search for the branch I left in the road. As my ambulance slams shut, I shudder, and then break into a cold sweat when the medic plugs an IV needle into my arm.

I sink into a daze, visualizing swarms of attackers in vicious pursuit. Their faces contort into rage and desire, clawing closer and closer. But I can't run or hide.

What seems like a long time later, I awake from the nightmare and find myself still in the ambulance. The medic says I was rescued twenty miles outside of Olympia, and Shane seven miles farther out. I cry in relief that they found him.

Although there's a hospital nearby, by order of the health department, CDC, and for all I know Homeland Security, the ambulance takes me to Florence Bishop Children's, my home away from home.

They roll me into the emergency department for stitches to my knee and bandages on my feet. Not surprisingly, Dr. Culdicott arrives within the hour.

She picks up my chart. "Any fainting spells or other symptoms?"

"No. How's Shane?"

"Very weak. He's been in and out of consciousness." Her eyes remained glued to the tablet.

From the set of her jaw it's clear what Shane's diagnosis is. "Can I talk to him? Just for a minute?" I desperately have to tell him how much I need him to get better. How much I . . . I don't know. I just have to talk to him.

"We'll see."

"Maybe Nova Genetics has something in the works you can use on him before it's too late." The ringing in my ears shifts pitch. "And I'll take it too."

She sighs. "Dr. Gordon has kept us apprised of the research." After a long breath, she continues, "Unfortunately, one of the chimps they've been testing their new drug on died the day before yesterday."

This knocks the breath out of me. Dr. Gordon should've said something. "Which one? Ruby?"

"I'm sorry. I don't know."

My heart thuds at the thought of losing any of those sweet animals. "But just because Nova Genetics' preliminary cure didn't work in chimps doesn't mean it won't work in humans, right?"

Her gaze is steady. "Aislyn, we're doing everything we can."

Mom bursts into the room, almost barreling the doctor over. In the past few days, her face has become even more gaunt. God, what I've put her through.

She squeezes me so hard I think the IV might pop off. "Oh, sweetie. What happened?"

Where to begin?

A tall policeman joins us and asks if I'm ready to answer his questions. Of course. The sooner they find these vampires, the better to prevent them from blood-jacking someone else, or worse, using Shane's and my blood to spread the CZ88 to more victims.

I give as complete an account as I can while Mom hovers to the side, her face going paler with every new detail of my story. When I get to the part where the creeps forcibly drew my blood, I think she'll faint.

"I'm okay, really." The IV drip has done wonders. My mouth no longer feels dry and my energy is rising.

The policeman eventually excuses himself and I hug Mom again. Dr. Culdicott returns to tell me Shane's condition is too serious for anyone but immediate family to visit him. By now, I believe I should qualify as family, but the docs don't see it that way.

Dr. Culdicott also says she's going to keep me here under observation until morning. No arguing.

An orderly wheels me to a room a few floors above, where I'm able to peel off my tattered party dress and take a sponge bath before putting on a hospital gown and robe, which feel luxurious in comparison.

I say to Mom, "I really need to see Shane."

She inhales deeply and pulls me into her arms. "I'm so sorry, sweetie. While you were in the bathroom, Dr. Culdicott stopped by to say he's gone into a coma."

My rib cage seems to implode. I can't believe the gene transfer has taken such a drastic turn in Shane too. After all this time, I'd almost begun to believe he and I might have a less lethal version. Maybe his health nosedived because those assholes stole his blood, putting his body through too much trauma. If they're ever caught, I'll throttle them until their leader's silky voice shatters.

Mom tries to comfort me, but all I want is to dive under the blanket. After a while, she lets me be, and I doze off for a few hours, dreaming dreams where I'm held down and stuck with needles.

In the morning, Mom hands me a change of clothes that she picked up. I take a careful shower, letting the steam empty every pore before I pat my pink skin dry.

When I'm done, the policeman has returned, along with a table full of pictures from the fundraiser. He asks me to point out anyone who seemed suspicious, and I immediately zero in on the guy who lasered me with the evil eye. The policeman thanks me and takes off.

With that taken care of, Dr. Culdicott releases me from the hospital with the usual warnings. Of course, I avoid telling her about the whistling in my ears. And, after I beg once again to see Shane, she finally allows me to spend a minute with him.

In the ICU, his family hovers around with puffy eyes. Shane, who's always loomed so large, appears small against the mountain of machines hooked up to him.

I swallow back tears and take one of his hands. "You better get up. *The Shane Show* and all its stupid girls need you. So do I."

His face, which I've come to know so well, doesn't register anything. That's perhaps the most frightening of all, seeing features that are normally so animated now unbearably still. I'd kill for one of his smirks.

A nurse informs me it's time to leave.

I inform her I need to see the rest of my friends. After some hurried discussion with family members, I'm allowed to visit everyone except Xavier, but only for a moment each. That's long enough to painfully remind me they're all still lost someplace far away.

Mom leads us from their ward through a winding set of corridors in the basement to the parking garage. As we drive off, we pass at least a dozen news cameras. I duck below the window line until we're well on our way.

We only stop for a moment to pick up Sammy. But when we pull up to our house, I wish we'd camped out longer at my aunt and uncle's. A horde of reporters lurks in front of our yard. Mom honks for them to make room for the car. They do, just enough, but their cameras butt up to the windows as we roll by.

I shrink from the commotion, a bolt of panic shooting through me. Are all these people really reporters? What if someone is out to steal me away again and drain the rest of my blood?

A dark-haired guy with the same build as the skinny guy in the woods yells, "Hey, Aislyn! Did they catch the people who abducted you? Have the doctors found a cure?"

I bury my face in my hands and huddle low. In jerky starts and stops that have my belly churning, Mom pulls into the garage. I don't realize I've been holding my breath until the door clangs down behind us.

Inside, several wrapped gifts sit on the dining room table. Mom places her hands on my shoulders. "I know this is horrible timing, but happy birthday, sweetie, one day late."

I hug her for the hundredth time. "Oh, Mom."

Sammy hugs me too. "Too bad seventeen doesn't make you legal for anything."

Not that that's stopped me recently.

Mom clamps me to her again. Finally, I pull away and say, "I'm sorry. I don't think I can open presents. Not today."

"I understand." Her gaze is forlorn.

I excuse myself and stumble upstairs and into my bed. The room and my ears are almost quiet. Or maybe my inner anguish out-roars above all else. I burrow between the sheets and escape into a deep sleep.

It's late afternoon before I return to consciousness with a start. Instinctively, I tug at my wrist and dart my head around, expecting to be horse-tied or abandoned at the side of a road. It takes a full minute to calm down in the knowledge that I'm home, safe. Well, as safe as I can be with CZ88 lurking in my cells.

Since my phone was stolen by the sickos who turned my blood into smoothies, or whatever they've done with it, I scoot to the landline in the hallway and leave voicemails for Jack and Evie, letting them know I'm okay.

Downstairs, Mom serves a curry chicken and rice dinner. The birthday gifts are no longer in sight, but Sammy's eyes keep darting to the china cabinet.

Dinner's spicy aroma takes me back to memories of sitting snugly around the table with Mom, Dad, and Sammy, the diving accident in an unimagined future, along with killer DNA and blood-jackers. Even Sammy rarely coughed in those days, since his lungs were still relatively undamaged. I shake my head sharply. Dwelling on the past only makes the present more painful.

After dinner, the phone rings, and it's Evie. Breathlessly, she asks a thousand questions at once. I bark, "Get your butt over here and I'll give you the full rundown." I give Jack the same message when he calls a minute afterward.

Evie and Jack arrive together an hour later. We hug silently before climbing to my room, where we sit knee to knee on my bed. The constant looks between them make it clear they've been discussing their crazy friend, but Jack tries to keep things mellow by asking about a pair of wooden shadow puppets hanging on the wall.

"From when I went to Indonesia." I wonder for the thousandth time if the microbes I picked up on that trip saved my life.

Evie stabs a finger at me. "Well, you aren't going anywhere else or talking to strangers for a long time. You hear me?"

Jack grabs my wrist, right where fresh bruises bloom from the ropes. "You stick with us." So much for staying mellow.

My torso seems to shrivel. "I'm not planning any foreign travel, if that's what you guys mean. But I was hoping one of you would come with me to Cle Elum."

Evie wrinkles her nose. "Where's that? And why are you whispering?"

"It's a couple of hours east and is where Dr. Sternfield's mother lives."

Jack's grasp on me becomes too tight for comfort. "You're still on that? Aislyn, look what happened after you and Shane went off on your latest adventure."

"That wasn't an adventure. We were raising money for a cure."

Evie's gaze is skeptical. "C'mon. I saw the pics of you, all dolled up like Cinderella and mixing with the glam crowd."

I remove Jack's hand from my wrist and rub where it aches.

"There was a time you would've paid me to go to a party."

She says, "That was before people stole your blood."

Jack adds, "You need to stay home and get better, not chase down someone you think is lying about someone else who's dead."

I drop my eyes from his face, not wanting to read what's there. In a small voice, I say, "But what else can I do to fix this?"

Evie, after giving Jack a lightning-quick glance, says, "Why not call the researchers and see if they have any sane ideas? I bet there's a lot you can do behind the scenes, out of the limelight."

I sputter, "You're jealous of the publicity, aren't you?"

Evie seems to rise a foot taller than her five-foot frame. Her eyes steam. "I'm hardly jealous of someone hell-bent on destroying herself."

I face Jack. "You think I want to destroy myself?"

He swallows. "I think you're someone who's not counting on the people she should."

I can't believe they're turning on me like this. I never faced so much hostility from my friends before the CZ88. Fighting against the dizzying heat in my face, I say, "And what do the people I *should* count on want me to do? Sit around, behind closed curtains, and discuss who's doing who or what sorry band is being interviewed on the radio station?"

Jack's nostrils flare. "Our lives might not be as exciting as yours or Shane's, but they're important."

Evie says, "You used to think so too before you became a household name who shows up on the news every night."

"You guys think this is all glamour and fame?"

Jack's face is empty of the tenderness I'm used to. "You think we're all shallow and boring?"

"Of course not. We just have different priorities."

He jumps off the bed. "Different priorities, huh? Evie and I have both taken a ton of crap for even hanging out with you. And you thank us by trying to drag us into your suicidal schemes. Yeah, I'd say we have different priorities."

Evie stands up too. "Maybe we better take our priorities somewhere else while you show off for the reporters. I hope you realize how outrageous you're being, before it's too late."

They stomp off downstairs. For a moment, I'm tempted to chase after them, but it wouldn't do any good. I force myself to breathe deeply, trying to calm down. I can't dwell on their mistaken impressions—it would paralyze me from doing what needs to be done. Because, in spite of what everyone says, I know the best path to follow. Even if it pisses off the universe.

I get online to prepare, quickly finding the info I need. I study it and grab the right tools to load into my backpack before going to bed. If only my thoughts would stop swirling around Jack's and Evie's accusations.

Hours later, my internal clock wakes me five minutes before the alarm I set. I quietly dress and tiptoe downstairs, where I run straight into Mom. Damn.

She hovers over the table with a cup of coffee. "You're up early."

"Couldn't sleep." My planning hadn't accounted for interference from Mom. I grab a muffin and gobble while I come up with a way to salvage my mission.

"What would you like to do this lovely day?" she asks.

"Maybe just stay inside after all the craziness." I stretch into a big yawn. "Boy, all I needed was food. Bet I could sleep until lunchtime now."

She nods. "Good. You need the rest."

Perfect. As unobtrusively as possible I reach into the cupboard for a couple of granola bars. "Would you mind asking Sammy not to wake me? I'm serious about sleeping until noon. Probably much later. I don't even want to answer the phone." I stretch again and rub my eyes.

Relief softens her features. "That's an excellent idea. Pleasant dreams."

Yawning loudly, I heave my body upstairs. Okay, if I'm going to make a move, I need to do it before the reporters show up.

Heading out the front door isn't an option. Hmm. The windows on one wall of my bedroom face the side of the house. In wistful daydreams of escape as a kid, I thought climbing down would be doable. Theoretically. Now I need to test that theory.

I pack the granola bars along with a water bottle and the stuff I collected last night. Even though I'm sure Mom will warn Sammy not to disturb me, I lock the door. I also write a note explaining how crucial it is for me to question Mrs. Sternfield. I tape the note to my laptop in case Mom unlocks my door in a panic later on. Hopefully, I'll return soon enough to prevent that from happening.

I leave a radio playing softly and rub my hands together. After putting on my sneakers and taking a deep breath, I climb out of my window. Whoa, the second story seems much higher when you're balanced outside it on a half-inch ledge. Much higher.

Legs shaking, I call upon whatever daredevil genes I inherited from Dad as I reach for the rain gutter. Will it bear my weight? It wobbles but holds fast. Clutching it, I toe the bricks, level by level, and slowly climb down. A woodpecker goes to work on the madrona tree a few yards away, startling me. I claw at the rain gutter, causing it to rattle. Inhaling deeply, I take another step down, and then another. Five feet from the ground, I lose my grip and fall, landing hard on my butt.

Whew, stop for a breath. As I brush dirt from my shorts, I glance around to make sure no one's watching, and then run from tree to tree until I'm at the edge of the front yard. Quietly, I unlock my car and put it in neutral to push it forward to the neighbor's before starting the engine. Hopefully, no one will notice that my car isn't in its normal spot later.

I get in and take off, not able to breathe normally for ten blocks. Once I'm sure I'm not being followed, I turn on the stereo and crank up my favorite playlist. Not that it does much to improve my anxiety or guilt. People have given Jack, Evie, and my family grief because of me. Sammy's out of the AV719 trial. Mom's a stressed-out mess.

The list is overwhelming. I want to be the one who fixes the chaos I've caused.

Two hours later, at eight a.m., I cruise around the cul-de-sac in front of Mrs. Sternfield's house. There's no movement from her house or any of the others. Now what? It's not like I'll try to break in while she's here. Shoulda factored the early hour on a weekend into my planning. Maybe Jack and Evie had a tiny point about my impulses taking front seat to my brain lately.

I drive out to the main road and pull into the lot at the trailhead where I parked with Shane the last time. Oh, God, Shane, you'd better recover. My insides seem to go hollow and the aching loneliness of missing him threatens to undo me.

Panting, I wrap my arms around myself, rocking against the seat. I've seen too many victims of CZ88 slip off one by one, some with a scream, others a whimper. All while I stood by helplessly. And now it's just me, alone with my sorrow, fear, and guilt. After all, Dr. Sternfield didn't forcibly jam a needle into me the way the blood-jackers did. I made the decision with only the tiniest prompting. And now my family and friends are suffering alongside me. At any moment, I could join the CZ88 victims, trapped in a coma and waiting for a rescue that might never arrive.

Which is why, no matter how much I hurt, I can never give up.

Charisma Feared As a Potential Bio-Weapon

John Rasmusson, *Hilton News*

The recent abduction of two teens, where attackers stole significant amounts of their blood, has citizens fearing a potential terrorist threat. According to our sources, Aislyn Hollings and Shane Elliott, who a month ago accepted the dangerous gene treatment known as Charisma, were kidnapped by a masked group of assailants, who "blood-jacked" the teens before abandoning them on a deserted road. Although Ms. Hollings's condition appears stable, Mr. Elliott now lies in a coma.

The purpose of the alleged blood-jacking is unknown, but theories abound, including the use of Charisma-tainted blood in weapons of terror. Sarah Dunsworth, a spokesperson for Survival America, stated, "We cannot be too vigilant when it comes to the safety of our country and those who scheme to attack it in a myriad of ways, including biological."

TWENTY-FOUR

I grab a granola bar and stare at the road. Every fiber of my body senses Mrs. Sternfield is the best chance for learning info that no one else holds. So I'll keep vigil and wait for my chance, whatever the consequences.

An hour later, a white Acura pulls out of the cul-de-sac. That seems like a car Mrs. Sternfield would drive. I squint for a glimpse of the driver. The silhouette is petite, probably a woman, but she passes too fast to be sure. Still, Mrs. Sternfield strikes me as the type to get an early start, weekend or not.

I drive back to her house and park two doors down. If the person in the Acura wasn't Mrs. Sternfield, and I end up arrested, I'll claim my symptoms are getting worse and causing erratic behavior. I've got plenty of ammo to play either the sympathy or the crazy card.

I stroll around the house, thumbs hooked in belt loops the way I imagine a meter reader would, even though it's Sunday. Unfortunately, every door is locked, and peeking into each window only reveals clutter-free furniture. No secret lab or chimp cages.

My head darts toward the neighbors' homes to see if anyone's watching. Is that a flutter of curtain? I wait, but no further sign of movement. I take a deep breath, thinking.

Okay, time for serious action. My brain goes cottony for a moment, whether from the insanity of what I'm about to do or from the remaining effects of blood loss, I can't say.

I huddle next to the back door, pull a small flat screwdriver out of my pocket, and, following the video instructions I looked up online, stick it into the lock, nudge it upward and twist. To my amazement, the door opens.

I tiptoe into the house, hoping Mrs. Sternfield hasn't set an alarm. Two steps into a hyacinth-blue kitchen that smells like croissants, I don't detect any sounds. A scan of the room shows not a dish out of place, nor anything else that would constitute evidence of gene therapy gone bad, unless the case of protein bars on the table has been modified somehow.

I tread softly through the first floor, starting with a lemon-polish-infused dining room. The table's set with two place mats, linen napkins, and a tea tray. She must be expecting a visitor. I pick up my pace, scanning a tidy living room and what appears to be an unused guest bedroom and bath.

Bracing myself, I make my way upstairs, startling whenever a floorboard beneath me squeaks, and only moving again after catching my breath. On the second floor, I glide through a bedroom decorated in off-white satin, and then home in on the second room, an office.

I power up her computer as I rummage through a stack of papers in the file bin. Most are bills, but there's a binder filled with press clippings. Fanning through them, I skim headlines screaming of Charisma and Dr. Sternfield's death. A morbid collection to remember one's daughter by, but no article includes anything I don't know.

The computer chimes to life with a tinny chord, and, happily, no password challenge. I set down the binder and hunt through computer folders, soon finding one titled "Charlotte." Bingo.

Before I can open it, the sound of the front door opening freezes me. Oh no. Already? As quietly as possible, I power off the computer and tiptoe to the hallway.

Heels click on wood and then echo on tile, followed by cupboards shutting and glass clinking against counters. I search in hope of finding an upstairs balcony I can climb down. No such luck. Swallowing back fear, I stare at the stairs leading to the foyer and front door, maybe twenty yards from where I stand. Could I run down and outside without being spotted from the kitchen? That seems like my best shot. Risky as it is.

My gaze lingers back on the office. If only I had more time to go through the Charlotte folder and examine the data Mrs. Sternfield considered worth saving. Something more than family photos, I'd bet.

Clanking rises from downstairs. It's only a matter of time before she heads up here. When the sound of running water begins, it's my cue to leave.

I slip off my shoes and skitter down the steps to the door, past boxes of fruit. Unfortunately, the door creaks as I open it, drawing a "Is someone there?" from the kitchen. I pull the door mostly shut behind me, in the hopes she'll think she left it open, and sprint across the yard and down the street until I'm at my car. Fumbling for my keys, I unlock my door and hop inside, panting. Only after I rev my engine do I check the rearview mirror to see Mrs. Sternfield reach the edge of her driveway, hands on hips and looking around.

I rumble off, hoping against hope she hasn't gotten a glimpse of me or recognized my car. Another peek in my mirror shows her turning around and heading back toward the house. Still, I scrunch my body low as I pass a neighbor walking his pit bull.

At the entrance to the cul-de-sac, I slow down to turn back onto the main road. A small pickup truck coming from the opposite direction stops at the same intersection. I glance at the other driver and jolt when I recognize a familiar face. Dr. Dulcet.

What the hell? I sink lower into the seat. My heart races as I drive off.

My mind spinning, I head once again into the trailhead lot and park. Off in the distance the pickup truck is already out of sight, no doubt at Mrs. Sternfield's. He must be her guest for tea. But it isn't a social visit, I'm sure of it. He must want info out of her too. But will she give it up? If only I were a true spy, with microphones and tracking devices.

For what seems like endless minutes, I stare at the street leading to Mrs. Sternfield's house, wishing my gaze could laser through all that stands between me and her door. I shift and wiggle, trying to find a comfortable position, but it's useless.

Right now they could be discussing insider information in the race for a cure. What's her price? As if trying to save lives isn't enough.

An hour later, the pickup truck leaves the cul-de-sac and Dr. Dulcet speeds past my hiding area. Now what? Return to Mrs. Sternfield and demand she tell me whatever she told him? It's not as if there are Internet instructions on interrogating hostile witnesses. Well, no online tutorials that I've sought out. Yet.

Dr. Dulcet has more incentive for finding a cure, so he's the one I should demand answers from, see if he's as up-front as he claims. I start the engine and trail the pickup truck.

We meander through winding roads, heading deeper into the mountains, where the trees meet over the street, casting it into permanent shadow. I follow him through the gloom, the back of my neck tingling. I dread ending up on another desolate road, yet I can't back down now.

At an unmarked intersection, he turns onto a gravel lane that leads into thick forest. My heart goes crazy as I contemplate following him along the almost-nonexistent road. On such a small path, he'd spot me for sure. Okay, think this through. Since it's unlikely this forest road will lead out to another street, waiting for him seems like a worthwhile gamble.

Backtracking, I park on a turn-about. I'm getting good at this surveillance thing. Sure wish my phone hadn't been stolen by the blood-jackers, though.

I find a floppy hat to hide my face before settling down for the wait. It's ten minutes before another car goes by, giving me time to ruminate about the damn ringing in my ears. Are Shane and the others able to dream, or is the racket in their heads driving them insane?

Forty minutes later, the pickup pokes from the gravel road and speeds past my parking spot. Clearly, he wasn't out here long enough for an outdoor sport. So, why, then? It has to be related to the falseness in Mrs. Sternfield's expressions and her appearance in hiking clothes a week earlier.

Given I don't have a partner in crime, following Dr. Dulcet from the safety of my car is awfully tempting. But if there's a secret in the woods, it may not be there long. And it's not like Jack or Evie'll be coming back here with me.

Taking a deep breath, I start my car and head down the unmarked road.

When the bumpy terrain becomes so rough I fear being able to get out again, I stop. Should I continue on foot? What if I run into another pack of blood-jackers? Or worse?

A pain shoots behind my eyes. If I don't investigate what's going on out here, there's an excellent chance I'll die anyway. That gets me out of the car.

I lock everything tight, and pick up a wrist-thick stick for protection. Armed, I tromp forward through damp, chilly shade. All I wear is a T-shirt and shorts. Obviously, I have more to learn about this surveillance stuff than I thought.

A breeze sweeps through the foliage, rustling leaves and twigs. Whenever a branch snaps or bird calls, I duck for cover, heart racing until I'm sure it isn't another human. When each sound dies, I smack my palm with the stick in mock bravery, but my soul seems to wither. The blood-jackers stole something far more valuable than my blood and phone.

Around the next bend, I smell something. Smoke? I peek

through the trees trying to make out where it comes from, and that's when I spot the cabin. A beautifully constructed building of broad planks that reminds me of something on the vacation channel. But why is Dr. Dulcet wasting time here?

I creep closer, keeping behind shrubbery for cover.

I sigh. The idea of waiting out here in the damp for what could be hours seems too stupid to contemplate. But so is confronting whoever's in the cabin about what Dr. Dulcet's up to.

Frustrated, I toss a rock at the door. It misses, but thunks against the wall. Good enough. Let's see what happens. I hide behind a broad fern.

A moment later, the window next to the door opens and a head pokes out. Then sticks out farther. I recognize that head. It can't be.

My insides fill with rage and shock, yet also an incongruous twinge of hope. Because Dr. Sternfield is alive.

TWENTY-FIVE

She peers around, frowning. I step out of the bushes.

"You look good for a corpse," I say, barely able to control the urge to race over and drag her by the hair back to Tacoma.

Her expression goes steely and her eyes scan back and forth. "Are you alone?"

I pat my pocket as if I'm carrying a phone. "Not for long."

She shakes her head apologetically. "No reception out here, I'm afraid." Her face withdraws into the cabin and a few moments later, she opens the door and steps out.

A coldness plants itself at the base of my spine with exactly how stupid I've been to come out here alone. It's just me and the doctor who treated unsuspecting people with killer genes. And that's the good scenario. In the bad one, she has friends with her.

I clutch the stick behind my back, and keep my distance. "Look, I don't care about exposing you or getting anyone in trouble. I just want me and my friends not to die. Please, make things right."

Her hand rests upon a hip clad in top-of-the-line hiking shorts. "Don't you think I want that too?"

"Then why've you been playing dead? You should be leading the research team."

"You honestly believe I'd be allowed to do any research? Maybe if folks had kept quiet and avoided the media circus, I could've helped." She shakes her head in disgust.

"The media never bothered you before. And what did you expect when your experimental subjects went into comas and died? How could you test something so dangerous on us?"

She sighs and takes a few steps forward. "The preliminary trial in Portland was going fine. What happened afterward was totally unforeseen. I truly wanted to make things better for you guys. And for a while, anyway, it worked. Aren't you finally the girl you dreamed of being?"

"I'm the girl who could go comatose at any moment. What kind of life is that?"

She hovers about ten feet away. Close enough for me to see a sheen of sweat on her temple. Her eyes track a hawk soaring above the trees, and then her gaze snaps back to me.

"Wasn't it worth the risk to enjoy even a few days of life to its fullest rather than enduring a long existence of mediocrity?"

Mediocrity. Of course, that's all I represented to her. "That's the kind of trade-off you don't get to decide for anyone else. I looked up to you, saw you as the type of researcher I wanted to be someday. You were just a con woman."

She brushes a three-hundred-dollar suede boot over a patch of clover. "I'm sorry, Aislyn. It really wasn't a con. And the science behind Charisma still holds tremendous promise."

I try reading her, but the myriad of emotions flickering across her features don't add up to a comprehensible whole. I inch backward. "If CZ88's so great, why didn't you take it yourself?"

Her eyes seem to swallow the shadows cast by the trees. "If I needed to improve myself that way, I would've." She takes a long breath. "Every great scientific breakthrough comes with setbacks. You know that. And there are those with resources who still support what I do. You could work with us. I always appreciated your insights, and I'm so close to nailing a cure. One that would let you keep your sociability."

A flutter of hope beckons, as real as the crow staring at us from its perch in the pine tree. The person most likely to fix everything is here, offering a chance I'd thought was lost. To keep the parts of CZ88 that've been so life-changing, yet remove the parts that could be life-ending. Win-win.

If I can trust her.

I stare at her face, so sure, so smug. Of what? That she can convince me again? Her manipulation has always been made easy by her smarts, I'll bet. At the top of her class, the most brilliant one at Nova Genetics, their star. Never confined to *mediocrity*. What would it be like to be so freakishly smart? Sure, I've always felt intelligent, but she operates at a different level, almost as if . . . Suddenly, a thought so crazy, yet so fitting, hits me.

My mouth opens involuntarily. "Oh my God. You *have* been enhanced. But not with CZ88."

She squints and a rising heat seems to shimmer off her skin. Finally, clear emotions spread across her features: surprise, and, more intensely, shame. It isn't an emotion I've seen on her before and she wears it like an ill-fitting shoe.

I say, "That's why you're special. Why your IQ is way outside of the norm."

She crouches a few inches as if she's about to spring. Only then do I realize she's also been hiding one arm behind her back. I jump sideways and swing my stick just as she lunges forward with a syringe pointed like an ice pick.

Holy crap! Hasn't she killed enough people with her damn needles? I whip the branch, hitting her in the thigh, but not before she scrapes my forearm with the syringe.

She bounces from one foot to the other like a tennis player waiting for a serve. "You're not going to bash my head in. That would take more of a warrior gene than God or science granted you."

I keep my distance, panting. My vision begins to go fuzzy. "What's in the syringe?"

"Just a little sedative. For horses. A girl's best friend out in these parts. The drug, not the horses." She eyes my arm. I glance at the tiny scrape, bubbling with pinpricks of blood. A surface wound. Hopefully. But I feel woozy.

She coos, "Let yourself go, Aislyn. Once you've had some rest, we can discuss this more sensibly."

I take a step backward. "So when did you get the alteration that made you smart?"

She leans forward, swinging the syringe. "The gene modification was only an extra boost. I was always smart." A pulling around her eyes and the tightness of her voice suggest a deep hurt.

"But maybe not smart enough, huh?" I take another wobbly step back, clutching the branch in front of my chest. "Did your dad force you to be his guinea pig?" It would explain her abandonment of his company now, when he most needs her to take responsibility for the mess she created, and why she's working with VidaLexor to find a cure, if that's what she's really doing out here.

The nearby crow squawks as Dr. Sternfield races forward, plunging the syringe toward my chest. I smack her arm with the branch, causing a sickening crack that sends her spinning around but also causes the branch to fly out of my hand.

In a second, she hurls herself at me again. Only this time I have no weapon. I don't dare turn around and run, terrified of a needle in my back. So I kick out toward her chest, praying I'll avoid the syringe. She stumbles back, but stabs at my calf, embedding the needle a half inch. As her thumb goes for the plunger, I grab her forearm and push her to the ground.

My vision is going dark, the way it did when the blood-jackers siphoned me. How long do I have? Seconds?

With the last of my energy, I throw myself onto her arm and yank the needle out of my leg. As I lose consciousness, I stab it toward her thigh, hoping against hope that she gets more of the drug than me.

When I awake, the sky has darkened to a blue-black twilight. Oh hell, Mom and Sammy must be frantic.

The body under me is warm, but still. Gingerly, I feel around for the syringe, which is still jammed into Dr. Sternfield's thigh. I pull it out and throw the evil thing into the foliage.

With a groggy head, I stumble through the faint light toward the cabin, stopping to vomit in the bushes. Inside, I flip a switch on the wall, revealing the doctor's lair. It might not have cell reception, but it has electricity. Inside is an array of tables filled with notes, a computer, lab equipment, cases of food I recognize from her mother's house, and a refrigerator filled with racks of vials. Scrambling, I tear open a supply cabinet and dig around until I find a rope.

I lumber outside to tie up Dr. Sternfield before she comes at me again, but the ground where we'd lain is bare. To my right, there's a thrashing in the trees. If she contacts someone to help her, to keep me silent, oh, God, no.

I chase after the cracking branches and catch up to Dr. Sternfield as she reaches a small clearing where a Jeep's parked. Balling my fist, I bring it down on her back and once more we're on the ground wrestling. She gnashes her teeth, and clearly has desperation on her side.

I may not have the warrior gene, but I have the upper body of someone who's spent years perfecting her butterfly stroke. More importantly, it's my life on the line.

"You bitch!" I wallop her upside the head and flip her over to loop the rope around her wrists as I sit on her legs. "You don't know me at all."

She screams and twists until I jam an elbow into her kidney. That knocks the air out of her long enough for me to pull the rope down to her ankles as well. With more knots than necessary, I tie her up as tightly as I was the night before last.

She grunts. "Now what?"

I rock her to the side and check her pockets. "There's no way I can carry you into the Jeep and I don't trust you enough to untie you." I pull the keys from her pocket. "So get comfy."

She whips back and forth, eyes in panic mode. "No, Aislyn. I was serious about working together. And I really am just inches away from a cure. That's what Dr. Dulcet's been paying me to do. No one else has the slightest inkling of which DNA to modify. If the police take me in, all my work comes to a halt. You just need to trust me."

I don't need her super IQ to know what a bad plan that is. "If you want me to believe you, name the genes you manipulated."

She rattles off three genes.

I sigh. "The researchers already identified those."

"Well, I'm not giving you the complete formula until you release me. But I can guarantee the other researchers won't figure it out."

"Why not? They've done multiple genomic scans on all of us, and located the viral vector you used to deliver your crappy combo of gene mods. There are a lot of smart doctors besides you, even if they haven't been genetically modified."

She smolders. "They've had almost a month. And they've

only found the obvious candidates. You won't find what you need."

"How can you be so sure?" In that moment, I remember something she once said about one scientist's trash being another's treasure. And hadn't Xavier scribbled *JUNK* on his notes? Maybe that wasn't because he thought his guesses were useless. What if he realized that the search was limited too narrowly? To genes. But about fifty percent of our DNA is considered "junk" because it doesn't code for protein-creating sequences.

My breathing becomes very rapid. "You altered our junk DNA too, to regulate our genes somehow."

Her smugness is replaced by tangible, raging anxiety. "Don't be ridiculous."

"No, what's ridiculous is how easy I can read you, thanks to Charisma. Gotta love the irony, huh?"

I run back into the cabin and grab her computer along with boxes I fill with the vials from her refrigerator. She's been busy. To keep the vials cool, I stuff bags of frozen berries from her freezer between them.

As Dr. Sternfield hollers obscenities alternated with offers, I take five trips to clear the cabin of anything that resembles research. On my final scan of her secret lab, I spot a well-worn copy of *Flowers for Algernon*. Figures. I leave it for her.

With the last load in the Jeep, I throw a blanket onto Dr. Sternfield and ignore her pleas as I drive off into the last evening.

At the nearest town, I'm tempted to pull in to the sheriff's station, but the urge to drive straight to Tacoma is stronger. My compromise is to stop at a gas station along the way to make an anonymous call to the police, letting them know that a criminal doctor who's been on the news is wrapped up and waiting for them at a nearby cabin. Of course, I'll have a lot to answer for, but my priority is to get this research into the hands of someone I can trust. Dr. Culdicott isn't the warmest doctor on the planet, but she's my go-to person.

Less than two hours later, I park at Florence Bishop Children's. My body trembles as I hurry into the emergency department. I explain to the receptionist that it's urgent I speak to Dr. Culdicott. She nods as if she's heard it all before, and insists I take a seat in the waiting room. Same-old, same-old.

Ten minutes later, Dr. Culdicott surges through the door, and, as soon as she hears my story, summons an orderly to help us load all the research notes, vials, and laptop from the Jeep onto a cart and into her private office.

My stomach growls; my head aches. Trying to ignore both, I say, "Tell the researchers they need to examine changes to junk DNA too."

She nods and has some demands of her own, which include contacting Mom and calling the police. I don't know who I'm more scared of. Well, yes I do, and she barges in first.

"Aislyn, what on earth were you thinking? Are you hellbent on getting killed?"

I hold up my palms in surrender. "But I was right, Mom! And I found Dr. Sternfield. She's alive, and she's been doing research. I may have even found a cure she's been working on."

Mom gulps a few breaths like she's about to hyperventilate and then rasps, "A cure?" She lowers her head and shakes like she can't believe it. Then she starts crying.

I grab her heaving shoulders. "It'll be okay, Mom. See, I wanted to fix things for everyone, to prove— I'm sorry for scaring you."

She's still sobbing and I'm still holding her when a tall female officer with hair in tight cornrows comes into the office with Dr. Culdicott.

The officer introduces herself and opens a notebook. "The sheriff's team found the cabin and your vehicle, but there's no doctor and it appears her premises have been ransacked."

My blood drains to my feet. "She can't be gone. I, uh, after she drugged me, I tied her up."

The policewoman's eyebrows rise. "We need to hear both sides of this story."

Dr. Culdicott, who's been watching with a frown, says, "We have reason to believe the doctor was withholding crucial evidence toward a cure that could save the lives of over two hundred people."

The police officer speaks to me. "So you admit to breaking into the doctor's cabin after you incapacitated her?"

"No, the door was open and I—"

Mom inserts herself between the policewoman and me. "She's not saying anything until we've got a lawyer. You should know better than to interrogate a minor. Especially one who's just been through such a traumatic experience."

Dr. Culdicott opens the door and uses her military commander's voice. "Ms. Hollings is correct. As her doctor, I insist Aislyn get some rest. I will be happy to testify, should it come to it, that there are dangerous sedatives in her system and injuries consistent with an attack."

The policewoman realizes she's outgunned and leaves with a promise to be in touch. After the door closes, Mom and Dr. Culdicott actually high-five each other.

I'm not as jubilant. If there was a chance of curing the CZ88 in the way I wanted it cured, that chance fled with Dr. Sternfield. Unless there's treasure in those vials and computer notes.

It's before I'm allowed to leave. As eager as I am to escape this place, I insist we see Shane and the others after midnight; screw the official visiting hours. Stopping at each bedside I say, "Hold on, hold on."

On the way home, between sighs and tears, Mom informs me that I'm grounded for the foreseeable future. All I can do is laugh. My room is the only place I want to be tonight. I think Mom would bolt my door and windows if she could. But she needn't worry. I'm done running away.

Five Countries Ban US Travelers
Jonah Walters, US Wire Service

Due to fears of the contagious gene therapy CZ88, the following countries have banned US tourists until further notice: Egypt, Iraq, Qatar, Singapore, and Turks/Caicos Islands. These are the same countries that deny visas to people living with HIV. To date, CZ88 has infected 273 people, resulting in 49 deaths and over 200 patients in comas.

TWENTY-SIX

It takes me a full day to sleep off the remaining sluggishness from the sedative. A low buzzing in my ears takes its place, like a determined mosquito, never letting me forget what's inside my body.

As soon as I'm conscious, Mom tells me Jack and Evie have called a dozen times, begging to come over. I decide to take that as a good sign.

Jack makes it to my house first. He hesitates in front of me for a moment, and then we dive into each other's arms. My body floods with warmth.

Eyes full of tears, I say, "I'm so sorry for making you worry and feel left out of my plans."

He rests his forehead on mine. "I should've gone with you to Cle Elum, no matter how crazy it sounded. Shane did."

"Anyway, you know I made my choice long ago." I run a finger along his collarbone, noticing he smells a little of chlorine, the way I always did when I could still go to pools. Well, if the research notes I risked my life for pan out, maybe we'll enjoy some late-night swims together.

In the middle of that delicious thought, Evie barges in. "You're already on the news!"

"Oh crap," I say. "It wasn't on purpose. And if they ask for an interview, I'll make sure you're there to prep me."

She tugs at my hair. "What you need is weapons prep. I can't believe you hunted down the crazy doc. Thank God you're okay."

I sniff. "Well, you don't have to worry about weapons and wild chases anymore. I'm not going anywhere."

In unison, she and Jack yell, "Promise?"

Hours later, Mom announces that Dr. Sternfield still hasn't been found, but Mrs. Sternfield and Dr. Dulcet have been brought in for questioning. The more useful news is that the researchers have found mounds of valuable information from the computer and vials, stuff Dr. Sternfield had been testing before she went missing.

The next day, Dr. Culdicott puts Mom and me on speaker-phone and has a geneticist explain how CZ88 includes two viral vectors, the second of which was found in the vials I grabbed. Dr. Sternfield needed two vectors to pack all of the gene modifications she wanted to make, and used a combination of techniques, such as sending snippets of RNA to modify genes rather than introducing whole genes every time. Even the material used to fill out the viruses, the "stuffing," which most researchers would consider "junk," had genetic instructions embedded within it.

Most of what he explains after that goes way over my head, but his excitement is obvious.

"So, bottom line?" Mom asks when the guy takes a breath.

He clears his throat. "No promises. But Dr. Sternfield mapped out several possible means of reversing the process, and even launched the development work, with a plan to sell it to the highest bidder, from what I can gather."

Mom leans toward the phone. "How long to finish and test it?"

"Months, most likely. We'll keep you informed every step of the way."

Mom and I stare bleakly at each other. Do I have that long? Do Shane, Chloe, and the others? But I force myself into a smile for Mom's sake and say, "The good guys know what they're doing. And there are more of them than there are Dr. Sternfields. Sometimes taking a risk is less risky than not taking one."

Mom's jaw tightens. We both know I've shifted the conversation to Sammy. But she doesn't dismiss what I say out of hand. We both have to believe that I've given the scientists enough to work with. Because there isn't any more.

During July and August, the buzzing in my head remains an incessant irritant. On the darkest of nights, a tiny part of me insanely wishes I'd just go into a coma already so I could escape the never-ending what-ifs. But come morning I shake off my despair and am thankful for another day.

While I try to ignore my symptoms, the researchers keep in touch via e-mails and conference calls. Even Dr. Dulcet offers to help, insisting he'd only urged Dr. Sternfield to turn herself in and work on a cure. Since there isn't enough evidence to prove he did anything illegal, the government task force accepts his scientific input under the strictest controls. Mrs. Sternfield, on the other hand, has been charged with aiding and abetting, since the police have evidence she sent the fake suicide video to the news stations and rented the cabin where her daughter hid out.

Meanwhile, I live a life where I'm afraid to get my hopes up. And afraid not to.

But I know how I want to spend whatever time I have—with my family, Jack, and Evie. Now that I'm done chasing down fugitives, the people I love aren't in a state of constant annoyance with me. Still, "normal life" isn't easy. Often I find myself biting the insides of my cheeks in frustration. The worst is when Evie and Rafe insist upon double dates with me and Jack. It's not that they're constantly on top of each other, but I can't help noticing the stolen kisses, even when they think they're being secretive. Yet there's no way I'll ask her to stifle her joy on my behalf. If Shane were conscious, I'm sure he'd offer some choice and salacious advice. Seeing his pale face get thinner every time I visit him and the others in the hospital gets harder to bear. But I still go there weekly, and will not let myself, or anyone else, forget about them.

Despite the challenge of facing impending doom, my own life thrives in odd ways. News programs fly me and the handful of others who've been infected by CZ88 but remain conscious to New York and LA for whirlwind interviews. They call us "miracle" cases. I use my miracle status to speak up for gene therapy, especially in treating cystic fibrosis.

My existence, such as it is, can make a difference.

At the end of August, Chloe's dad sends me a message. HAVE YOU SEEN THIS? He includes a link to a story about a gene therapy trial that uses a modified form of the HIV virus to attack cancer.

I text him: AMAZING! THERE'S HOPE FOR EVERY-THING.

He replies: DAMN RIGHT THERE IS.

Yes, he and I have become pals.

He follows up with: HEARD THAT ONE OF THE CREEPS WHO KIDNAPPED YOU DIED.

I actually feel sorry for the woman, who drove the getaway van. Jail would have been enough of a punishment. Turns out one of my blood-jackers was the scary guy from the fund-raiser, and their leader, with the smooth voice, was the guy who'd tried to bust into my homecoming party with a six-pack of beer. After injecting the tainted blood, their whole gang ended up in comas. Given how contagious the blood-borne path is, I wonder if Dr. Sternfield was infected after I stuck her with the syringe she'd used on me. Even if the police never catch her, the CZ88 might.

And maybe the CZ88 would catch up with me too. I've been through countless exams to figure out whether I have some crazy immunity or if those odds that were stacked against me and made me so shy are also the cause of my good fortune now. It could be I started from such a different base-line that the changes in my biochemistry have further to go before reaching the threshold that'll send me into a coma, which only begs the question, "How long do I have?"

TWENTY-SEVEN

In September, after intense online petitioning leads to real-life protests, and a number of speeches by the ACLU, my school decides I can attend my senior year, as much of it as I'm conscious for, anyway. That ruling revs up the hate mail and protests at Nova Genetics. However, gene therapy is here to stay.

A week before Halloween, when I plan to dress up as Madame Curie, the morning crackles with crisp air. Jack holds my hand as we drive to school.

Sammy yells from the backseat, "How many gene therapists does it take to change a lightbulb?"

I say, "No idea."

"None. They send viruses to do their work."

Jack and I groan. But those viruses are doing a good job

on Sammy. There are days when he goes the whole ride without coughing. And his lung capacity has gone up twenty percent since Mom allowed him into the expanded AV719 trial, which she only did after patients in the previous trial showed rapid improvement. With no side effects.

Jack's hair blows from the wide-open windows. Autumn's here, but I crave fresh air more than ever these days. Still, being outside comes with its own price. Even though the blood-jackers have been incapacitated, and Homeland Security ruled out bio-terrorist threats, I keep a constant vigil in the rearview mirror, and check out everyone around me, especially strangers who get too close.

Jack taps on the steering wheel. "So, you up for apple-picking next weekend?"

My cheeks are getting numb from the cold air, but I don't turn my face from the window. "Evie and Rafe want to go too."

Jack gives a tiny grunt. "I'm guessing there's a hayloft?"

I shrug.

We stop in front of Sammy's school and say good-bye to him before continuing on. Five blocks from the high school, my phone buzzes. Probably Evie wanting last-minute help with calculus. I'm happy some things have remained a constant in my life. We even drew our customary school map to calculate the maximum contact opportunities between ourselves, this year adding boyfriends to the equation.

But the text on my phone is from Mom. A message I've prayed for even if I've been afraid to let myself really expect it.

My face must betray my shock.

Jack pulls over. "What?"

I stare out the windshield, not seeing anything. "The cure is ready."

He grabs me into a hug, his breath making my neck tingle. "That's fantastic."

My body feels numb within his arms. "Yeah. It would be great not to worry about going into a coma or passing on what I have, but—"

"But what?"

I clamp my eyes shut, burying my face into his chest. "I don't want to go back to being shy again. Of not knowing how to feel around you. Of not being able to speak up for kids like Sammy." Of course, I tried to persuade the researchers to figure out a win-win cure where I'd get to keep the Charisma part of CZ88, but even my glowing personality couldn't make a strong enough case for them to take that chance.

Jack holds me tightly. "If the cure takes back the social stuff, you still know me and I know you. It can't undo that. You were never shy around Evie and your other close friends, right? And the real you managed to make itself known to those of us who paid attention. Believe me, I always did."

I pull up my head and nod, wondering for the millionth

time how much of our personality resides in our DNA and how much is learned behavior. For the past months, my brain has used synapses that ride the paths of confidence. Maybe that'll be mine to keep if I'm cured. Maybe it won't.

He squeezes my hands. "Hey, if things get tough, you can always go back to texting me until you see things haven't changed, okay?" He kisses my cheek. "Besides, you're forgetting the upside of getting cured, I think." His eyebrows rise along with the corners of those luscious lips I've been aching to kiss.

Ah, yes. A flutter whisks through my chest and down to my belly. All I can do is smile, no doubt blushing as badly as I used to.

He says, "Something to think about while you're in the hospital all alone tonight."

I suddenly find it difficult to speak. "Ooh, boy." My voice squeaks in a way it hasn't since before the CZ88. Who needs a cure? Just thinking about being with Jack has me changing already.

"So, should I take you straight there?" he asks.

"Let me call my mom."

They plan to administer the drug this afternoon, so Mom will take me at lunchtime. Until then, I plow through the motions of a school day, needing constant nudging from Evie to remind me where to go.

She puts a finger to her lips. "Maybe you should do one last diva-y thing before the cure."

"C'mon, I've never been a diva."

She gives a ten-point eye-roll. "If the TV news coverage fits . . ."

I'm not going to argue. Not today. "Any ideas?"

"Hmm."

"Never mind. I know what I'm going to do." I march into Dr. Lin's science room, where most of the class shuffles around their lab tables.

"Dr. Lin," I say, projecting my voice to the back of the room.

The class pauses their chattering.

Dr. Lin looks up with his eyes but keeps his face pointed down toward a set of magnets he's sorting. "Good morning, Aislyn."

"At the science fair, you asked about my project's relevance and where I'd draw the line."

He raises his eyebrows. "I did."

"Well, I couldn't answer then, and I might not be able to tomorrow, but I'd like to try now."

He narrows his eyes in a way that makes it seem like he's tempted to hit the panic button under his desktop. "Class begins in two minutes."

"I'll risk the tardy. So, here goes." I face the classroom.

"My project's relevance was to shine a light on the incredible possibilities of gene therapy. Once we truly understand how to manipulate our DNA, we can change the whole game in terms of quality and quantity of life. What could be more relevant than that?"

A girl in the back of the room yells, "My boyfriend's abs."

Dr. Lin starts to add something, but I cut him off. "As for where I'd draw the line of which enhancements to make and which to ban, I don't know. We shouldn't allow extreme experiments like the one I got involved in, but as to how much we allow humans to change themselves, it's a moving target. It's okay to admit we don't have the answers yet. But once the future's been seen, it can't be unseen."

Dr. Lin says, "Since you feel so strongly about this, you can lead a discussion this afternoon when you get to class."

"Actually, I'll be out after lunch, at the hospital."

He stares for a few seconds before blinking, as if he's going to record his impressions of me in a lab book. "If it makes any difference to you, I voted for your project at the state competition."

"Really? Well, thanks. Um, I'd better get to class."

"Good luck, Aislyn."

The rest of the morning I chat with as many friends as possible, raise my hand at every opportunity, and hug Jack after each class. If school can be half this good when I get back, I'll be happy. A crowd sees me off when Mom picks me up.

On the way to the hospital, my legs can't stop trembling. I remind myself there's no guarantee any of this'll work. In fact, the "cure" could have unexpected side effects, or end up worse than the treatment. Not for the first time, I speculate that the "Valley of Death" between animal and clinical trials isn't just littered with unfunded projects, but with the people who've undergone experimental cures that failed drastically. No, that kind of thinking only leads to a racing pulse and nothing good.

I check my phone one last time in the parking lot. Jack's sent ten texts, all of which say: FOR ME, YOU'LL ALWAYS BE "THAT GIRL."

Oh, how I hope he's right.

Mom sticks with me through the check-in process. Once I'm installed in a tiny room, Dr. Culdicott and a gene therapy specialist named Dr. Cho show up. By mutual agreement, a small camera crew discreetly captures the moment. I smile their way. If these are my last moments of being brave, I want them to inspire folks.

Goose bumps rise on my arms. "Have the others gotten the cure already?"

Dr. Cho smiles tightly. "What we *hope* is a cure, Aislyn. You're the last one to receive it at this hospital."

"Can I see them?" I've visited these guys regularly, mostly

to sit and hold Shane's hand, while I tell him about all the people he can harass when he gets better. I plan to be there when he does.

Dr. Culdicott says, "Of course."

Dr. Cho washes up and gloves his hands. "Ready?"

Ready? God, it's hard to imagine how eager I was to receive the CZ88 back in June. Now it seems a whole lifetime has passed. A lump plays in my throat and my body slumps. For too many others, a lifetime *has* passed.

I clench the blanket I sit on and force myself to sit upright. "Ready."

He wipes my arm. Unlike what Dr. Sternfield gave us, the cure requires two injections today and there might be a follow-up. I flinch with each needle jab. Probably will for the rest of my life. When the doctor is done, he advises me to relax. Yeah, right.

He and Dr. Culdicott promise to check in later. That leaves the camera crew time for interviews with Mom and me. They've paid us top dollar to capture my possible metamorphosis back into shy-girl. Oh well, better this than Mom working extra hours to raise college money. Fortunately, the families of the other teens have signed on for the documentary too, so the crew leaves to film them.

My room suddenly seems too quiet. There isn't much in the way of entertainment. Not that Dr. Gordon had time to think of that between working with the task force to find a cure and pushing the police to find his daughter. I have a difficult time looking him in the eye these days anyway. On the one hand, he seems genuinely concerned about making things right; on the other, whatever gene therapy he forced upon Dr. Sternfield helped make her what she is.

Mom pulls up a chair. Her expression is overly bright, trying unsuccessfully to mask her worry. Will I still be able to read her this well if the cure takes hold? I hope not. Witnessing everyone's emotions is exhausting.

I place my hands on her trembling ones and give my best version of a perky-daughter face. "I feel fine. In fact, I have a great book, so you don't have to wait around here."

She brushes a piece of lint from the bed. "How about I stay for a bit? We could go to the cafeteria for a feast."

I smile. "Fine, if that's how you want to spend Friday night."

We nibble on overcooked pasta, salad that's been refrigerated too long, and bowls of lime Jell-O that are just right. I lean back and consider my next words. "You know, whatever happens with this cure, you need to get a life, Mom."

She coughs. "What do you mean? I have everything I want with you and Sammy."

"You deserve more. Dad's been gone a long, long while. It's time you considered dating."

Her coughing turns to choking. "Uh, honey, let's take things one step at a time."

I hand her my napkin. "I just wanted to get that idea out there while I still have this not exactly inhibited personality."

Nodding, she wipes her lips. "I'll take it into consideration."

I plan to start drafting an online ad ASAP. It'll be fun to channel my inner Evie to give Mom's wardrobe a makeover.

Back in the room, the doctors pop in to look me over. No changes yet. But then, it might take days or weeks to detect a difference. When the doctors leave, Mom says she'll head out to check on Sammy, as long as I'm okay. I assure her I am.

As soon as she's gone, I shuffle to the elevator in slippers made of the same stuff they use to make disposable diapers, and visit the ward with Sebastian, Xavier, Jesse, and Shane. In their comatose state, they've been relegated once again to a boys-only room.

I clap my hands. "You guys call this a party?"

They lie on their backs, the way they always do. Their family members have set up chairs on the other side of the room for the documentary interviews. Shane's mom waves to me and puts her fingers to her lips since the camera's rolling.

I start at Sebastian's bed, running my fingers along his blanket. When I remember his body in fluid motion, creating something beautiful even in a drab hospital room, my throat catches. Oh, to see him perform a pirouette on stage. Just once. Moving from his bed to Jesse's, I whisper to each of them, "Wake up."

At Shane's bed, I take a seat and grab his hand. "When you get out of here, you'd better keep the nice-guy part of your DNA. Or I'll beat you silly." I tap his knee. "And don't expect me to fix you up with any of my friends, even if you're virus-free." I rise and kiss his cheek.

With the camera still running, the family members ask how I'm feeling so far. I haven't noticed any specific changes, physically or personality-wise. Not yet, anyway. They nod somberly and I make my way next door to Chloe's room. Her mom and little sister sit at a table playing Go Fish. Fortunately, the documentary crew is done with them for now, so we have a little peace.

Bailey gives me a Sammy-wide smile. "Wanna play?"

It's five games before Bailey lets us take a break. "How much longer before Chloe wakes up?" she asks, limping to her sister's bed.

Her mother says, "Honey, we don't know. Could be a long time."

Bailey puts her face next to Chloe's. "But her eyelids seem twitchy."

"I know, sweets, I'm sure they do." She joins Bailey, playing with her younger daughter's braid. "One more card game before I take you home to bed?"

Bailey pouts. "No. I wanna talk to Chloe and Aislyn."

We set chairs around Chloe to tell her what we've been up to, as if she's part of the conversation. How could this crazy vibrant girl have been still for four long months? I clutch her hand, which has become so boney. Maybe the doctors will let me paint her nails a bright lime green. She'd like that.

Chloe squeezes back.

"Oh my God," I say. "I think her hand moved."

Bailey jumps. "Look at her eyes. I told you they were twitching!"

Sure enough, Chloe's eyelids flicker and even blink open for a moment before quickly snapping shut as if the light hurts them.

Chloe's mom hovers right above Chloe. "Honey, baby girl, are you awake?"

Chloe's face spasms, and this time her eyes open and stay open. Her mouth does too. "Uh-huh," she says.

Chloe's mom calls out toward the hallway as she madly presses the button for the nurse. "Someone get over here! My daughter's waking up! My daughter's waking up!"

I stare at my friend, my heartbeat going crazy. Is this really happening?

Chloe manages to get a word out as her eyes dart around the room. "Jesse?"

We explode with hoots and shouts. Nurses and doctors and parents and camera-people flood inside. I back up to give them space.

The cure is actually working.

The boys' parents must have the same thought, because we all run back to their room to see if any of them are waking up. No luck. But we hug each other with hope.

Scrambling to the room's phone, I call Mom to share the news. She screams with delight and says she'll head back this instant.

The rest of the evening is a swarm of laughter and giddiness. Chloe revels in the attention, asking when she can do a newscast for "her" TV station. We celebrate long past official visiting hours, until the nurses demand everyone leave so Chloe can get some sleep.

As much as she and I beg to be roomies once again, the docs insist Chloe stay in her room, which is more heavily monitored. I guess that makes sense. Still, my room feels terribly lonely that night.

The next morning, I wake up just before sunrise, excited to see what the day holds. It takes me several minutes to detect the startling noise in my head. Silence. The ringing in my ears is entirely gone. Oh my God. My breath hiccups and tears roll down my cheeks. For the first time since June, I have true, precious hope for a future.

I quickly shower, dress, and run upstairs toward rooms that burst with glee. Sebastian, Xavier, and Jesse regained consciousness overnight. I flit between their room and Chloe's as the party from yesterday grows in size and volume. Our camera crew returns with a couple extra members, which seems to speed Chloe's post-coma recovery. The only person missing is Shane, who still lies unresponsive. It has to be only a matter of time, yet every hour without him becomes more excruciating.

Dr. Cho and a team of researchers put all of us through a zillion tests, drawing blood and taking DNA swabs. By that evening, they say with assurance that the viral load in our bloodstream has decreased dramatically. There's no way they can test whether the genes in our brains have changed without taking tissue from that region. But the best proof is that my friends are out of their comas. As far as personality changes, we'll have to wait and see.

Am I acting differently? Hard to say. These people are so familiar to me, how could I be shy around them? Maybe the true test will be how I feel around strangers, or with Jack. For now, my chest bursts with happiness. Except when I catch a glimpse of Shane's parents, who huddle by his bed, waiting so hopefully I have to look away.

Given the change in the others, as well as in the patients scattered in other hospitals, who were given the cure this afternoon, the researchers ask that I stay one more night to allow them to document our progress in detail. Not that I have as much progress as the others to report. But my body's chemistry is of major interest to them since only five percent of us didn't go into a coma.

So we chat and joke until ten p.m., when the staff asks anyone who isn't a patient to please go home. The families finally agree an hour later. I know they'll return long before visiting hours start up at eight.

When it's just us "victims" left in the boys' room, we take turns encouraging Shane to wake up and join us. But his body remains so still.

Chloe has me roll her to his bedside, and places a hand on his forehead. "His temperature feels good. And his coloring looks normal."

I clear my throat. "All of your coloring looked pretty normal the whole time, just faded tans."

The others stare at me. Chloe shakes her head. "How come you never went into a coma?"

I bite my lip, feeling guilty for something that isn't my fault. "I've thought a lot about it, and all I can say is that it's luck, maybe due to weird antibodies. But I did have symptoms, and without the cure, I probably would've gotten sick eventually, just like Shane."

We all gaze his way. If only his lip would twitch or his eyelids flicker. But what happens instead is the monitor next to him begins to beep, first lightly and then louder and louder. A nurse rushes into the room and checks it. Her mouth presses into a tight line and she runs from the room, ignoring our shouts of "What's wrong?" in her wake.

In moments, she returns with a doctor I don't recognize, who begins an exam as the beeping on the machine grows to a wail. Another doctor joins the first and then one of the researchers we'd been partying with earlier hovers with crossed arms.

The nurse shoos us away from the bed. "You kids need to make room."

Our bodies quiver and our eyes dart to each other. After frantic minutes of instructions shouted by the first doctor, a gurney steals Shane away. How could this be happening? The festive mood dives into a belly-churning fear. Chloe and I refuse to leave the boys' room despite the nurses' demands.

Chloe grasps Jesse so hard he winces. "He has to get better, he has to."

I sit next to Sebastian, holding one of his hands while Xavier clutches the other. We wait numbly as whatever courses through our bodies also courses through Shane's.

Finally, hours later, Dr. Culdicott returns. On that battle-weary face flows something that sends my senses into a vortex of hurt. Tears.

My spirits plummet. This couldn't be. It. Could. Not. Be. "No!" I yell.

Dr. Culdicott wipes her cheeks. "I'm so, so sorry."

TWENTY-EIGHT

Everything in my world goes darker and heavier in the hours that follow Shane's death. By the next morning, the sky has lowered and the rain clouds burst forth. Whenever I think I can't cry any more, I do. Shane, oh, Shane.

I'm released from the hospital the following day, and the others are released shortly thereafter. On the morning of Shane's funeral, the sky shines the same deep blue as his eyes. It's the kind of cobalt-skied October day that begs you to run through cornfield mazes and drink freshly pressed cider.

Shane's parents asked me to prepare a eulogy. For the first time in months, the thought of public speaking has my stomach twisting. But I remind myself that I've spoken in front of groups and to thousands online without fainting. There's no reason to return to my former panic-stricken days of never letting myself be heard. And I want to be heard when it comes to my sweet friend.

That doesn't mean I don't feel a twinge as I walk to the podium at the front of the church. But I don't run away.

With my fists clenched, I take a deep breath and speak to the large crowd in front of me. "I met Shane almost five months ago, and it was clear we would never become friends. Except we did."

Murmurs ripple through the crowd. I continue, "I got a chance to know the guy Shane was at heart. The one who could turn every little fear into a laugh, and help you figure out what to do with the biggest terrors of all. When we were in the hospital together, it was his idea to make videos to send to all of the people we loved, so that we could say good-bye on our own terms. The way Shane did everything." I take a breath. "You get to know someone really well, really fast when you hear them delivering what they believe are their final messages."

Images of Shane holding my hand in a hospital bed, joking with Sammy online, and wading in the waters off the peninsula flash through my brain. It takes all I have to go on. "I wish now I'd made a video for him, to say how much I came to love *The Shane Show*. The real one beneath the hype. It was funny and sweet and loyal and never, ever predictable. There'll never be another one like it."

Fearing my grief will flood out at any moment, I finish with, "Shane accepted the Charisma to become irresistible, and, you know what? He was."

I gaze out to the crowd with blurry eyes. Teenage girls are well represented among funeral-goers. I imagine Shane's spirit hovering above and mumbling, "What a waste." With an inward smile at that thought, I make my way back to my seat, where "loverboy" waits with a hug.

For the next few weeks, I spend a lot of time in my room either keeping up with homework or chatting with Jack and Evie. It isn't that I'm resorting to my old wallflower ways, more that I need to grieve alone. Evie doesn't bug me about the parties I'm missing. Jack doesn't insist on alone-alone time.

On a positive note, the blood tests show that both of the viruses in the CZ88 have been eradicated in all of the patients. So we're no longer contagious. Presumably, our altered DNA has been repaired in our cell tissue as well, which is supported by our improved physical health and debatable personality changes.

While seeking a cure, the task force shared my own genomic sequence with seven reputable research organizations, all of which have offered me in-depth reports of how I can expect my body to function as I age. Part of me is tempted to learn whether I'll go gray early or be at risk for various diseases. But the wiser part of me puts the reports aside. It's way more important to relish being seventeen.

Not that I've done much relishing lately. Sure, Jack and Evie come over with more and more frequency, but mostly it turns into failed attempts to cheer me up.

On Jack's visits at least, I find he was right about how my "knowing him" wouldn't change with the cure. Our friendship has worn away enough grooves in my psyche for me to feel comfortable around him forever. This supports what the hospital counselor insists upon, that I don't need to return to ground zero as far as inhibitions go. My behavior these past months was amped up by the altered DNA, but by performing the behaviors, they in turn rewired my brain, the way exposure therapy can make changes that are proven via brain scans. The trick is to keep practicing.

On a bone-chilling night before Thanksgiving, Jack invites me to go with him to a party at Drew Collier's house. Evie will be there too and even though she doesn't dangle quotas over my head anymore, she urges me to give it a go. Practice, practice, practice.

So I do.

Jack takes my hand as we stroll up the walkway. "It'll be okay, and if it's not, I understand you like certain breakfast cereals."

I smile. "Just don't flirt with Alexandra."

His eyebrows rise. "I never—"

I play-punch him. "I know."

When we enter, a light snaps on and dozens of kids yell, "Surprise!"

Jack nudges me forward. "We never properly celebrated your seventeenth."

Everyone launches into a rowdy chorus of "Happy Birthday." I choke back tears as I remember Shane's rendition of "Happy Birthday, Dear Badass."

But I need to focus on the here and now. And the fact that I'm badass enough not to run from the attention. Because I always had the strength not to run. Well, almost always, but I've forgiven myself for the one time I did.

I wipe away a tear that I hope everyone interprets as happiness, and, truthfully, a good part of it is. "Thanks, you guys. Seventeen's been interesting so far. But I hear the real excitement starts at eighteen." Now, there's a scary thought.

Jack and I nestle in next to a couple of kids who visited my house when we pulled out the waterslide. They seemed to have genuinely had fun that day. But there's no way to know for sure. Since I got the cure, I still get a feel for the social vibes people give off, but it's more like something I've learned rather than intuitive. And now my shyness is a whisper in the background that makes it nice to be alone, yet doesn't suffocate me.

The new Aislyn is someone I can live with.

I turn away from the others and focus on Jack. He wraps his arms around me. Not caring who watches, I draw his face closer and kiss him hard on the lips. And then harder. He's warm and delicious and mine. Worth every second of the wait. My heart races, my body goes weak, and my skin tingles.

When we pull away, panting, one of the kids nearby yells, "Get a room."

Evie, pulling Rafe behind her, rushes over to us. "Don't you guys look cuddly."

I place my cheek against Jack's. "And I didn't even have to drink three beers for courage."

Evie rolls her eyes. "What kind of refreshments do they have, anyway?"

We get up to scope out the kitchen. Besides a huge birthday cake, there are the usual suspects—a keg and a stack of red cups. A bunch of kids hover near the door to the backyard, laughing and passing around little packets of something.

Evie raises her eyebrows and struts over to them. "What's going on?"

A girl who usually sits in the back row of World History turns around with a shiny expression and a giggle. I've never seen her so bubbly. Probably had a beer too many.

She rubs the spot between her nose and mouth as if she has the sniffles. "Drew picked up a few party favors from a rave downtown."

To emphasize her point, Drew comes in grinning broadly. "Wanna try a little C?" he asks. "Free samples. Makes you feel oh-so-friendly."

Jack waves him off. "Uh, no thanks."

We start back to the living room. I've never been to a rave, but I've heard about snorting drugs with "friend-making" abilities. Still, something tugs at my curiosity.

I turn back. "Um, could I see what C looks like?"

He gives me a wink. "Sure, you can 'see what it looks like.' But go to the bathroom if you want to do some, okay?"

I hold out my hand and he places a dose of C into it. Trembling, I open a yellow paper packet holding white powder. My heart pounds as I fold it up and examine the back side, knowing before I do what I'll find: a tiny pink heart stamped onto its center.

My knees tremble as I contemplate the odds that anyone but Dr. Sternfield is behind this new drug. Despite all that's happened, what disturbs me more is that I have an insane urge to take it, to experience the rush of being more than myself for just a night. This isn't full-blown gene therapy, after all; I could bloom without going into a coma.

I stare at the packet for a long moment, considering, my pulse racing faster and faster. But no. I hand it back.

With my head raised and eyes closed, I breathe. And breathe. On my own.

Author's Note
Gene Therapy and Viruses

Although Charisma is the story of one rogue scientist who takes many misguided shortcuts, the promise of gene therapy in real life is breath-taking. Ever since scientists began to understand which gene mutations were correlated with certain diseases, they've been on a quest to fix those genetic faults. That quest is finally bearing fruit.

A huge challenge in this regard is getting the "fixed" version of a gene to the right cells. Several delivery vehicles have been tried, but for me the most fascinating, and at the time of this writing the most common, way is to use viruses. We all know how well they spread when we don't want them to, so why not take advantage of their power and use it to spread some good?

To make this happen, scientists keep the infectious aspects of the virus but replace the disease-making DNA within it with good DNA designed to fix genetic problems (e.g., by either replacing or deactivating mutated genes, or by introducing a new gene that will help combat a disease). The "viral vectors" packed with good stuff can be introduced to a body in several ways: via an injection, intravenously directly to the tissues with defective cells, or by removing cells from the body and introducing the virus to them in a lab before returning them to the body.

One of the most fascinating facts I came across while researching this book was that a modified form of the HIV virus was being used to deliver treatment against certain types of cancer as well as HIV itself. There's a certain poetic justice in the idea that one of humankind's greatest scourges could be used to combat itself and another deadly disease.

Like many other promising treatments, gene therapy still faces many hurdles. Among them, the issue of viruses inadvertently triggering the body's immune system, its high cost in comparison to the number of patients who can be treated at this time, and the complexity in getting the right genes to the right place in sufficient quantities, and then activating them without disrupting good genes.

Nonetheless, I believe gene therapy holds great promise. If you'd like to learn more, there are many wonderful online resources (some interactive) and books. Spending hours and hours with this material has made me wish more than once that I'd taken biochemistry in college.

Acknowledgments

This book took much longer to complete than I expected. But supporting me all the way was my tireless editor, Heather Alexander. The final product would not be what it is without her.

As always, thanks to Ammi-Joan Paquette for her stellar representation. Thanks to Danielle Calotta for her captivating cover design, to Maya Tatsukawa for designing the book's interior, and Regina Castillo for saving me from grammatical and other errors. A rip-roaring thanks to Draga Malesevic, Kim Ryan, and Donne Forrest from Penguin's subrights department, who've brought my books to readers around the world.

Thanks also to the many critiquers who gave me their valuable input when this project was nothing more than a handful of rough opening chapters and a synopsis. They include:

Jaye Robin Brown, Kelly Dyksterhouse, Dani Farrell, Tara Grogan-Stivers, Annika de Groot, Lee Harris, Kristi Helvig, Joanne Linden, Christine Putnam, Michelle Ray, Lesley Reece, Mary Louise Sanchez, Niki Schoenfeldt, Meradeth

Houston Snow (who also beta read), Pam Vickers, and Laura Hamilton Waxman.

Thanks to Ryan Tjoa, the first beta reader for this book, and to Rachel Chamberlain, my drop-everything-and-review beta reader for every manuscript I send her way.

Thanks to Dr. Ricki Lewis for responding to my questions about gene therapy, to Dr. Paulene Quigley for taking the time to meet with me and answer more questions about gene therapy, and Dr. Anthony Fiore for his help in understanding how epidemics are handled. Any errors I made on the above topics are mine alone.

Thanks to my patient and amazing kids. I hope I'm always as enthusiastic about your dreams as you are of mine.

And, finally, thanks to James, who makes pretty much all the rest possible with his counsel, cheerleading, and love.